"You're wrong, you know," he said slowly, watching her breasts rising and falling, rising and falling.

"You don't want to like me, but you do."

She gasped. "I never said—"

"And now you're wondering if I'm worth the risk of making love."

He was serious! Stunned, all Barbara could do was gasp again.

"Okay." He grimaced his endearing, self-effacing grimace. "Making love's the wrong expression. Making...whatever. You've never done that before, have you, mystery lady? Well, let me tell you something, neither have I. They say it can kill you, you know, this thing of casual sex, and I don't have any reason to doubt them. Until this moment I never imagined it mattering."

Looking away, he laughed with a shred of amusement. "But now it does matter—God, it matters." He returned his eyes to her. "So, now you tell me, Miss Cinderella-Come-Lately-To-The-Ball, what happens when the clock strikes twelve?"

Dear Reader,

Sophisticated but sensitive, savvy yet unabashedly sentimental—that's today's woman, today's romance reader—you! And Silhouette Special Editions are written expressly to reward your quest for substantial, emotionally involving love stories.

So take a leisurely stroll under the cover's lavender arch into a garden of romantic delights. Pick and choose among titles if you must—we hope you'll soon equate all six Special Editions each month with consistently gratifying romantic reading.

Watch for sparkling new stories from your Silhouette favorites—Nora Roberts, Tracy Sinclair, Ginna Gray, Lindsay McKenna, Curtiss Ann Matlock, among others—along with some exciting newcomers to Silhouette, such as Karen Keast and Patricia Coughlin. Be on the lookout, too, for the new Silhouette Classics, a distinctive collection of bestselling Special Editions and Silhouette Intimate Moments now brought back to the stands—two each month—by popular demand.

On behalf of all the authors and editors of Special Editions,
Warmest wishes,

Leslie Kazanjian
Senior Editor

LINDA SHAW
Disarray

Silhouette Special Edition

Published by Silhouette Books New York

America's Publisher of Contemporary Romance

SILHOUETTE BOOKS
300 East 42nd St., New York, N.Y. 10017

Copyright © 1988 by Linda Shaw Ltd.

ISBN: 0-373-09450-7

First Silhouette Books printing April 1988

America's Publisher of Contemporary Romance

Printed in the U.S.A.

Books by Linda Shaw

Silhouette Special Edition

December's Wine #19
All She Ever Wanted #43
After the Rain #67
Way of the Willow #97
A Thistle in the Spring #121
A Love Song and You #151
One Pale, Fawn Glove #224
Kisses Don't Count #276
Something About Summer #325
Fire at Dawn #367
Santiago Heat #403
Disarray #450

Silhouette Intimate Moments

The Sweet Rush of April #78

LINDA SHAW,

the mother of three, lives with her husband in Keene, Texas. A prolific author of both contemporary and historical fiction, when Linda isn't writing romantic novels, she's practicing or teaching the piano, violin or viola.

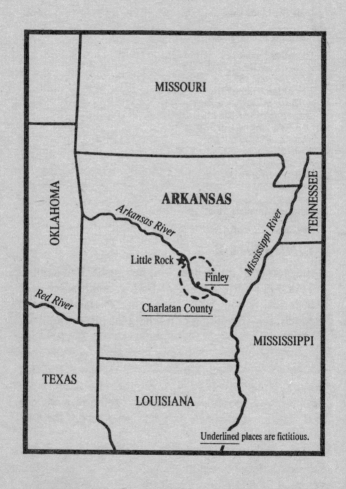

MISSOURI

OKLAHOMA

ARKANSAS

Arkansas River

TENNESSEE

Little Rock ★

Finley

Mississippi River

Red River

Charlatan County

MISSISSIPPI

TEXAS

LOUISIANA

Underlined places are fictitious.

Chapter One

"Breaking his oath and resolution, like a twist of rotten silk." Shakespeare.

If only it had happened during the romance of King Arthur and Camelot, Barbara thought with a sigh the old-timers around the courthouse would have called hangdog.

Excalibur and Lancelot and all that purity and Holy Grail business. Or at the turn of the century, when a man's word could cause shoot-outs in the streets and a woman's honor could unsheathe swords in the first mist of dawn. At least, in the sweetness of summer, when the sky was alive with blue and the sun was beating in and out of the pines and pale, fragile orchids were nestled cozily in the banks of the river.

Then she could have joined a convent. Or she could have killed herself with quiet dignity in the attic. Then, in later years, Julia and Granna could take out her portrait and reminisce with the boarders at Sunday dinner.

Sweet Emma Parker would adore the drama of that. "Barbara was such a fine artiste," she would recall as she lovingly fingered the porcelain brooch at her throat. "One of my best piano students. Curving her fingers on the keys and lifting at the ends of phrases precisely so. And her staccatos? Sheer perfection. She could have played in the Tchaikovsky competitions, you know. Tsk-tsk, such a pity..."

Mr. Katt and Edward Wheeler would look at each other with the tacit hostility that hadn't varied an iota in all the years they'd taken room and board in Julia Regent's house.

"Yes, Miss Emma," Mr. Katt would agree in his protective basso profundo, as if he were gathering evidence in one of his investigations. (And also because he'd had a yen for sweet Emma Parker for the past forty years.)

"Barbara was a good, upright citizen, all right. She never broke the rules and took care of public property. In all the years I was sheriff of Charlatan County, I don't think she got one traffic ticket. A fine young woman. It doesn't stand to reason..."

Edward Wheeler probably wouldn't say anything. Edward had a space between his center teeth, which tended to make him lisp, something he was more than a trifle sensitive about and which always made Mr. Katt certain that the small, nearsighted accountant for Charlatan County was hiding something.

Barbara glimpsed her reflection in the night-silvered mirror of Lucy's car window. Again she sighed. It wasn't the turn of the century. King Arthur was dead, long live the king. And Finley wasn't Camelot; it was Arkansas.

It wasn't even summer. It was three o'clock in the morning, and outside, on the first day of spring, snow was banked against the houses on Castle Park Road like freakish, scooped-out clamshells. Uptown, trees that had yesterday been lacy with buds were now huddling together for warmth, and the courthouse square was stiff and shivering. The whole county was wearing its ice-crusted telephone wires like a woman committing the faux pas of wearing all her diamond necklaces at once.

But then, everything was wrong side out. Her own mother, Julia Regent, one of the kindest women in the world, was sitting in her room wondering what she would say to people. Lucy Levitt, her very best friend, was hunched over her steering wheel like a geriatric case.

"Can you see where you're going?" Barbara asked.

Lucy reached up to scrub at the condensation on the windshield with a wadded, tear-soaked Kleenex. "Does it matter?"

"Only if you're a sled dog."

"We could probably make better time if I were." Lucy laughed briefly.

They both smiled to prolong the amusement, but their moods slipped gradually back to the bleak task at hand.

At last a steeple pierced the night. Lucy gamely aimed the car at it. The tire chains played a brief little cha-cha as they laid out a trail across the parking lot of the First Lutheran Church.

Barbara reminded herself to be strong. She must remember who she was now. How many thousands of times had she heard *that* since the day she was born twenty-five years ago?

"Barbara Lee Regent, you're the great-great-granddaughter of Thaddeus T. Finley, and don't you ever forget it."

She had all that matchless Southern blood running through her veins, after all. Her middle name had been passed down from General Robert E. Lee himself, because one hundred and ten years before, Robert's wife, a dear friend of Thaddeus's Marie, once stopped off in Finley to help select the site where the old stone courthouse stood like a sentry guarding the Arkansas River.

Of course, Finley had a new courthouse now, one that really looked like a courthouse. The old one had become the Annex. She and Lucy had adjoining offices there. On Lucy's door the sign read County Employment Office, on her own, Human Resources.

Since the iron foundry had closed, her own business at Human Resources was booming. Forty percent unemployment. Bad conditions becoming worse. People and families falling apart. She had carried on in the fine old Thaddeus T. tradition, naturally; above and beyond her adult reading classes and Big Sister duties, she'd organized working-mother support groups and family counseling to deal with the effects of prolonged unemployment. Night and day she worked on the industrial committee and on the community services committee and with the Charlatan County welfare office.

And now, because of one stupid, foolish mistake, one she couldn't believe she'd made, she stood to disappoint them all. She would shatter the Finley mystique. She would go down in history as "that woman."

She walked into the deserted church with Lucy and stood inhaling the cold perfume of wedding flowers and new candles. She arranged her face with a stoicism Thaddeus would have been proud of.

Lucy was more fortunate. She was only the mayor's daughter. She could sag against the church door, cover her face with mittened hands and sob bitterly.

"Oh, Barb," she grieved now, her words muffled with wool, "this wasn't a good idea."

"You have a better one?" Barbara hated the icy distance of her voice.

"We could hire someone."

"To do the dirty work?"

"It's too painful, Barb."

"It's the business of marriage to be painful."

The moment the shabby words were uttered, Barbara put her arms around Lucy's shoulders. "Hush now, Luce," she whispered tenderly into the knitted cap that made Lucy look like an adorable child on Christmas morning. "You're right, it is too painful. I shouldn't have brought you here." She kissed the tip of Lucy's ear. "I want you to go home now, sweetie. I'll get this done. It's no big deal, really. I'll see you at the office tomorrow."

Amazed, Lucy lifted her ruined face. She loved Barbara Regent more than any human alive. Maybe the Levitts were destined to love Finleys; her own widowed father had once proposed to Barbara's mother, Julia Regent.

But being Barbara's friend was hard. Barbara was good, and Barbara was smart. The trouble was, Barbara could never just kick back and shut her eyes to things. Maybe it went with the territory—working so closely with people, going into their homes, seeing much more of their bad than their good. Barbara was a champion of endless lost causes.

But everyone admired her. Most of the time Lucy wished she *were* Barbara. Except—and they had joked about it all their lives—Lucy had a prettier nose.

Barbara had always scoffed when the subject of her nose came up. "Do you honestly think I care about my nose? Workhorses don't have time to worry about mundane things like noses. Why, workhorses don't even know they have noses!"

That was one of the things Lucy liked most about Barbara. Barbara knew her looks were average, and she settled happily for that: average height, average weight, average waist and average breasts. And an average face— good bone structure and classic features that would age magnificently, but her nose did tend to have an endearing little Streisand protuberance.

Early on Barbara had cleverly learned the value of trade-offs, something Lucy had never been very good at. Barbara's hooked nose—"Not hooked, dear," Julia often gently reminded her daughter, "*aquiline*. You inherited your aquiline nose from your great-great-grandfather Finley."—was pleasantly offset by a wide mouth that was quick to smile and merry sapphire eyes that always seemed to know a delicious secret.

Barbara's best trick was to draw attention to her mouth with artfully applied gloss, and she emphasized her eyes with elaborate, funky glasses. She didn't have tons of clothes, but they were backbreakingly expensive. She accentuated them with Hermès scarves and antique shawls or Ralph Lauren jodhpur boots and pieces of Granna Finley's nineteenth-century jewelry.

If Barbara had a true glory, it was her hair. Practically every woman in Finley envied Barbara's hair, and some tried to get it out of a bottle at Kitty's Headline. A stunning, natural silver-blond color, it never needed to be permed or put through any of the customary tortures. With its midback length it took any style, and though Barbara clipped it, twisted it, frizzed it, moussed it or pulled it all up in a topknot, it collected all her "averages"—aquiline nose and all—and turned them into a cunning, eye-catching whole.

But now, in the cold, dark church, with her glory tucked beneath a depressing wool turban and her mood as stormy as that outdoors, Lucy thought there was little about Barbara that anyone would envy.

"The office?" she chided. "Tomorrow? You're insane, Barbara, d'you know that? I've always said you were a masochist, and this proves it. Through and through, you like to hurt."

Barbara smiled only because she knew it would make Lucy feel better. "I've worked hard for two years on this contract with Abrams and Bean, and out of the goodness of my heart, too, I might add." She laughed mirthlessly. "Now it's time to take the glory. It's mine, and I want it."

The oblique irony was lost on Lucy. "That contract won't keep you warm on lonely nights, Barbara Regent."

"Really? I would have sworn it whispered a few sweet nothings in my ear."

The cold draft blowing around their feet was as uncomfortable as the strained limits of their friendship.

"Don't make fun of me, Barb," whispered Lucy.

Barbara covered her mouth in regret. You don't call off a wedding twenty-four hours beforehand for no reason! Lucy had railed all afternoon, tear-streaked and exasperated with the bride. You don't call off a wedding! And if you do, you tell your maid of honor why!

But if Barbara told her secret, Lucy wouldn't despise John Woodward for what he'd done. She would wonder if something couldn't still be "worked out." Lucy was like that. Lucy could never bear it when things went wrong; Lucy had affairs with married men because she didn't want to hurt their feelings.

"I'm sorry, Luce," Barbara said, feeling like a criminal.

"At least you're Finley's heroine now," Lucy said with a sigh. "You've proved you could do what no one else in this town could do. You've coaxed Abrams and Bean to bring their new paper mill below the Mason-Dixon line.

Right here. To our little town. Maybe people won't talk so very much."

People wouldn't talk? In Finley? To keep from bursting into hysterical laughter Barbara stooped and began rolling up the rustling white satin runner the florist had stretched the length of the center aisle. People were already talking. But not about the called-off wedding.

"Hey, princess." The muffled, drunken whisper came from her telephone receiver late one night. "Say, I just thought I'd call and say hello. I didn't wake you up, did I?"

Half asleep, she wasn't able to get all the circuits working in her brain. She pulled up onto an elbow and scrubbed her face. "Who is this?"

"Aw, why don't you just call me an admirer?"

Awake now, she fumbled for the light beside her bed. "Who is this? I'm not talking to anyone I don't know."

"Now that don't really matter, does it, princess? You jus' tell old John for me that he's marryin' himself a prime piece of goods, and I oughta know. But, hey, I like it. Lip-smackin' little rear you got there, princess. 'Course, I'm partial to rears myself. Always have been. I might clue you in on one thing, though. If you'd take it all off while you're sunbathin' up on that fancy deck of yours, you wouldn't have that little white strip goin' round. Know what I mean? Not that I mind, understand . . ."

Lightning, in all its killing, destructive glory, could not have horrified Barbara more. She felt as if it had struck deep inside her. Somehow, some way, the vile man knew. He had seen the photographs. But how? *How* had he seen them?

She proved an even greater naïveté by whispering, "Why are you saying these things to me?"

His laughter had turned her blood cold. "I think you oughta ask John that question, princess. He knows. And he shows and tells, ain't that handy? Ole John, he's a shower and teller, that's what he is. Look, gotta go, princess, but I tell you what. If you ever get tired of gettin' it on with ole John, just let me know. I can make you feel real good—"

"Damn it, who is this? Don't hang—"

Click.

No, Barbara didn't dare tell Lucy the truth, not yet, and she clutched her friend's words as if they were a medicine to heal her battered soul.

In a way she actually was Finley's heroine. *She* was the one who had refused to give up when doors started slamming shut. *She* was the one who had convinced Abrams and Bean's corporate heads to come south, though they were impossibly condescending; *she* bore the sting of waspish secretaries and the power-swollen egos of flunkies, insecure middlemen too frightened for their jobs to make quick decisions, thereby delaying her for weeks on end.

Thanks to her, the engineer was committed now: one Lewis A. Paccachio. She had his résumé in her desk. Wheels of progress. A paper mill was coming to Finley.

But jobs only put food on the table. Scandal was the real bread and butter of narrow-minded towns. She would be the morsel they would chew on for months, years.

"So you think people won't talk, eh?" Barbara rose, her arms spilling white satin and her soul spilling its fears. "Where have you been the last twenty-five years of your life, Luce?"

Lucy wasn't used to such rancor in her friend. "You need a vacation, Barbara."

"Run?" *Yes, run, Barbara, as fast as you can. Leave this town before it's too late.* She shook her head. "No."

"But a vacation isn't running, darling."

"I can't leave the mill project."

"Darn it, Barbara, the mill project can get along without you for a few days."

"In less than a month, people will be pouring into this town." Barbara pretended jaded resignation to disguise the misery unraveling in her chest. "The engineer's flying in from West Berlin in a couple of weeks. I just can't take off, Luce. It'll screw everything up."

Lucy had no opinions about that.

"Mr. Pac-cach-i-o." Barbara rolled the name around in her mouth for a moment, then grimaced. "Can you imagine the redneck jokes Finley will conjure up for 'Paccachio'?" She tried to picture what the man would look like. It didn't matter, as long as Paccachio put the town to work. Once that was done and she knew everything would be all right, *then* she would leave, and Finley could talk about her until the Arkansas River ran uphill.

"I expect Paccachio can't wait to get here and show all us country hicks how it's done," she declared as she discarded her musings. "You don't think I would go on vacation and miss that, sweet child?"

Lucy wanted to remind Barbara that if things had gone as they were supposed to, she and John Woodward would've been on their honeymoon tomorrow.

"Then lead on," she said with dour resignation. "Let's get this over with."

Lucy reached behind them to flip on the light switch. The fluorescent lights stammered in the coldness, and Barbara, stepping swiftly nearer, touched the switch with a gloved fingertip.

"Hard deeds are best done in the dark," she whispered.

Lucy watched Barbara draw two folded garbage bags from the pocket of her coat. Like some doppelgänger, some ghostly counterpart of her once sparkling, vivacious self, she moved through the church with only the streetlight's sad glow to guide her.

Taking one of the bags, Lucy numbly followed from pew to pew. With frozen fingers she collected white satin streamers and bows and tiny sprigs of baby's breath and stuffed them into the bag. And the exquisite white rosebuds that had been repeated in the bridal bouquet.

Together they moved to the candle holders and stood on tiptoe to pluck the fragile white tapers from their fittings. The candles made protesting *thunks* as they struck one another in the bag and broke into pieces.

"I couldn't be so cool about it," Lucy mumbled.

But Barbara didn't hear. In a separate part of herself, she was burning with fury and pain each time a candle broke and a rose petal was crushed. Some savage, uncivilized part of her thirsted for revenge upon John Woodward. No one would take the time to consider that John was a professional photographer, nor the fact that the photos were not lewd but fine, artistic work. Nor that she and John had dated for four years. *It was between you and me, John!*

She couldn't even hope for justice in the natural order of things, could she? Culprits never paid for their crimes. It was an incontestable fact of life: the small were historically stepped upon by the large, the poor were trampled by the rich, the trusting were crushed by the exploiters, and women who gave to men in blind trust paid the highest price of all.

Fight back, Barbara. Don't just take it like a wimp.

Fight back with what? My good name? That won't last long.

Find the power.

Power? She had no power! Money was power. Great beauty was power. Genius was power. Innocence was power, and goodness knows, she wasn't innocent.

Now, What's-his-face Paccachio—*he* had power. At least twenty pieces of material in her files had Paccachio's name on them, proving how powerful he was: Mr. Paccachio this and Mr. Paccachio that, Mr. Paccachio had been with the company for fifteen years, Mr. Paccachio had traveled all over the world for Abrams and Bean, Mr. Paccachio's credits included aircraft factories and embassy complexes, energy plants and government projects and hotel chains and on and on and on. Mr. Paccachio was a virtual phenomenon!

All of which put the great Mr. Paccachio in the group who stepped upon the small and trampled the poor and crushed the trusting, didn't it? She could see him now—living it up in fine old style in West Berlin, making all his money and spending it on expensive German cuisine and German beer, a gorgeous fräulein on each arm, no doubt. While she, great-great-granddaughter of Thaddeus T. Finley, was running amok in Arkansas!

What a vile mood she was in. But she couldn't help it; at three o'clock in the morning the truth was like a bath of acid. She had made a terrible, terrible mistake with her life, and if she could have cleaned away the stain, she would have scrubbed herself with sand. But chipping at her bones with a chisel wouldn't have purged her. Knowing her failure was the grain of sand in the oyster's shell; it was relentless and merciless, and it polished a fine, cutting edge on her resentment for Mr. Lewis A. Paccachio. Without ever having laid eyes on him, she thought she hated the man.

At three o'clock in the morning, while the snow was blowing along Castle Park Road and Barbara was having the worst day of her life, the sun was climbing to a splendid zenith over West Berlin.

There, among the soaring glass-and-steel structures of the city that some called the most decadent in the world, business executives were rushing to their appointments, smart leather attaché cases swinging in their hands. Along the older, twisting, cobbled lanes, shopkeepers were taking leisurely coffee breaks beneath ivy-covered Gothic spires.

At the spanking new Regency Hotel the picture-taking was already in progress. Allie Tremaine would be on-site all morning. For an astronomical amount of money the public relations crew she headed would film a piece on Abrams and Bean and spirit all the information back to New York in time to affect the next day's statistics on Wall Street.

Since the first segment of the propaganda project required the engineers, the head honchos of Abrams and Bean and the financiers, it was Allie's job to collect them beneath one roof. She was presently working around landscapers who were installing last-minute exterior lights in the clumps of dwarf spruce while, inside, decorators were hysterically trying to finish the carpet around the newly installed hotel personnel, most of whom hadn't a fig's worth of knowledge about what they were doing yet.

The U.S. officials were arriving in limousines that glided, whisper-smooth, beneath the canopies. A Mercedes-Benz and a Jaguar purred to a halt. Doors swept open to spill the German money men.

Allie stepped with disregard over cables and elbowed her way through management hired by the hotel.

"Gentlemen, please." She raised her voice to a metallic decibel. "Listen up, everyone. Please read your cards and see where you're supposed to be." Under her breath she added crudely, "Then get your butts over there."

The executives were much too involved with matters of prestige and professional mistrust to notice. They gazed around themselves to see who was watching, and they straightened their lapels with fidgeting hands.

Cursing them all, turning so that the breeze caught the silk of her pink suit and threw out the strands of her jet-black hair, Allie spotted her cameraman watching buxom German girls through the lens of his camera.

Walking over, she said from behind an abrasive smile, "Curtis, if you don't get off your skinny duff and help me get these execs in place, we'll be late for our appointment with the chancellor."

No love had ever been lost between Curtis Gregory and Allie Tremaine. Allie placed cameramen on a general par with golf caddies and waiters, none of whom she would waste a smile upon.

Turning, Curtis gave her a slow, immune grin. "Havin' a problem?" His brows wiggled Groucho Marx style. "Sir?"

With an impatient stamp of her pink pump, Allie glared. "Stick it in your ear, Curtis," she hissed. "Now get in there and find the engineers. It's ten o'clock, for pity's sake!"

Pleased with himself, Curtis blandly lowered his mini-cam and shuffled through a gleaming door that would, in a very few days, be manned by a uniformed attendant. He fished a flask from his pocket and expertly pried out the stopper with his thumb as he walked.

Two men passed, carrying a framed painting the size of a wall. Curtis tuned his radar for Reception, tossing down a shot of smooth bourbon as he went. Behind the reception desk a clerk shifted his gaze up from his bifocals and caught a strong whiff of liquor. He narrowed his eyes in disapproval; Americans were so disgustingly lacking in self-discipline.

"Does that thing work?" Curtis blithely indicated the switchboard.

The man gave a pained look and said through his nose, "Of course it works, sir."

"Would you crank it up then and page Mr. Lewis Paccachio and Bumper O'Banyon?"

Before the clerk could comply, a tall, rangy man lazily detached himself from one end of the marble-topped counter. From the deep center of the bourbon's glow, Curtis watched him move forward—not a particularly handsome man but a magnetic one who had only to walk into a room for people to feel his formidable presence. Deeply tanned, with indolent unconcern for the flurry around him, he was hooking a pair of sunglasses to the breast pocket of his suit, anchoring them by an earpiece.

Curtis grinned. He and Paccachio went way back. The man had to be at least thirty-eight, maybe thirty-nine, but he never seemed to age, and he appeared no more at ease in a suit than he had five years ago when they'd first met in the Philippines. The scar had still been new in Manila, angry and red, but now it was a thin white line zigzagging out of a quarter-size patch of snowy hair at his temple. He seemed at ease with it now, though it scored his left temple and shot down the side of his jaw, where it splintered into his neck and disappeared beneath the stiffly starched blue of his collar. Rather than marring him, however, the scar tended to trigger images of rakish New Orleans gam-

blers or bloodthirsty pirates off the coast of the Hebrides.
Coupled with lady-killer dimples that winked even when
he talked, it was a very nifty item, Paccachio's scar.

"Curtis," he said, extending his hand in a friendly way.
"How's the Japanese coming?"

Laughing, Curtis blushed. "Now you know I don't
catch on to languages the way you do, Mr. Paccachio."

The older man grinned. "Well, I think it helps when
you're going to starve if you don't." He indicated the other
side of the lobby with a nudge of his chin. "If you're
looking for Bumper, you'll probably find him by the cigarette machine."

Laughing, Curtis turned down the corners of his mouth.
"I knew it. He couldn't quit."

"Oh, he did, he did." Lewis chuckled. "Now he just
buys them and folds, spindles and mutilates. Bumper isn't
very happy today, Curtis. He had to cancel a flight just to
make this gig."

"We'll make it as painless as possible, Mr. Paccachio, I
promise. If you'll go outside and look for Allie, she'll tell
you what to do. Thirty minutes, max." As he started to
walk away, he looked back, winking. "If she tells you
otherwise, tell her to . . . tell her that *I* said to stick it in her
ear."

With pleasure, Lewis thought as he strolled across the
seething hotel lobby and stepped through the door into the
blinding sunlight. Allie Tremaine was a man-hater, but her
ambitions outweighed her hatreds. The only man in the
corporation she hadn't slept with was probably himself.
He'd once told her that if she worked hard enough she
would someday screw herself all the way to the bottom.
She had not forgiven, nor had she forgotten.

He was reaching for his sunglasses when he glimpsed the
twinkle of her gold bracelet. He winced. Maybe he was

getting over Sunny; for some reason Allie didn't turn him off so badly today.

She approached him on a stunning pair of legs, consulting a clipboard as she came, and he considered letting everything go and being attracted; he *tried* to be attracted.

"Mr. Paccachio," she said as she walked up, shuffling papers with long, soft fingers that had never done a hard day's work in their life. "We're so glad you could work us into your busy schedule."

Smiling thinly, Lewis didn't offer to shake her hand. "It wasn't a problem, Ms. Tremaine."

"Otherwise you wouldn't have?"

"You got it."

Lewis raised a brow and expected Allie to give one of her famous snorts and stalk off. Instead she smiled, and Lewis could feel the wheels spinning in her mind. She sensed something was different about him. She was wondering if she had anything to gain, careerwise, by getting him into bed.

Her kind of flesh appraisal was very much out of vogue these days, he could have reminded her, and if there was one thing Allie had, deep in her genetic material, it was an appreciation of vogue.

"Where's Mr. O'Banyon?" she asked. "He was supposed to be here at ten o'clock."

"He'll be along."

"We don't have all day." As if he had just used up his allotted five minutes, she consulted her wristwatch—a Gucci, Lewis noted wryly. She studied a script with penciled notes scribbled in the margins. He glimpsed his own name in red. He squinted at the group of men waiting beside the front canopy.

She said, pretending to be preoccupied, "Ah, I was meaning to ask you, Mr. Paccachio, will you be going back to the States after this is over? After the photography session today?"

Curious to see if he'd heard the underlying invitation in her tone or if his ego was playing tricks, Lewis narrowed his eyes until they were slits against the sun and let the sharp lemon scent of her fragrance fill his nose. Her skin seemed almost iridescent in the sunlight. How easy it was to imagine how darkly nippled her breasts would be, how blackly thatched the curls at the apex of her legs.

She smoothed the side of one hip with her hand, and her appraisal strayed to his waist, where the vest buttoned about his ribs. Her pink lips parted. If he'd reached out and touched her, she wouldn't have pulled away. It wasn't worth the trouble.

"I'll be going back tomorrow," he said blandly, and wondered if he should begin to worry about his lack of interest in women. "My family's . . . The boys are with me."

Allie gave him a pursed little smile as she ran that information through her brain, wrote him off as a loss and dismissed him with a swivel of her lovely hips. She walked off toward the executives. "Well, have a nice trip, Mr. Paccachio."

Bitch! Like a sullen child, Lewis strode to where a lavish sign bore the heavy brass letters, REGENCY HOTEL. The men were gazing into the open sky at his own construction.

It's a plane! It's a bird! he wanted to cup his hands and mockingly hawk.

"Over here, Lewis!" Reuben Abrams waved the arm of a fine Italian suit. "I want you to meet the men whose money you've been spending."

Lewis nodded blandly. People were the same the world over; they wanted the best of your labor at dirt-cheap prices. Harry Bean waited with his hand draped through his lapels like Napoleon returning from the campaign.

"We're very pleased, Mr. Paccachio," he said, and deigned to remove his manicured, diamond-crusted fingers. "Very pleased, indeed."

Lewis wondered how many of those diamonds his own fifteen years of hard labor had bought. "Thank you, Mr. Bean."

"It turned out much better than we expected," said another man.

"And only a week behind schedule. I think that's phenomenal."

After giving the strangers the usual necessary seconds to stop staring at the scar, Lewis curled one side of his mouth in mild self-deprecation. "You can't rush quality," he intoned, as was expected of him.

"Exactly."

Behind him Allie Tremaine's diplomatic voice asked, as if she didn't know and hadn't known for the past two years, "Where's the next big job now, Mr. Abrams?"

As Reuben Abrams leaned toward the foisted microphone, Lewis glanced aside to see Bumper O'Banyon reluctantly join the group. Curtis Gregory, having taken his cue from Allie, was moving in to focus.

"Actually, we have several things going, Allie," Abrams explained to the lens, clearing his throat importantly. "A large aircraft facility in Japan, as you know. And we have two power plants beginning construction in the States, one in Texas and one in Nevada. Then there's the paper mill in south Arkansas, of course. Mr. Paccachio, here—" Reuben clapped a magnanimous hand upon

Lewis's shoulder "—has just contracted for that. I'm sure he'll do us a fine job."

Of course you're sure, you greedy bastard, Lewis thought bitterly and smiled. *And you don't give a good damn about why I took a colossal cut in pay to go to this godforsaken place to build the damn thing.*

The hand upon his shoulder briefly mauled his suit, and Reuben Abrams's voice assumed a fatherly tone. "You're going to like Arkansas, Lewis. I went down myself a few weeks back. Fine place, fine place."

As Abrams gestured expansively, Lewis withdrew his shoulder. He said, "You liked it, eh?"

"You bet. It has everything—scenery, a slower pace, that great hometown feeling where everyone turns out for Little League. Talk about your peace and quiet—everybody loves everybody, just one big happy family. Fine mayor—a good man. A woman's in charge of their committee, you know."

Lewis wasn't sure why he put a hokey expression on his face. Maybe because he knew that Reuben Abrams also believed in UFOs and was so out of touch that he thought his own wife didn't know why Allie Tremaine was on the payroll.

"Is that a fact?" he said.

"Not actually in charge," Reuben corrected himself, "but she's done the legwork. When we first began negotiating, I learned early on that if we wanted quick responses to go to her. Good head on her shoulders."

Lewis stole a glance at O'Banyon and knew exactly what the older engineer was thinking as he rolled his eyes.

"I'm looking forward to meeting her, sir," Lewis lied.

"Good man."

Allie Tremaine was waving at Curtis to stop the camera. "Arkansas, Mr. Paccachio?" she purred, and moved closer to indicate that he should adjust the knot of his tie, which had twisted askew. "You're actually going to Arkansas?"

Smiling coldly, Lewis thrust his arm in warning for Allie to keep her hands off him. He adjusted the tie and strained his neck against the bit of the collar. "What's wrong with Arkansas?"

"Why, nothing, of course."

"Arkansas appeals to me just now."

Frowning, but getting the message loud and clear, Allie moved on to the more promising corporate giants who were happy to explain their business with the respect she deserved.

"Arkansas, Lew?" Bumper O'Banyon mimicked Allie in his gravelly voice. Laughing, he said, "You really are going to take that little hick job, aren't you? With all those hillbillies?"

Bumper O'Banyon was the only man Lewis knew who could look as if he were standing up when he was still sitting down. Bumper had a beer belly and a wide gash of a mouth and small, boxer's ears. His nickname came from his floor-bouncing days, but his real name was James. His nose had been fractured more times than he could remember, but his heart was pure gold.

Lewis said, "You got a problem with that, O'Banyon?"

"Me? Good ole Bumper?"

Bumper probed around in his inner breast pocket for a new pack of chewing gum and pulled out a fresh stick. He offered one to Lewis, and Lewis shook his head. As was Bumper's habit, he slipped it into Lewis's pocket, anyway.

"Hell, no, Lew," he said. "I was just wonderin' what Sunny thinks of goin' to live in the Ozarks, that's all."

Sunshine glinted off a panel of glass and flashed into Lewis's eyes. Taking out his sunglasses, he fit them on his face. No one knew yet. No one in the company knew that he'd awakened one morning and looked over at Sunny's side of the bed to find it empty.

He didn't quite believe it himself—his mad dash through the rented flat in his skivvies, snatching open closets and jerking drawers off their tracks, shaking his three sons awake, bundling them into the car and sprinting half-dressed down the front walk of the apartment building they'd lived for the past two years.

He had battled traffic all the way to the airport while a trio of intelligent, smooth-skinned faces stared back at him from the rearview mirror as if they'd been drafted and thrust into the front line of combat, empty-handed.

Great crystal tears were trembling upon Rick's lashes. At eleven, he hadn't yet learned how to accept life's crimes against innocence. "My head hurts," he said from where he slumped, heartbroken, upon his spine.

"Yeah." Charlie, thirteen, had nearly disappeared into the floorboard, and his one syllable translated from international adolescentese to mean: *My whole life's a foul-up. So why aren't you doing something about it?*

At fifteen, Steven availed himself of the Fifth Amendment and said nothing, but his eyes were grave.

"Yeah, well..." Lewis mumbled. The boys didn't yet know how many ways a man could prostitute himself in the name of the sacred "family unit."

When Rick leaned forward, hungry for reassurance, Lewis's heart threatened to burst. He laid his hand compassionately upon the neck of his youngest son and lied through his teeth. "It'll be all right, Rick. You'll see."

"No, it won't. She's gone. Didn't she love us?"

"Shut up, stupid," Steven growled at his brother.

Charlie, caught in the middle as usual, worried his braces with his tongue and said, "Yeah. Shut up, stupid."

"I just wish she hadn't left." Rick sobbed with unashamed hopelessness.

"I wish I could tell you she'll change her mind." Lewis divided his attention between the congested highway and them. "But whether she does or not has nothing whatsoever to do with you kids. You have to believe that. And you can't forget that she loves you very much, and this . . . this—"

Catching sight of his own disbelief in the rearview mirror, Lewis snapped his mouth shut. By some miracle, he found a parking place, and when he twisted on the seat, he winced from the accusations of their faces.

"Look, guys," he began uncertainly. "I know you'd like to come inside with me—"

"You mean, we can't?"

Lewis pleaded silently with his oldest son to help him. "I'm not sure she'll still be here, Steven. And if she is, I really don't want you all to have to hear what we might say."

"We've heard you fight before," Steven sullenly declared, and ducked his head.

"Which is all the more reason I don't want you to hear it again!" Lewis bit his tongue as three pairs of solemn eyes threw darts into his chest.

"I'm sorry." Lewis pinched the bridge of his nose. "Look, there won't be any fighting, I promise."

"Are you going to ask her to come back?"

"I'll get down on my knees and grovel, Steven." And for the sake of those three precious boys, he would.

With a look of male commiseration, Steve told his father that he understood much more about men and women than Lewis could possibly guess. "All she wanted was to stay in one place, you know. The most we ever stayed in one place was three years."

"Yes, I know."

Sighing, Lewis bleakly opened the car door. Without making all the rash promises that were in his heart to say, he climbed out and dodged traffic, leaving a trail of unhappy pedestrians behind him as he sprinted through the terminal doors.

After a frustrating battle with a ticket agent that got him nowhere, Lewis finally leaned across the counter and came within an inch of grabbing the man by the necktie. "Do you remember her or not, buddy?" he snarled.

"I think she went that way, sir," the man choked.

Leaving the agent complaining to his associate, Lewis spun on his heel and strode hotly through the terminal like a man with mad dogs yipping at his heels. As he went, he rehearsed futile speeches and demeaning acts of contrition. He would remind her of the Arkansas job. He'd already accepted it, for heaven's sake. She knew that. In a matter of weeks they would be back in the States.

The company had said Finley was a quaint, picturesque little town nestled in the loblolly pines along the Arkansas River. It would be peaceful and quiet there—none of the rat race and the nasty little head games people played. He would play things differently this time. He'd buy Sunny a *real* house on a *real* street. Maybe that would calm her down some, give her some stability. She could join the P.T.A. and grow roses and gossip. The boys could join the football team and ruin their knees.

In the first seconds when he saw her, he stumbled to a halt. Sunny always had been one of the most beautiful women he'd ever seen. Her lovely head was bent, and her face was hidden behind a shimmering curtain of silky brown hair. At the memories of how many ways she'd found to waste that beauty—on men and booze and God knew what else—such an anger rose in his throat, he didn't know whether to rush up and throw his arms about her and kiss her, or jerk her up and shake her.

She didn't see him as he approached. Lewis wondered, as he gazed down at the crown of her head and teetered upon the edge of some gaping chasm in his life, if he hadn't known all along that this final moment of reckoning would come. And he also wondered at the phenomenal stupidity of a man who could kid himself for sixteen long years.

She looked up. "Lew."

Lewis watched her trace the path of the scar with dazed, teary eyes. Sometimes she said it made him look romantic and debonair, especially when he put on a tux, but he knew she said that to escape her guilt. Maybe that was when it all began to get away from them, when he was down there in the pitch-black water beneath the pier, snatching her from the jaws of death.

No. It had ended even before that. There were times when he thought it started ending the day it began.

"Sunny," he said softly as he stooped beside the swirl of her skirt and ignored the heads that turned curiously to see. "Please. You can't do this, Sunny."

But she had. She'd gotten one of those quick, heathen ends to a sixteen-year-old investment. Now he smiled unhappily at Bumper.

"Yeah, it's pretty hard imagining Sunny in Arkansas, all right," he said, and shrugged. "Hey, what're you going to do next? Take that Saudi job?"

Bumper turned down the sides of his mouth like a clown. "Too much hassle with the State Department on

that one. I really don't know yet, Lew. Go to L.A. Or
Dallas. Job shop, I guess."

"Why don't you come to Arkansas?"

The big man hesitated, as if he were having difficulty
connecting Arkansas with jobs. "*Arkansas?* Well, I don't
know, Lew..."

"The pay's terrible."

"Aw, it's just that—"

"Look, you can stay with us until you find a place."
Lewis tapped his scar with a fingertip. "You heard what
Abrams said, Bumper. A nice little woman's in charge.
Maybe you'll do yourself some good. I bet she secretly
likes Saturday night wrestling."

Bumper grinned, and Lewis gazed dramatically at the
sky and struck his chest with both fists, drawing in a deep
breath. "Clean livin' in small towns, Bumper. Clean livin',
pure hearts and vitamin C."

When Bumper O'Banyon laughed, the whole world took
notice. Now he threw back his great, shaggy head and
roared, making all the executives nearby raise their brows
with distaste.

He was still chuckling when he took a fresh focus upon
his friend's sober expression. "Good Lord Almighty,
you're serious, aren't you, Lew?"

"Dead."

Thinking of the weeks of apartment-hunting in L.A. he
would have to go through, Bumper heaved a thunderous
sigh. Then he thought of Sunny Paccachio's cooking. Before his mouth started to water, he dismissed the thought;
somehow he didn't think Sunny was doing much cooking
these days. Lewis was way too thin.

He scoured a beefy hand over his jaw, giving the momentary impression that he'd pushed his nose to the side.

"What th' heck?" he rumbled, and laughed deep in his belly. "When do we leave?"

Chapter Two

"Sorrow concealed, like an oven stopp'd, doth burn the heart to cinders." Shakespeare

And don't forget the wheelchair for Mrs. Frank's mother," Barbara reminded the county health nurse at noon Friday, three weeks after she and Lucy had sneaked into the First Lutheran Church like thieves and stripped it of the wedding flowers.

"Barbara, I really appreciate your helping me on this."

"Glad to do it, June."

"Listen, I was so sorry to hear about you and John. Is everything okay with you?"

For a moment Barbara's emotions pressed the rewind button. She closed her eyes, then took a deep breath of resolve. This was part of it, something she would have to live with for a long time: the wobbles of the head, the suppressed smirks, the hectoring silences that said, I heard it was all your fault.

"Yes," she said mildly. "I'm fine."

"Good. Let me know if there's anything I can do."

"Okay, June."

"Have a nice day, then."

"Thanks. You, too."

Barbara replaced the receiver and pushed back from the desk in her tiny office. There had been times the last weeks when she thought some kind of animal was slithering around inside her, hungrily gnawing through her nerves and chewing away her senses. But the truth was, she was actually beginning to heal. There had been no more drunken telephone calls in the middle of the night. She hadn't seen John or his family, and they hadn't seen her. And—one of her more high-profile nightmares—not a single person had walked into her mother's real-estate office and demanded, "Julia, what's all this filthy rotten gossip we hear about your daughter?"

Rising, Barbara replaced the file in the metal cabinet and hummed several bars of nonsense. Music? She smiled. She really was on the mend.

She was also due for her lunch break, and she'd been watching the clock all morning. Slipping into her duster-length jacket that spilled silk to the hem of her skirt, she stuffed a lovely orange into her shoulder bag and locked her office door. As she passed Lucy's office she rapped smartly on the window.

"Lucy," she called breezily, "I'm taking an extra half hour for lunch today. In case anyone calls, I'll be at Kitty's."

Turning, she walked resolutely down the hall toward the front door of the Annex, her footsteps a brisk murmur on the old worn tile, *You're going to be okay, you're going to be okay, you're going to be okay.*

Lucy's voice floated down the empty hall like a mist. "Barbara, wait a minute. No, finish filling out your form, Mr. Phelps, I'll be right back. Barbara . . ."

The familiar sound of Lucy's high heels made Barbara tilt her face to the ceiling in mock exasperation and turn around.

Lucy marched up, her face as prettily pink as her bouncy earrings. A fragrant cloud of Sin followed her. "What's up?" she asked, huffing.

Barbara arranged a smile appropriate for mending fences and reached back to grasp the long silvery braid that spilled down her back. She laid it across the space below her nose like a mustache.

"You're getting a nose job?" Lucy's eyes widened to saucer size.

"Silly, I'm getting my hair trimmed."

"The beauty shop?" Lucy placed her hand to Barbara's forehead. "You're not well. You're even smiling. Now I know you're sick."

Barbara pulled a face. "Infectious split ends."

"And you wore that great Bonnie Strauss outfit just to get your hair trimmed? You've got something split, all right. Your personality."

"One has to take excitement where one can find it, I always say." Laughing, Barbara lifted the open sides of her tie-dyed silk skirt so the flirtatious petticoat was visible all around. "Great, huh?"

"I hate you, Barbara Regent."

They both admired the total effect of the matching tie-dyed jacket with its flowing sleeves folded to Barbara's elbows and the low-cut halter top, also silk. Her feet were smartly shod in terra-khaki sling-back shoes.

"Are the shoes right?" Barbara asked with a sudden seizure of uncertainty.

Lucy laughed. "Perfect, Imelda."

Barbara shook her finger, then peered at it. "Since I'm on such a roll, maybe I'll get reckless and have a manicure. What color do you think? Something racy—" she assumed a sunken-cheeked model's pose "—or something that makes an elegant statement?"

"Don't get cute. This was my idea in the first place."

"Was it?" Teasing, Barbara tried another laugh and was surprised to find how easily it came. She liked it and tossed her head. "Then how about lending me ten dollars?"

At Lucy's sudden blink, followed by a fit of rippling giggles, Barbara's laughter emerged, too, full-blown and wonderfully minus any effort whatsoever. They laughed until, in a fit of theater, Lucy clasped both Barbara's hands in her own.

"God, Barbara—" she was melodramatically grave "—I begged you to get some therapy."

"You're so-oo easy." Barbara giggled, relishing the enjoyment of their familiar game of matching obscure quotes with even more obscure films, then matching the film's score with the composer. "Sydney Pollack in *Tootsie*."

"Composer? Quick, quick."

"Dave Grusin. Don't you know you can't master the master?"

"But I've been working so hard," Lucy whined.

"'Well, keep at it, Windows. Keep at it.'"

Lifting a forefinger to her temple, Lucy pondered. "Don't tell me, don't tell me. Ah . . . *Eddie and the Cruisers*."

"Wrong."

"*Risky Business*."

"Nope."

"Barbara!"

"*The Thing*. Enrico Morricone, composer. I gotta go, Luce."

To look at them, Barbara thought as she hugged her friend, one would not have guessed that she still hadn't confided in Lucy why she'd called off the wedding. *Be patient with me, my dear friend,* she wanted to say, but she walked instead to the Annex door, pushed it open and paused to turn in the opening.

"If anyone has a spaz attack while I'm gone," she called, "come over to Kitty's and get me."

Lucy waved her on. "What could happen?"

An Abrams and Bean truck rumbled deafeningly down Main Street, its muffler sloughing and slurping as it lugged a piece of earth-moving equipment out to the site of the mill where, so Lucy's father had reported in yesterday's *Finley Crier*, Mr. Paccachio had now arrived and was preparing to do his thing.

Barbara was forced to wait until the truck passed. "I don't know, Miss Levitt." She blew on the tips of her fingers and brushed them upon the lapel of her jacket in self-congratulation. "But as you can plainly see, Finley is in the midst of economic growth out here. Anything could happen."

"Go do something constructive."

Barbara intended to do exactly that.

Lewis Paccachio was bored. In only three days he was bored in a way he had never been bored before—bored with Arkansas, bored with his sons, bored with himself and, most of all, bored with his own loneliness.

He stood in the doorway of a mobile home office that had been pulled hastily onto the site. His hands were stuffed into the pockets of his work jeans. His back was hunched beneath an old, faded Levi's jacket, and he gazed from beneath the shadow of a billed cap.

In all directions, bulldozers, graders, earth-movers and backhoes were at work clearing land and piling brush, cutting roads and digging ditches for water lines and sewer systems. The power company was sinking poles for the electric lines. Scattered around the perimeter were huge Abrams and Bean rigs containing construction paraphernalia.

And he had the gall to be bored. Fishing a pair of leather gloves from his hip pocket, he sighed and started lankily out across the scraped land to examine the water line.

Over the noise of the equipment, a coughing muffler attracted his attention. Turning, he saw an antiquated Ford pickup parking alongside one of the company vehicles. He couldn't begin to estimate the number of trucks he'd seen with the same decal of Waylon Jennings or a Confederate flag on the rear window, the predictable macho gun rack mounted across the glass and rifles resting in the brackets.

Three men sat in the front seat of this truck. Two more hunkered on the bed. Climbing out of the passenger side, a man ground a cigarette out with the toe of his boot and walked across the hard-packed dirt toward him.

He was probably one of the most handsome men Lewis had seen in a long time—the kind of cocky, blond-haired hunk that hustled his way into women's bedrooms on a paying basis. On his jaw was the fashionable stubble of beard, and his plaid shirt was tucked into lean-hipped jeans. Over it he wore a sleeveless, quilted vest.

He might have been thirty. "I'm lookin' for a Mr. Pacatcho," he drawled when he was near enough to talk.

Lewis imagined the man running illegal whiskey on dark nights. Removing his gloves, he slipped them back into his hip pocket and extended his hand. "I'm Lewis Pacca-chio."

"Simon Bodine, Mr. Pacatcho. Glad t'meetcha."

"What can I do for you?"

Simon Bodine flashed a dazzling, ten-volt smile. "Hey, I talked to the lady in town. You know? Ms. Regent? She said I should give you this."

"Regent?"

Lewis was accepting the creased slip of paper as a stir at the truck distracted him. The men were climbing out and slouching against the fenders, their feet crossed at the ankles and their faces closed as if wooden shutters had been pulled together.

Uneasiness crawled like a caterpillar up the length of Lewis's spine. "Your truck?"

Bodine shrugged. "Me and my buddies are lookin' for work. That's why Ms. Regent sent us out here. You know, from over at the Annex. She's a good friend of mine." He crossed his fingers in the sign of closeness. "She said to ask for you personally, that you'd give us a job."

Irked, Lewis wanted to say that being a good friend of Ms. Regent didn't cut any ice with him, but he murmured politely, "Is that a fact?"

Bodine glanced over his shoulder at his friends and made a ceremony out of retrieving a folded cap from his pocket and fitting it onto his head so that the ends of his blond hair spiked from beneath the edges.

Lewis opened the note.

Dear Mr. Paccachio,

This will introduce Simon Bodine. Though this office isn't directly connected with employment, Human Resources has been working with Mr. Bodine's family in other ways. He's eager to get to work, and I feel certain you can find a place for him in construction. I'm looking forward to meeting you, since I've heard so many nice things about you.

Cordially,
B. Regent

Corporation politics had never been a matter of much concern to Lewis. He didn't like power games, and he shied clear of situations that would require him to play kissy-face or polish apples for the teacher.

Well, Ms. B. Regent, he thought, imagining someone as venomously likeable as P.R. maven Allie Tremaine, *you might have done just fine dealing with the desk jockeys, but this turf is mine, and you're sticking your female nose where it doesn't belong.*

Letting out his breath, he pondered the road graders in the distance. "Mr. Bodine, I think I should explain that we've only been on the site two days. I'm really not in a position to begin hiring just now."

The younger man shifted his weight and spit into the dirt. A scowl marred his features when he looked up. "You're puttin' me on, right?"

Sidelong, Lewis glimpsed, in the distance, pennons of dust streaming over the treetops where the new road was being cleared. Bumper and the boys: his own idea, of course, bringing them out from school, wanting them to feel involved in his job since they were going to have considerably less spending money in their pockets. And also because his bruised ego could use the help.

"Why should I put you on?" he said.

Bodine scratched the stubble on his chin. "You're not hirin'?"

Lewis shook his head. "Not right now."

"Then I think we've got us a little communication problem here, Mr. Pacatcho."

A tendon jerked sharply behind Lewis's eyes. "How's that?"

"Looks t'me like you've done a lot of hirin'."

Overhead, clouds momentarily blocked out the sun. Lewis was developing a distinct dislike for Mr. Simon Bodine, and he wanted him off the site. Now.

"The men you see," he grudgingly explained, "have been contracted for this job for months, Mr. Bodine. Some of them have worked with me all over the world. I can assure you there'll be plenty of job opportunities for the county once the plant construction reaches a certain point. But right now, I'm not hiring."

Lewis could have added that Abrams and Bean's policy was to use their own crews on construction, to be supplemented by locals only as residual day labor. He was surprised that Ms. Regent wasn't aware of that fact; it didn't say much for her being on top of the job.

The Suburban was coming into view, skimming across the cleared expanse, dust rolling. Hardly had it stopped than the doors flew open and three jeans-clad bodies tumbled out. Lewis wished Bumper hadn't chosen this particular moment to return with the boys.

Bodine seemed fascinated by the youngsters, and he drawled around his grin, "I guess you wouldn't mind telling me where these contracted men come from." He jabbed a thumb over his shoulder toward the machinery.

"As a matter of fact, I would mind."

"Discrimination." Bodine's grin suddenly grew ugly. "Is that what you're tryin' to tell me, Mr. Pacatcho?"

Several things were going on at once now, all of them beyond Lewis's ability to control. One of the men at the truck, having apparently received the sign from Bodine, had reached into the cab and lifted a rifle from the rack. He and the other three men continued to walk forward: The Magnificent Four. His own sons, having run ahead of Bumper O'Banyon, were completely unaware of anything but the good time they planned to have horsing around.

Bumper, however, had hesitated and was sizing up the situation. *Get them the hell out of here!* Lewis wanted to shout, though as yet he wasn't quite sure why.

"Hi, Dad," called Rick as he raced up and came to a laughing, skidding halt, thick red dust settling upon the hems of his jeans.

Charlie, with his typical congenial fashion, was strolling behind his younger brother, sucking on his braces. He wasn't looking at his father; he was measuring the man with the rifle.

As he trailed along in their wake, Steven wasn't thoughtful and he wasn't smiling. He was worried. "Hey, Dad," he called as Lewis shot him a warning look to keep back.

Cursing Ms. B. Regent for putting him into such an awkward situation, Lewis held out a cautioning hand.

"The way I see it, Mr. Pacatcho—" Bodine spit in the dirt again and spread his feet to a more cocky breadth "—you Yanks came down here just to use our land and our river and whatever else Ms. Regent promised you. But once you got it, there ain't no work, and there ain't gonna be no work."

"Dad?" Rick realized that he'd stumbled into trouble. He looked back to consult with Bumper O'Banyon.

Motioning for the boys to remain where they were, Lewis was anxious to put an end to the matter. "Can you operate a backhoe, Mr. Bodine?"

"Ah…" The blonde removed his cap and scratched his head. "Naw, can't say that I can, Mr. Pacatcho."

"Can you operate a bulldozer or a road grader?"

"Nope."

"Can you read a blueprint?"

"Hey, I could learn, though."

Bodine's cronies were forming a loose flank now. They had one thing on their mind—unemployment—and to try to reason with them would have been like tossing a lighted match into a pool of gasoline, Lewis knew. Thanks a lot, Ms. B. Regent!

"I don't think it matters too much what I can do, Mr. Pacatcho." Bodine's grin was that of a bobcat. "What I do think is that you'd be really smart to hire me and my buddies. Now, Ms. Regent promised it, and you gotta deliver. You'll find we're prompt. Hunger makes you very prompt, Mr. Pacatcho. We'll be ready to start first thing Monday morning."

Lewis stared at the ground, his face set with flint and his nerves stretched like wire. The last thing he wanted was to create a situation that could blow up in all their faces.

Slapping at his pocket for a pen, he found one and angrily spread the note on his thigh. With furious strokes, he wrote,

Dear Ms. Regent,

In the future, when you have people you'd like to see hired by my company, you'd do well to remember that I'm the one who makes those decisions. If you'll do me this one little favor, I'm sure we'll get along just fine.

Cordially,
L. Paccachio

Taking a grip on his temper, he folded the paper and thrust it at Bodine, adding tightly, "If you'll come and see me in about three months, Mr. Bodine, we might have something to talk about. Now if you'll excuse me..."

Simon Bodine, Lewis realized a fraction too late, was a scavenger. Out of necessity he had become an animal who has learned to attack from the rear, going straight for the crippling tendon. Before Lewis guessed that he would dare, Simon closed the distance between himself and Rick and laid his hand upon the mass of soft boyish curls.

Lewis started, as if someone had jabbed him with a needle. Frightened, Rick knew better than to infuriate a man older and larger than he was; with a daring, wide-eyed look at his dad, he remained exactly where he was, trembling.

Lewis's hands shook from the force of the anger coursing through him. He stepped forward to take Rick's hand, but when the rifle barrel rose from the ground and, in horrifying slow motion, came to rest between himself and his own son, blinding rage swept through him like the flash of napalm.

"Careful now, boy." The armed man chuckled in a shockingly high-pitched voice. His large belly quivered. "Watch where you're goin'."

Rick was terrified. The men from the truck waited like salivating dogs straining on their leashes, and Lewis envisioned himself snatching the gun and impaling the man upon its barrel. His exterior, however, was one of perfect control. He waited, his eyes riveted to the mocking blue ones of Simon Bodine.

"Dad?"

"Do as he says, Rick," he commanded, his voice soft and dry as sand.

Thunder rumbled across the nearby hills. The clouds that had been collecting all afternoon spread a thick haze. It could have ended quite differently, but Simon Bodine, his scavenger instincts working, seemed to know that the timing was wrong. He flicked his fingers at the man with the rifle.

Instantly the barrel lowered to the ground, and Rick scrambled into the sure, safe harbor of his father's arms. Feeling the trembling of his son, Lewis gripped the boy in a fierce embrace and propelled him toward Bumper.

"I'll catch a ride back into town with one of the guys, Rick," he said, his voice low and rough. Then to O'Banyon, he hissed, "Get them outta here, Bump."

Bumper swept his arms with a motion that included the four trespassers. "Are you sure?"

"I want to stay with you," Steven mumbled, worried. "That dude's crazy, Dad."

Lewis's concern was only for them. He laid a hand upon his son's shoulder and pressed it with a surge of love. "I'll be all right, Steven. I'll see you later tonight. Go on, now. Take care of Rick."

His authority was final. With a few hostile looks at the man with the rifle, the boys trudged glumly back to the Suburban with Bumper. Not until it was spinning out a cloud of red dust did Lewis allow the aftermath of weakness to wash over him. He turned to the men who waited, and the veins in his neck felt as if they would burst. Inside, where his heart was, the dull ache made him the promise that someday Simon Bodine would belong to him.

"Hey, listen, man," Bodine said, and shrugged congenially at his buddies. "Chino didn't mean nothin', did you, Chino?" To Lewis he said, "Chino's a little simple, if you get my drift."

"The drift I get," Lewis said in a near whisper as a stone settled heavily in his throat, "is that if you ever, ever come onto this property with a weapon again, Mr. Bodine, I'm going to have you arrested. You tell that to your pal Chino.''

Bodine blinked, and a surly sneer turned down the edges of his handsome mouth. ''Now, now, there's no need t'get riled up, Mr. Pacatcho.''

Lewis's voice was deadly. He had never been more riled up, and he'd never been more sincere. ''And if you ever touch one of my sons again, Mr. Bodine, they'll have to arrest *me*, because I'll kill you. Now take that paper back to your good friend, Ms. Regent, and you tell her for me that she'll do us all one hell of a favor by staying out of the construction business.''

Kitty's Headline was tucked cozily beneath a red-and-white striped awning in a niche off the courthouse square, between Bracey Fillerman's hardware store and the Laundromat where the Federal Express truck always made its turnaround.

Nature, in a delirious hurry to redeem itself after the freak snowstorm, had put on a gorgeous display of green. On her way to Kitty's, Barbara glimpsed tulips and jonquils nodding cheerfully from the courthouse lawn. Bridal wreath and Rose of Sharon around the square had made a new beginning, too. From the lace of the huge pecan trees that shaded Main Street, jays were haggling fiercely with the sparrows over the best available homesites.

The bell over Kitty's door jingled merrily when Barbara entered. Hesitating, she craned to see into the back. ''Kitty? Are you here?''

''Be there in a minute, darlin'. Just come on in and sit down.''

Barbara moved happily inside and glanced around. Kitty's tiny salon looked like something out of a fifties ladies' magazine. Some of the clippings thumbtacked to her walls probably *were* from the fifties, and Barbara took it all in, the way a person would do who's been away from home for a long time. Her gaze came to rest, in the reflection of the mirror, upon Mary Woodward and her sister, Catherine, John's aunts on his father's side.

The two women were seated on Kitty's faded settee and had obviously been watching Barbara from the moment she'd walked in. Both sets of stout legs were crossed at the ankles. On their faces was the same old harassed weariness as always, that of having been given the greatest of all burdens to bear—removing the mote from Finley's moral eye.

"Why, Barbara dear," Mary said, and smiled at Barbara's own reflection. "How nice to see you. Kitty's in the back, finishing with Helen."

As she spun around, Barbara's hard-won smile died a brutal death. She wondered if it were possible to get gracefully out the way she'd come in. Or out any way at all. How much did they know about the canceled wedding? What had John told them?

"Hello, Mary," she forced herself to say. "You're looking well today. Catherine, how's your back?"

"It pains me something awful, dear," Catherine whined. "Whenever there's a storm brewing, I always know."

Smiling thinly, Barbara glanced through Kitty's plate-glass window. "A storm? Today?"

Catherine's pink mouth pursed, and Barbara didn't think any man's eyes could have stripped her to nakedness the way the sisters' were doing. She imagined them having seen the photographs, looking in disgust at the pose of her kneeling, her bare breasts sloping forward. Had they sneered at the sight of her naked back, her weight shifted to one hip so that her buttocks were artistically captured

by the heavy shadows? Or the half-turn so that her profile, her curve of shoulder and breast were in alignment
with the bone of her pelvis, showing only the barest, most
subtle hint of flaxen curls above her legs?

A hideous embarrassment washed over her.

"Oh, Catherine's never wrong about storms," Mary
informed her. "She feels them in her bones. Our father
always used to say it was her special talent."

Barbara stepped numbly to the counter and leaned upon
it. "You say Kitty's giving Helen a perm?"

"It's been six months." Mary's smile informed Barbara that she should have known Helen would be getting
her permanent today.

"I see," Barbara said.

But she didn't really. The Woodwards had never liked
the Finleys. Now that the engagement was off, why
couldn't the sisters simply say they had always despised
Julia because her great-grandfather had built the town and
theirs hadn't?

The silence was broken by an occasional murmur and
soft laugh from behind the floral draperies. Presently,
Mary cleared her throat.

Startled, Barbara winced.

Mary said, with a saccharine smile, "How's your dear
mother, Barbara? We haven't seen Julia since the re-
hearsal dinner. The night before the—"

The omission was worse than the word. Barbara was
desperate to escape.

"Everyone's busy getting ready for Granna's birthday
party," she tonelessly replied, pretending to look at her
wristwatch again. "If you two ladies would excuse me, I
think—"

"Ah, yes. Dear Estelle would be . . . let's see, now . . .
Barbara?"

"What?" Barbara practically shrieked.

"Estelle," Mary sighed. "Where's your mind, child?"

Catherine explained in a more confiding way, "Mary wanted to know how old Estelle was, dear."

"Granna's seventy-four."

Catherine said, "Well, wish Estelle well for us, dear. I suppose there'll be the usual picnic in the park."

"Everyone at the house is busy planning for it." How *was* she going to get away from the women?

"I suppose we won't be going this year, will we, Mary? Since the wedding's off."

"Oh, Catherine, do hush!" Mary snapped.

By now the waistband of Barbara's skirt was soggy with sweat. Her mouth was full of cotton, and her head was beginning to ache. Raising her voice, she called, "Kitty?"

"Nearly through, darlin'," Kitty's voice rang out. "Just make yourself at home."

Catherine had accepted her sister's approach. "Wish your mother well, too, Barbara, dear," she said meekly.

Barbara thought it would have taken a hammer and chisel to put another smile on her face. "Thank you, Catherine. Look, would you tell Kitty for me that I'll come back later?" She took several steps in the direction of the door.

"Of course, dear," Mary answered, "and I want you to know I received your lovely note along with the returned towels. You didn't need to have them delivered, you know. I would've been more than happy to drop by and pick them up."

"And I got the returned glasses, too, dear," Catherine chimed in. "They weren't chipped or anything."

Barbara closed her fingers about the doorknob. If she didn't get away from the women, she would disintegrate with the next "dear." Just as Barbara twisted the knob,

Kitty poked her head through the draperies and waved a vinyl-gloved hand.

"Oh, Barbara, darlin'," she chirped in her sparrow's voice, "I was afraid you'd left. Helen's at the sink, darlin'. You know how nervous she gets. But I'll be through in a sec. Joe brought me the new *Family Circle* in yesterday's mail. If Mary and Catherine are finished with it, why don't you just kick up your heels and relax, darlin'."

Barbara could have said that she would probably never relax again for the rest of her life. But the thin, spindly woman disappeared through the drapes, then reappeared without warning, only her head poking through the folds.

"Darlin'," she added earnestly, "I can't tell you how sorry I was to hear about you and John. And I got the napkins back, along with your note. Such a shame, darlin'. You know, it's so hard for a woman to be alone these days. Ask me, I know. Raised two kids by myself. Listen," she waved, "it's hard, but you can do it if you set your mind to it."

The Woodward sisters had risen and proceeded to walk about the waiting room. At the mention of John's name they turned in unison and neared the counter. Mary's head was lowered, like that of a bull about to charge.

Here it comes, Barbara thought sickly as her palm grew slick upon the knob. *Judgment Day.*

"Tom tells me you made quite a showing for yourself on the industrial committee, Barbara, dear," she murmured. "We think it's wonderful. You've been like family to us, and we've been following your progress with great interest."

"We weren't being nosy, dear," Catherine was quick to add, "but Tom is our brother, after all, and he does tell us everything."

Mary said, "Tom assures us that, without you, the paper mill wouldn't even be coming to Charlatan County. Of course, we all hope, our poor John included, that you can handle the responsibility that goes along with such an undertaking."

Barbara blinked at them in confusion. "What responsibility?"

"It is fearsome, dear."

Catherine bobbed her head like a jack-in-the-box. "Fearsome, Barbara."

Barbara narrowed her eyes until Mary looked like a dwarf through the thick forest of her lashes. "Why don't you go ahead and say what you're getting at, Mary? Just be done with it."

There was a murmur of remonstrance from Catherine, but Mary cut in with an ascending tone. "Finley will change now, you know—what with all these people pouring in. Heaven only knows who they are and where they're from. All those qualities we've guarded so devoutly over the years—godliness, innocence, purity—will be lost now, never to be regained."

Barbara wanted to laugh in Mary's face. No innocence existed in Charlatan County. Finley had as many drunks, drugs, adulteries, abortions, meanness and violence as any town in the country.

"Having three-fourths of our working force on unemployment hasn't exactly made this town a model community, Mary," she said coldly.

"Better to be out of work and go hungry than to go down the bad road, my dear. Most of the men coming in—and I know this from Tom, you understand, not from firsthand knowledge—are taking rooms at the county line, where the liquor is. But you can never depend on them staying there. Soon they'll be infiltrating like communists, and you can be sure they'll bring their awful drugs with them. And their X-rated movies and pornographic filth. Of course, I don't suppose that type of thing shocks you, does it, Barbara, since you have your own circulating around town? Oh, look at our sweet Helen. Doesn't she look pretty? Look, Catherine, didn't Kitty do a splendid job?''

The most demoralizing part of it, Barbara thought as she stumbled backward against the door and instinctively pressed her hand upon her heart, was that a strain of truth wove through what Mary had said. If it hadn't, she could have screamed at them both to prove such a rotten lie.

But she found herself stupidly smelling the miasma that followed Helen McAfee into the room, and she watched the Woodward sisters flutter over her, clucking and brooding as if Helen were a fifty-five-year-old chick.

Helen turned in a slow circle to be admired and complimented on her new blue hair that was sprayed to the consistency of an army helmet. A pain buzzed in the back of Barbara's skull. As they gathered up their parcels, she stared down at her silk outfit. The petticoat mocked her now. Her shoes taunted her, as did the thrust of her breasts beneath the loose, low-scooped neck and the faint impression of her nipples that she had smiled at in the mirror's reflection this morning.

This morning? Had it been only this morning when she'd stood in the doorway of the Annex and watched the trucks passing on their way out to Lewis A. Paccachio?

Before the trio of women left, Mary passed close by and dropped her voice to a pious murmur. "Barbara, dear, John told us everything. You know, don't you, that in his heart he's forgiven you? He's not a vindictive man, Barbara. If you'd talk to him and tell him how much you regret having those pictures made, I feel certain he'd take you back. He told me so. We were all so happy when you two became engaged, you know. It seemed so fitting—your family and his family...well, you think about it, dear. And don't forget that we're praying for you. Even if you and John don't get back together, you'll always be in our prayers."

The bell jingled for several seconds—like a fire alarm, Barbara thought. Then the beauty shop was a crypt. Barbara knew she would never get out alive.

Kitty availed herself of the break to light up a cigarette, and she waved at Barbara through the smoke. "You want to take off that pretty blouse for me, darlin'? Just put on one of those wraparounds so we won't get hair down your back."

As she waited for Barbara to change into a robe, Kitty kept up a running commentary about the ongoing feud she was having with the football coach at the high school. Then she commenced upon the town's closed foundry and what it would mean for the paper mill to be completed.

When she had positioned herself behind the chair, she met Barbara's reflection in the mirror and crinkled up her face in the smile that Barbara had always thought was the nicest thing about Kitty—a smile that smudged the lines her worthless ex-husband had placed there.

"Now!" Kitty said briskly as she lifted the heavy silver braid and began loosening it. "What can we do for you today, darlin'? A nice conditionin' and blow-dry to make you feel better?"

How could you, John?

I...I was a little drunk, Barbara. Hell, I never meant...

The golden boy, Barbara thought bitterly as she gazed at her reflection. She'd been done in by Finley's golden high school quarterback. She would go down in history as the slut who turned Finley into a den of pornographers, pimps and junkies.

"Cut it off," she said quietly.

Kitty's thin face showed no expression at all. She blinked once, twice, then opened her mouth and shut it. "What?"

Barbara moistened her dry lips and said gently, "You heard me, Kitty."

"But—"

"I want it short. Very short."

"But, darlin'—"

"I want . . . one of those punk things, you know? Make me look like Billy Idol. Anything, but just off—all of it."

Kitty looked as if she had been struck openhanded across the face. Barbara guessed if she wanted to sweeten the gossip, she couldn't have chosen a better way to do it.

"Only your hairdresser knows for sure, eh, Kitty?" she said tonelessly.

"Oh, Barbara," whispered Kitty. "Oh, dear girl. Are you sure that's what you want?"

Barbara couldn't tell Kitty of all the thousands of times she had heard, "Barbara isn't beautiful, but wouldn't you just kill for her hair?" Or John's husky, "There's nothing that turns me on like your hair, babe."

With merciless self-will, Barbara held the beautician's look. A knot the size of her fist seemed to lodge in the center of her throat, and she guessed Lucy would probably never speak to her again after this. And her mother? Julia would be appalled.

"Are you sure, sweetie?" Kitty repeated.

Because she knew she couldn't speak without tears, Barbara bobbed her head up and down. Yes. Very sure.

With both hands, Kitty lifted the silky tresses that had been the greatest challenge of her professional career. Then she fetched her tiny scissors from the drawer and fit them over her fingers.

Hands trembling, lips trembling, she lifted the first gleaming lock and whimpered, "Barbara?"

"Do it." Barbara's voice was like stone.

Kitty drew in a long, slow breath and let it out even more slowly.

"Sweet Jesus," she said under her breath, not daring to look at Barbara's reflection again, "forgive me for what I'm about to do."

Chapter Three

"Like two doomed ships that pass in storm, we had crossed each other's way." Wilde

It had been the last fragile barrier between herself and ugliness. Barbara, in a state midway between horror and fascination, stared at the strange person who blinked back at her from Kitty's mirror.

"What d'you think?" Kitty asked as she stood ankle-deep in hair.

"I like it," Barbara lied.

And she didn't know whether to laugh or cry about it; if she cried, she wouldn't know if the tears were for her poor hair or her outrage at Mary and Catherine Woodward. Or John. Or her seemingly determined efforts to self-destruct.

A visceral blast of self-pity welled in her as she retraced her steps back to the Annex. "At least things have to go uphill from here," she muttered grimly as she walked through the door.

Wrong. Slouched low upon his spine in a chair outside her locked door, his booted feet propped on the wall and crossed at the ankles, a cap covering his face as if he were sleeping, was Simon Bodine. She had never been especially fond of Simon, but she did like his family, and she knew what desperate straits they were in. And he'd certainly been persistent about seeking employment. That persistence had finally prompted her, against her better judgment, to give him a note of introduction to Lewis Paccachio.

Her noise brought his feet to the floor with a slam, and he lazily unfolded himself to follow her inside. When Barbara turned, he lifted his cap, a satyr's grin on his handsome face. It was then, as his cap was suspended in midair, that he noticed her hair.

"Well, now," he purred in husky fascination, his lips twitching as he took in the whole effect, "what have we got here, _mama_!"

How perfectly fitting that the swan should have turned into an ugly duckling, Barbara thought sourly. And how distasteful Simon Bodine was. She punched out her words. "May I do something for you, Mr. Bodine?"

"Mr. Bodine?" He bridled sardonically. "Aw, come on."

"Si-mon!"

One by one he patted his pockets, as if he couldn't quite remember what he'd come for. "Let's see... Oh, yeah, here it is."

He fished out the same note Barbara had written the day before and extended it between his second and third fingers. Taking care not to be snookered into grasping a finger instead of the paper, Barbara unfolded the note and read Lewis Paccachio's reply scrawled brashly across the bottom.

Amazement widened her eyes. Dumbfounded, she jerked up her head. "What in heaven's name *happened* out there?" Infuriated, exasperated, wondering why she'd ever felt stupid for resenting the hateful engineer, she hurled the paper to her desk and threw her bag after it. "What did you say to the man to warrant this?"

Even in high school, when he was the "bad boy" all the girls whispered about, Simon's chuckles had been the most flagrant sexual propositions around. He pulled a grinning face and moved his eyes from the toes of Barbara's terra-khaki shoes to the fluff of her new hair.

"Beats the hell outta me," he drawled.

Barbara dragged a hand over the unfamiliar hair. How dare the engineer insult her so? This man, this Paccachio whom she'd done everything but get down on her knees and beg to come to Charlatan County? And had just been held responsible for his sins?

The note caught an updraft from the open window and sailed across the room to come to rest at the base of the lady palm. Barbara didn't care. It could sail to China. Paccachio could sail to China!

Sinking into her chair, she buried her face in her hands in total disheartenment. Simon peeled himself from the edge of her desk.

He said, "Allow me."

Sauntering to the plant, he scooped up the note and ambled around to her side of the desk. Leaning forward so that his nose practically brushed the end of her own when she slowly lifted her head, he slipped the paper beneath the neckline's low binding so that it nestled in her cleavage.

"Here ya go, princess," he said huskily. "Better hang on to this. Evidence."

Princess? An even hotter fire blazed in Barbara's mind. Had he called her *princess*? *Lip-smackin' little rear you got there, princess. I think you oughta ask John, princess. Gotta go, princess.*

She felt as though she'd just been wakened from sleep, one so deep that it could have killed her. The drunken voice on the phone had been Simon Bodine's! She was certain of it. She had to do something. She had only seconds in which to do it. But what?

"And by the way," he was adding as he gave the piece of paper an added tap that pushed it deeper between her breasts, "did I mention that I dig your hair? Primo stuff, princess. Listen, you don't have to give me an answer now or anything, but since you and Woodward aren't doin' your thing anymore, what d'you say the two of us go out sometime? I know a real funky place across the county line where we can have a coupl'a beers, do a little dancin'."

Snatching the note from her blouse, Barbara straightened in her chair and clumsily leaned away from him. Reaching into her drawer she placed her hand upon anything it could find and withdrew a leather-bound book of telephone numbers.

She flicked distractedly at the tab index. Her course could consist of several things; she could pretend she didn't have the slightest idea what he was talking about, or she could let it pass and do nothing. Or she could dispense with the fencing and get right down to the terms of blackmail. For that was what it was, wasn't it? When the small-town razzing was peeled away, it was one person having information about another one.

Deep in her heart she guessed she'd already been given the terms. Simon Bodine wanted to go out with her. He wanted her.

Shivering, she threw down the telephone book and reached past Simon for a stack of forms in her In box. She pretended to be absorbed in something so important that she could give him only half her attention. "Actually, Mr. Bodine," she said, "I'm not doing much dating these days."

At first he didn't reply. Straightening, he hooked his thumbs in the loops of his beltless jeans and let the fingers of one hand caress his fly. Presently he said, "Is that a fact, princess?"

Barbara quickly cleared her throat and kept her head down. "I wish you wouldn't call me that."

Laughing, he moved back onto his side of the room. He fiddled idly with a picture on the wall. "I declare, I don't know what to think about you, princess. A guy tries to be nice, and you just give him the big brush. Ya know, you keep to yourself too much. Now you start goin' out with me, I'll teach you how t'have fun. I know you can have fun if ya try. I saw you havin' fun, remember?"

The floor felt as if it were falling away from Barbara's feet. The ceiling was a million miles away.

Grinning, Simon leaned so far across her desk that he was practically reclining upon it. Propping on an elbow, he snaked a long, sensual finger to hook the top of her glasses and pull them low on the bridge of her nose. "Ya know what, princess?"

Barbara heard her own horrified breath draw in.

"My favorite picture—oh, by the way, did I tell ya I thought they were real artsy? I'm no connoisseur of art, you understand, but I really like what you did with the shawl."

Barbara wanted to lunge from her chair, but she couldn't move. "Get out of here!" she hissed. "Get out of here, or I'll—"

His laughter was as obscene as the insinuations he'd made. Straightening, he jerked his vest into place and resettled his cap. "Or you'll what, princess?"

Never had Barbara felt so at the mercy of life. But she had it coming—oh, yes, she had it coming—and it crippled her. It kept her in her chair when she should have been planting the heel of her hand upon his insolent face. Spinning around in her chair so she could look out the window, she asked in a cold, small voice, "What do you want?"

"Want?" Simon laughed softly. "Besides a piece of the most delicious cake in town? I'll tell ya what, princess, let's make a deal, you and me. You get me a job with your good buddy out there at the paper mill, Pacatcho, and you get jobs for my friends, and maybe, just maybe I'll be so busy I won't have time to think about all the good stuff hidden away under my mattress."

Dear God. John had not only showed Simon the pictures, he was so drunk that he'd let the villain actually get his hands on them.

Barbara laid her hand across her mouth. Beyond the window, children were riding their bicycles home from school, and high school boys were making the drag around the courthouse in their trucks, the girls beside them giggling and squealing at each other.

"Well?" he demanded, and actually had the gall to step behind her chair and lean over its back.

Barbara's hatred for him was a cold circle in the pit of her stomach. "I'll talk to Mr. Paccachio," she muttered frigidly.

"Talk?" He blew a stream of warm air into her hair. "Well, *I* talked, princess, and Pacatcho, he don't listen. But I'll tell ya one thing, if he don't, there're a lot of people in this town who will. Know what I mean? So you go on and talk, princess. Talk your sexy little head off. But you come up with results, ya hear?"

The terms could hardly have been clearer. Barbara hugged her waist and swore that Simon Bodine would not see her crumble. "I'll see what I can do."

"What?"

"I said I'll see what I can do!" She spat the words and spun around in her chair. She hurled herself out of it and braced herself at the opposite side of her desk, glaring at him. "Now get out of this office, Simon Bodine. Get out, and don't you ever come back."

Laughing softly, he shuffled backward to the door and, cupping one hand on the frame, leaned the upper part of his body out into the hall. He reconnoitered first one way, then another.

Looking back, he made a kissing motion with his mouth. "You don't need to get back to me, princess. I got your number. Know what I mean?" He mockingly tipped his cap. "I'll be in touch."

Barbara drove too fast along Spur 109 to the site of the paper mill. The mind was a funny thing; once it reached its saturation of grief, it blessedly shut down until the overflow could run off.

She hardly felt a thing as she drove and watched the sky turn more and more gray. It was metallic now, throbbing, like her own helplessness. Rims of haze hovered over the highway. That would be the worst insult of all, wouldn't it? If Catherine Woodward's bones proved true and it stormed after all?

Adjusting the rearview mirror of her Mustang, Barbara caught sight of the wind ruffling her hair. It was Paccachio's fault—all that silver fluff. It had to be his fault!

The nearer she got to the river, the flatter the hills became. The seams of the old road were a steady *ca-thunk, ca-thunk, ca-thunk* against the tires now. She flicked on the radio to find a weather forecast but got a squawk of static instead. Beyond her, the pavement ended suddenly. She hit the gravel too hard and jarred herself to the core.

For a mile she bounced along the corrugated roadbed. It was difficult to imagine that in two years it would be a lovely two-lane road threading through the countryside. When she reached the site she was exhausted. She was careful to keep out of the way of machinery, and she parked in a clearing beside the other parked vehicles, most of them trucks.

For a moment she watched the great, noisy, yellow, monster machines at play, but raindrops were spattering her windshield, and the workmen, also, had an eye on the weather. Most were returning from the field. One by one, khaki-clad drivers climbed down from the machinery and, gathering up their Styrofoam water jugs and removing their hats, wiped their grimy faces and headed to the trucks parked alongside her Mustang.

It didn't take long for some of the larger trucks to begin pulling off the site and head for the pavement. As newly worked as the soil was, a good soaking would bury a truck to its axles.

As men pulled into line and waited for their turn, they lit cigarettes in their cupped hands while clouds of dust swallowed them. Having no clear idea of what she would say to Paccachio once she found him, Barbara got out of the car and waited until two men reached the pickup that was parked closest beside her.

From a distance, as they approached, one of them removed his cap and called, grinning, "What can we do for you, ma'am?"

With one hand Barbara held down her silk skirt and petticoat, with the other she cupped her mouth. "Where's the man in charge?"

"Paccachio?"

She lifted her shoulder in a bland way. The men conferred as they approached the truck. The driver climbed in, and the other man shouted to workmen nearby, "Where th' hell's Paccachio? Anybody seen 'im?"

"He was out with the surveyors, last I knew," a man hollered back.

With a grinding of gears, the driver of the pickup inched his way forward to wait for his place in the line of outgoing traffic. "I don't know where he is, ma'am," the first man called over the roof of the truck. "He may have gotten a ride back into town." He smiled. "Maybe we can help?"

Disappointed, deflated, Barbara smiled and shook her head. "That's all right, thanks."

He laughed. "Well, say, if there's anything *I* can do…"

Barbara could have burst into tears.

"Well, take it easy," he called. "Looks like you're gonna get wet."

She was already wet. She was drowning.

Some of the large semis were creating small typhoons of dust as they pulled out. Choking on it, coughing, Barbara trudged back to her car, climbed in and shut the door. There was nothing she could do but drive back to town.

Well, crumb. Sighing, she put the car in gear and waited her turn. Men took her apart as they drove past, and in her present state Barbara didn't know whether to love them for building Charlatan County a paper mill or to hate them because they weren't sharing the wealth.

Weary of waiting, weary of worrying, weary of living, Barbara defied the rig snarling its way toward her from one of the side areas and whipped into the snaking convoy in front of him.

Immediately dust engulfed her, and the trucker behind rudely blared his opinion of what she'd done. The first huge droplets of rain starred the dusty windshield. "Great," she muttered. "Soup."

It descended then, before they could get off the site—a steel-gray sheet that dropped down upon the roof of her car like the curtain at the end of act one. Barbara switched on her headlights. The truck driver behind—he was undoubtedly cursing her now—gave a long, shrill blast of his horn that made her nearly rocket through the windshield.

"Hang on, will you?" She twisted back to glare at him, but that was stupid; visibility was a joke.

Her wheels spun briefly as she pulled onto the road she had just driven. The ruts were mushy now, and the trucks in front of her were making it worse. Behind her, the trucker's patience was at an end, and he pulled up hard on her bumper.

What did he expect her to do? Fly like a bird? Or swim like a duck?

Swearing that if she ever got her hands around Lewis Paccachio's neck he would never take another breath, she searched for a shoulder to pull over onto so that she could let the man have the road and be done with it.

She couldn't *see* the shoulder for the blinding rain. Anger forgotten, it was now a serious matter just to stay on the road at all. Ahead, taillights pulled away from her and blinked at her like adder's eyes as they disappeared over the top of the hill. She couldn't drive as fast as they did, and the driver behind her, thoroughly exasperated, pulled so close that it sounded as if he would move up into the front seat with her.

Frightened, she clutched the steering wheel as if it were a life preserver. When they were nearly a quarter mile from the site, in a thunderous roar of horsepower and a raucous blast of his horn, the trucker jammed his accelerator to the floor, squeezed his way onto her share of the road and, in a great tornado of mud, roared past.

It really wasn't her fault, Barbara told herself when her car fishtailed crazily and her tires lost what little traction they had. When the car turned crosswise with the road, she hit the brakes and fought to keep control. But that *was* her fault, and she realized it immediately.

The skid had gone too far. In the distance, the monster who had caused it all was reaching the crest of the rise toward the pavement. His taillights glowed red for a moment, then disappeared into the swiftly falling night while fate, as tenderly as a loving mother, placed the rear of Barbara's car gently and neatly into the ditch.

Feeling a dreary sympathy for Joel in *Risky Business* when he put his father's Porsche in Lake Michigan—score by Tangerine Dream, she parenthetically mocked herself—Barbara sat for a moment in total disbelief and listened to the rain pelting her car. She and the trucker had been the last to leave the site. There would be no more pickups and no more semis.

Presently she rolled down the passenger window and peered out at the damage. The car was sitting at a crazy angle—half on, half off the road. She might as well have been teetering on the edge of the Grand Canyon.

"Well, what now?" she asked herself aloud. "You can either sit here and wait until it gets too dark to do anything, or you can get out and screw this up along with everything else."

Barbara groped beneath the seat and found her umbrella. Gathering her jacket, skirt and petticoat into a tight fold at her side, she hesitated, took a deep breath, collected all her courage and kicked the door.

"Oh, God!"

By the time Barbara tumbled out of the car and wrestled with the umbrella, she was soaked to the skin. It wasn't only demoralizing, it was incapacitating. Shivering, she stumbled her way to the trunk and ruined her lovely terra-khaki shoes in the process.

"Don't look at them," she ordered, and after some moments of battling with the lock, threw open the trunk.

Never, in all Barbara's twenty-five years, had she jacked up a car. She learned several things when she did it now. First, no amount of acrobatics made it possible for a woman to hold an umbrella and operate a jack at the same time. Second, the value of silk goes down quite rapidly when compared to the chances of death by freezing. Third, and this was perhaps the most important, a person could *not*, after ruining her clothes, her nails and her innocence, tempt the gods by looking up at the sky and screaming, "See if I care! I don't care! Just kill me, I don't care!"

The gods took her at her word. After finally getting a jack under a bumper with hands so numb that they no longer felt connected to her body, and after hunting for and finding a rock and getting it into the space between the tire and the ground, the gods had a nasty way of ensuring that the whole wretched business could slide off the embankment into a pine tree—car, jack and all.

"No, no!"

Another thing Barbara learned: don't, under any circumstances, grab the bumper.

To keep from reaping the results of that sad miscalculation, she was forced to jump backward, and she landed on a bank of dirt left by one of the road graders, except that the dirt was now cream of tomato soup. She watched in horror as gallons of sloughy, chunky, red gunk closed over her lovely Bonnie Strauss outfit.

Bending her head, Barbara wept. She howled. She howled for every wretched, miserable, unfair thing that had happened to her the last several weeks.

Presently, however, even that afforded no relief. Freezing, dragging off her glasses and wiping her face, she heaved herself up and, taking her bag, opened the umbrella and began trudging doggedly toward the highway. She didn't even give a last look at the car. If anyone wanted the accursed thing, they were welcome to it.

It was when she reached the pavement and was scraping the mud from her shoes that she saw the rutted trail leading off into a stand of pine. Hesitating, she studied it for a moment. River people?

She wiped the rain off her glasses with a smeared finger. River people were a strange breed, somewhere between the social strata of hobos and city vagrants who constructed shacks beneath the overpasses of highways. River people came and went on the river bottoms, often without anyone knowing. Campers and tents were quite often pulled in and pulled out, and fishing sheds were thrown up overnight. Sometimes families lived in them, sometimes men on the run from the law.

Barbara considered the utility pole with its wires drooping over the trees. At this point she would be glad for the company of a junkyard dog. Pulling the umbrella low, she quickened her step.

The house was not a surprise when she came to it, tucked into a snarling tangle of grapevines and wild sumac. The steep roof was sheet iron, the kind of prewar design where all sides met at the top, leaving standing room in the attic. Its chimney was fairly intact, though the clapboard exterior was rotting through in places. A porch had once spanned the front, but part of it had also rotted away.

The entire structure had been placed upon three-foot piers in case of flood, and it didn't appear to have been lived in since Noah. Straining to see the faintest sign of habitation through the downpour, Barbara walked to the steps and placed a mud-caked foot upon the lowest.

"Hello!" she shouted over the rumble of thunder, and flinched as a flash of lightning answered her back.

A moment's wait. Nothing.

"Is anyone at home?" she yelled again. "Hello?"

Should she go inside? Should she wait out the storm here? Wasn't it better to keep walking? At least she stood a chance of being seen on the road.

The porch's ability to hold her up seemed a bit questionable, but it held, and a thrill of fear made Barbara shudder as she placed her hand on the handle of the front door.

At first the door didn't want to open. It screeched loudly as she forced it. She poked her head hesitantly inside. "Hello? My car's in the ditch down the road," she called. "I need someone to help me pull it out. Is anyone here?"

She stepped inside and for some seconds listened for a growl of outrage at her intrusion. She rehearsed a list of excuses for trespassing and looked around.

The last residents had left things in a sorry state. Little furry creatures of the night had systematically dispensed of the stuffing in a chair beside the fireplace. A piece of cracked linoleum hinted at faded colors of days gone by, and patches of water-stained wallpaper clung stubbornly to the walls. The single window of the front room was broken.

She shivered at the prospect of spending the night alone in such a place and peered up at the ceiling, where the rain was lashing the metal roof like an angry beast. Then, as she was hovering at the precipice of time and listening to the wind howling eerily through the cracks of the house, she knew he was there.

At first she didn't move. Gooseflesh pebbled her skin, and sweat broke out on her upper lip, but she waited for him to make a move. When he didn't, she turned and found him standing in a doorway—not the door she had come through but another at the back of the house.

He was a tall man, about six feet, and older than she by at least ten years. He appeared to take up a good deal of room as he stood there, his feet spaced, his legs muscled with warning, his hands braced on the facings as if it were his strength alone that supported the shack.

Wings of alarm beat in her mind. A sopping baseball cap was pulled low over his hair. She could hardly see his eyes, but she knew they were accusing her of trespassing, slashing her to ribbons. His left cheekbone and a long, resentful jaw were marred by the most evil scar she'd ever seen.

Neither of them spoke. Neither of them moved. What now? she wondered. Did she turn over the cards she'd been dealt and lay them facedown upon the table? Or did she play? She had little or nothing in her hand. So where did that put her? In only one place. She must bluff her way out of this. Heaven help her, the stakes were survival.

Chapter Four

"All undone, as earth from her bright body casts off night." Swinburne

Lewis Paccachio had always believed that deep in every man's heart lurked at least one secret fantasy he'd never told another living soul—a fantasy so dark and sinful that it merited instant disowning by his parents, exclusion from good restaurants, disqualification for credit cards and burning at the stake by every decent woman he'd ever met.

Something to the tune of being stranded on a deserted road one night and falling into the clutches of a wild, insatiable wanton who knew ways of giving pleasure to a man that hadn't been invented yet.

As he walked through the back door of the river shack and came face-to-face with its owner walking through the front, he knew he'd met the epitome of all his dreams.

She was *wild*! Though she stood half in shadow, eclipsed by dusk brought on too early by the storm, he was staggered by her feral, high-voltage disarray. She could have been a heroine in a western movie starring Gary Cooper—one of those where a gun-slinging woman drives a wagon loaded with ammunition and shoots Mexican soldiers from high atop mountains.

Wantonness couldn't be ruled out, either. Her incredible silver hair, plastered to her head like a glistening snood, made him want to sink in his hands and ruffle it. Her blouse, what he could see of it beneath the long, sopping duster affair that almost dragged the floor, would have been perfectly proper in a dry condition; now its low, scooped bodice clung to her bare breasts with a sensuality that was only slightly shy of criminal. Her skirt was even worse. Like some great, tie-dyed sheet caught at her middle, it was plastered back at the sides to show a petticoat glued to her thighs and dipping between them with a promise that literally set his teeth on edge.

The resemblance to his dream-woman was uncanny.

Say something, jerk, he told himself. He drew in a deep breath and let it out again.

"Who are you?" she challenged fiercely.

He stiffened with resentment. "Who are *you*?"

"That's none of your business. What're you doing here?"

"That's none of *your* business. What are *you* doing here?"

"None of your business!"

Stymied, Lewis removed his cap, tipped it in a ludicrous acceptance of the stalemate and fitted the soggy mass upon his head again. "I'm glad we had this little chat to clear things up."

Irritation marched briskly across her face, letting him know that she didn't approve of his teasing and had no intention of taking it.

He raked his lip with his teeth and tried to play down his presence with a shrug. "Ah, pardon me, lady—" calling her a lady was the blackest form of irony, but what the heck? "—one of us is a wee bit lost, I think."

"I'm not lost." She squinted fiercely through the muddy lenses of her glasses. "My car's in the ditch."

"Oh?"

She jerked the glasses from her face and, keeping her bag wadded with comical primness beneath an arm, smeared at the lenses with the sleeve covering her bent elbow. "Some idiot truck driver ran me off the road."

Lewis vacillated between an apology, sympathy and uproarious laughter. "That's a real shame," he said cheerfully.

It occurred to Lewis to wonder if he should be seriously concerned about having trespassed into her house. The way his luck was running—first Bodine had ruined his day, then he'd missed his ride into town and had started walking cross-country to reach the highway, and heaven had thrown up all over him—she would have one of those slow-talking mountain men tucked away somewhere. Maybe Simon Bodine himself was waiting outside the window this very moment with a double-barreled shotgun.

Glowering, she shoved the glasses onto her face again and pursed her lips in a way he found quite fascinating. "I was looking for someone to help."

She hesitated and snapped her mouth shut, not having intended to admit that she was alone, he knew. Lewis waited. If Sunny had been in her shoes, she would have made a flashing reassessment of the situation and presented her most winsome and fetching smile. She might have shifted her weight and lifted both palms skyward as if to say, "But thank goodness heaven has blessed me with a wonderful man who's going to make everything all right." That would have been his cue to lay his body down as a human sacrifice.

This woman wasn't Sunny. Definitely. He tugged awkwardly at the bill of his cap again.

"Is it a big one?" he asked.

"A big what?"

"Your car? Is it standard? Automatic?"

"Automatic."

"Where?"

She frowned. "On the steering wheel."

Lewis decided she and his son Charlie would make a great team. "I mean, where *is* it? Your car?"

"In the ditch!" she exclaimed with exasperation. "Where d'you think?"

He sighed.

She sighed.

Presently, with a flippancy that was beneath him, Lewis coughed discreetly into his fist and quipped, "I just hate it when the conversation drags, don't you?"

She was nibbling her upper lip. A very nice upper lip, he decided. She started once to speak, lifting a hand to the neckline of her blouse as she did, but she realized that the top had lost its shape and now revealed half her bosom. Her fingers fumbled to reposition it, though at this stage the matter was somewhat redundant.

"What?" Lewis blurted as he forcibly tore his eyes from the impression of cold, pebbled nipples.

Her look ricocheted around the confined space of the room. Angling her profile so he could see only the slope of her cheek, she said more guardedly, "Ah, I don't suppose . . . I don't suppose that you would—"

Stroking his scar, Lewis waited. "You don't suppose I'd what?"

"Have a telephone?" Straightening, she became quite intense. "It's rather stupid to ask, I realize, since you probably don't have electricity, but . . ."

A telephone? Electricity? *Him?* Did she think this was *his* house? That *he* would sink to the depths of living in this rubbish heap?

Insulted, Lewis spun on his heel and was about to stomp toward the door—she could damn well get her own car out of the ditch!—when, as if to ring the bell on round one, from directly above their heads a bolt of lightning slashed the sky like a brilliant scythe in the hand of God.

The room turned ruthlessly white for the space of a heartbeat. Almost quicker than Lewis's mind could follow, a splintering crack and the groaning of a great limb sent branches of a tree thundering to earth in an explosion of twigs. Glass splintered across the floor in all directions as one of the branches speared the window.

Screaming, she stumbled forward in an attempt to keep from being slashed by flying glass.

As he instinctively lunged toward her—to protect her, he supposed—it occurred to him to wonder just how much a person could trust that mysterious part of the brain that was responsible for recording all the thousands of impressions a person received every second, impressions that were computed so quickly that the eye was sometimes ignorant of having seen and the ear of having heard.

In that moment he supposed he saw her with the eye of his heart instead of his head, for while nature was throwing up a smoke screen, he was watching fear strip her completely of defenses and facade.

Gone now was the bristling porcupine with all its quills on red alert. Gone was the wild wanton. She wasn't a tough woman at all. To his even greater confusion, he saw she was incredibly innocent—not virginal, but innocent in a way that people nowadays connected to Victorian heroines. Whoever she was and whatever circumstances had sent her wandering around the river bottom by herself, they hadn't been of her making, he was sure.

The lightning was abruptly gone, and with it his own fragmented fancies. The room was filled with roll after roll of deafening thunder, and the walls seemed to tremble. Gasping, she covered her head with uplifted arms, unwittingly making herself an even more erotic silhouette than before.

Lewis felt like an intruder for seeing what she had gone to such elaborate pains to conceal. He stepped more gently toward her, and though she couldn't possibly have heard, she jerked her arms to her sides.

She threw back her head in a righteous challenge.

He stopped dead in his tracks. *Easy,* he warned himself, *you're way out of your depth here, Paccachio. Be very, very careful.*

Not even in her most brash moments had Barbara ever considered herself an expert on men, but she recognized one important fact about the man she had just stumbled upon. Be he drug smuggler or river rat or whatever terrible thing he was, he didn't go with the house any more than she did. Like herself, he had only come in out of the storm.

But whereas she was afraid and wanted only to get away—anywhere away!—he was intending to establish some awful squatter's rights or something. One of two disasters would occur, she figured: he would either assume his rights included whatever happened to be in the house at the time, namely herself, or he would see her as an obstacle in staking his claim.

In the lightning's brilliance she glimpsed the quickening of her suspicions in his scarred face. Whatever he wanted, he was quite capable of taking it.

"All right," she bluffed more rashly than before, and placed a space between her own feet just so he would know she meant business, too. "Let's get this over with. I want to know straight out what you're doing here. Right now, you tell me who you are."

She'd come off sounding like a throbbing potato!

"Maybe I'm Jack the Ripper." His reply was rough and slow and hoarse. Like a wolf that hadn't fed in days, he began slowly to stalk her.

Unnerved, Barbara licked her lips and determined not to let her anxiety show. "You're not Jack," she countered with what she hoped was a joking manner. "I know Jack. Jack has this curly red hair." She tugged at a dripping tendril of her own hair.

It was no use. The man could see in the dark. Barbara could feel the heat of his thoughts assaulting her, stripping her. She had to *do* something. In the movies, didn't women turn the tables? In novels, didn't the heroines use their swaying hips and whispery feet? Didn't they unfasten buttons and let their clothes slither into pools so they could make an offering of themselves, of their eager nipples and moist, tempting lips?

She considered the proximity of the door. It was a good ten feet away. It might as well have been a hundred and ten.

She shivered convulsively. The wolf in him smelled her fear. In mounting hysteria, she began inching in the direction of the door, but for every step she moved back, he took one forward that brought him dangerously nearer.

Swallowing, still hugging her silly bag, she tried to smile and extended her hand, palm out. "Look, I, uh—I've changed my mind about the telephone.'' She attempted a laugh, and it fell flat. "It's all right, though, perfectly all right. What I think I'll do is run along now. It was very nice meeting you. The house is all yours."

Barbara knew, as seconds ticked past with atomic precision, that everything was irrelevant now. In the cross fire of this one moment in earth's great history, nothing in the world existed for her except him—nothing in the past and nothing in the future, not John, not her shattered dreams. Life began and ended in the ravaged face of a stranger whose legs were long and very strong and whose boots knew everything it would take to overpower her.

She realized she was afraid to die. Dear Jesus, don't let her die.

Seconds passed, and more seconds. Without warning, then, they lunged together—she for the door, he for her. He was much faster, sprinting with a speed she hadn't dreamed was possible. He reached the door first.

"No!" Barbara screamed as he slammed a powerful fist against it and she whirled to confront him. "No!"

From the apex of her fear, in the next moments he seemed everywhere—on her, around her. As she struck wildly to fend him off, his cap was knocked from his head and he crushed her tightly to the door with the force of his weight. Her purse was knocked away; her glasses flew off her face. From deep in her hysteria, with her eyes flared wide, she watched his face fill her vision and felt his legs, iron hard and capable, strain tautly against her own.

She could almost count the long, thick lashes of his eyes and each tiny place where his whiskers grew. She could see the way his teeth were too crowded on the bottom and their edges that were smoothly irregular and brilliantly white. Beside the scar were the infinitesimal tracks of a surgeon's neat stitching.

His breath was blending with hers somewhere deep in her lungs. "Will you just hold it a minute?" he growled angrily between his teeth.

"Let me go!" Blindly, savagely, Barbara struck at nothing, at everything, over and over at his head, his sides, his thighs.

"Listen to me." He was dodging, grabbing at her hands, trying to capture her wrists. "Damn it!" he thundered when her fist connected smartly with the side of his head. "Be still!"

"Help!" But no one heard her weak, pitiful whimpers. "Somebody, help!"

He was too strong. So tired was she already, so beaten, so hopeless, like an exhausted, ill-matched fighter in the ring, Barbara did the only thing left to her, and that by instinct only: she melted against him until she felt herself falling through the floor to the very center of the earth. As her arms clasped his waist and her bones disintegrated, she became a part of him until she could not distinguish whose heart was beating in her breast, his or her own.

For one brief moment he relaxed his vigilance. He released her and dipped his chin in what Barbara supposed was an attempt to see if she had fainted. There, in that fragment of time, she revived enough to see her chance and to know it was the last she would ever get.

Wriggling from his arms, half running, half falling, she lunged across the room and grabbed her bag. Spinning, she hurled it at his head.

"Take it!" she cried. "Take the money!" With her legs shaking and out of sync with her own heartbeat, she raced to the door and darted through it.

A haze of rain swallowed her instantly. She could hardly see as she skittered down the steps and splashed across the boggy yard, but she heard his boots slamming heavily upon the steps, and she heard him swear as he came hard on her heels. When he caught her, his arm roped around her waist and she was jerked back against him so violently that her feet left the ground.

"Bastard!" she cursed him. "Monster! Oh, please."

Did she fall, or was she pushed? Barbara didn't know. She knew only that as his weight slammed into hers, thrusting her forward as one of his arms clapped hard across her breasts, she was being turned in his arms. Together they fell into the soft bed of mud, and she thought, as her breath was knocked out of her and as he pulled himself up, pinning her with his great man's weight, that he made some sound. She could not isolate the point where his assault became an apology. She wasn't absolutely sure that he meant for it to, but however it happened, he was retreating. His hands, instead of taking, were miraculously giving—slipping beneath her, lifting her, drawing her to her knees.

"My God," she heard him mutter as he pulled her to her feet and closed his hands strongly upon her shoulders, "what have I done to you?"

Lewis guessed that if he were observing this scene from a distance, watching a man bend over a beaten feminine figure to survey the evidence of his violence, he would have shown no mercy to such an animal, no mercy at all.

Cursing his own black heart and not quite certain how it had all happened, he drew her into the safe haven of his body. "Easy now," he said, and wrapped her protectively in an arm so that her head was tucked beneath his chin and her back was shielded from the rain's fury.

Yet she hardly seemed to notice that they were no longer struggling. He drew her toward the shack, and her feet followed her body obediently, but after moving through the slush to reach the porch she seemed unable to generate the strength to climb the steps.

Lifting one of her arms and draping it around his neck, Lewis scooped her up and penitently carried her into the house. Once inside, with his pulse throbbing in his veins, he hesitated before placing her upon her feet. How very small she was, how fragile and delicate. Cradled against his chest, with her head resting beneath his chin and the side of her breast pressed sweetly to his chest, he wondered how he possibly could have thought she was a stray.

Desire was unexpectedly hot in his throat and heavy in his groin—not the rapacious desire to take her but the need to truly know her. He couldn't remember the last time he'd even been that interested in a woman.

Swiftly he put her down. "You're okay now," he murmured, and awkwardly wiped rain—or were they tears?— from her cheeks with his fingertips.

Like a bedraggled mermaid pulled from the depths of the sea, she stood dazed, trembling. Without opening her eyes, she took one deep breath after another.

"It was a mistake," he insisted earnestly, wanting absolution so badly that he grazed a knuckle along the wet ledge of her jaw. "That's all it was. Craziness. I'm very sorry."

When she still didn't respond, Lewis let his breath out in a rush. Well, *hell*!

Closing his arms about her back, he held her close and rocked her back and forth in his arms as he would have rocked one of his own sons. "Shh, shh," he whispered in her ear as he stroked her back over and over, "it's okay, it's okay."

Presently he ducked his head to peer down at her. "Look, I'm not a criminal or a rapist or a murderer or anything else. I just came in out of the rain, and I thought for a minute that you lived here, and then I realized that you thought *I* lived here. And then, well, I was just trying to stop you from running outside and drowning yourself for nothing. It all got out of hand.''

He waited. ''Damn it, are you listening to me?''

More than he would ever know, Barbara wanted to say; she heard all his words, and she believed them, because the ring of truth was pure and unmistakable. But she had no strength to lift her lashes from her cheeks, much less explain.

Defeated, he released her shoulders and framed her face urgently between the roughness of his palms. He shook her head gently. ''I'm sorry. I didn't mean to yell at you. Are you all right?''

She took a great, ragged breath.

''Are-you-all-right?'' A whiplash jerked at the end of each word.

''Yes,'' Barbara gasped, and wished he would just stop badgering her and hold her again so she could place her head upon his shoulder and close her eyes. But genteel ladies didn't cling to strange men, did they? And she was— at least she had been once in her life—a lady.

Averting her face, she pushed back the muddy wisps of hair that clung, dripping, to her cheeks. ''I'm all right,'' she said in a thin, reedy voice. ''Really.''

To her surprise, he chuckled. And then he sighed the kind of sigh a man does when he's almost lost something he'd never valued before but has come to realize how drab his world would be without it.

''Good,'' he said with hoarse relief. ''I thought for a minute I was going to have to give you resuscitation.''

''Mouth to mouth, I suppose?'' she murmured without missing a beat.

He laughed, and she, still dazed, was surprised to discover her humor sneaking out of hiding. She covered her face with a hand.

"You know," he said, "you may not believe this, but I don't have one single corpse to my credit."

She angled a look of censure between her fingers. "Neither does my cat," she said, and lowered her hand, "but I don't argue the point when his claws are buried a half inch in my skin."

His chuckle was buried deep in his chest, but Barbara, instead of savoring it, was making a harried inspection of herself. It suddenly dawned on her that she'd just lost several hundred dollars worth of silk. Incredulous, she lifted the sides of her skirt, which were heavy with mud.

"Look at me!" she cried. "This was my best outfit! It's ruined! Just look at me!"

He was trying his damnedest, Lewis wanted wryly to say, but she wasn't exactly making it easy.

The desire he had felt moments before returned, but with a vengeance this time and complicated by an unfortunate blending of his original fantasy and all the minute information his brain had stored about her. She was utterly irresistible: earthy yet innocent, opinionated but shy, serious but impish.

He wondered if he'd ever wanted Sunny so badly in the beginning. He smiled, for no good reason except that he couldn't help it.

"I'm glad that amuses you," she said waspishly, and gave a vicious shake to her skirt. "Maybe you'd like to buy me another."

"Maybe I would," he drawled, and thought of several things he would like to do for her and to her. "In fact, I insist. But that's not what amuses me."

She was absorbed in the very charming feminine task of trying to make some order of her disarray, and Lewis didn't think he could continue to watch her without doing something completely foolish.

He raked water off his own clothes and halfheartedly stamped mud off his boots. Feeling for his cap and not finding it, he combed his fingers through his soaked hair, leaving it a mass of disorderly waves. Seconds later he glanced up to see her and realized she'd been watching him for some time.

He froze with one hand held inches from his hair, and Barbara, unable to catch her next breath as she stared at him staring at her, felt as if a trap had suddenly yawned beneath her feet. Deep within her, something stirred, and she felt stripped naked by his eyes that touched her from the shadows.

Turning, she groped through the darkness for the nearest wall, but he had unnerved her so badly that she could have been stepping onto land after a long time at sea. She stumbled, and he was instantly there to grip her arm.

At his touch, an even deeper awareness came to life, a warm, dark center of herself that she'd gone to great lengths to disguise by heaping debris upon its door.

She shrank from the familiarity of his touch as if burned by it. "I'm fine... thank you. I mean, I can see perfectly well."

"Your cat may see in the dark," he huskily disagreed, "but I have serious doubts about you. Oops, watch it. Be careful."

Her heart was in her throat, but she tried to laugh and despised the sound of it. Finding the wall, she gratefully let it bear her weight so she could slide down it to sit.

"My legs think they've been in the navy," she gasped lightly.

But Lewis was thinking that she looked more like the infantry than the navy—a poor, weary draftee who hadn't wanted to fight the war in the first place but who had accepted his duty to endure to the very end. If he hadn't already made so many miscalculations with her, he would have said that he would like to sit with her for a while, mud and all, and just...talk, get to know her, perhaps hold her hand and feel the comfortable presence of another human being.

He was too scarred by his failure with Sunny to consider such a vulnerable move. Besides, if he'd ever met a more hands-off woman, he didn't know who she was.

Outside, the electrical part of the storm was wearing down. The thunder was rolling farther and farther into the distance. A residual shiver traced its fingers down his spine as Lewis pondered the way her skirt was spilling upon the floor in a dark, haunting pool.

He said, turning away too abruptly, "I think I'll look around and see if there's anything to build a fire."

"Don't ask me for matches." Her voice was low, throaty. "I don't smoke."

He fished a book of matches from his pocket and felt to make sure they were dry. "Don't go anywhere."

"Are you insane?"

She looked up with a mild mockery that made Lewis's resolutions somersault. "At this point," he muttered, wondering if he was entering some strange post-divorce crisis the experts didn't know anything about, "that's still debatable."

When he was gone, Barbara drew her knees beneath her chin and wrapped her arms around them, resting her head upon them as he moved through the house. How quickly roles reversed themselves. If someone had burst into the house at this moment, she would have darted to the back, yelling and screaming for the protection of the man who had just sent her tearing out in the first place.

Soon he returned, carrying two broken chairs. She flinched as he swung one against the stones of the fireplace with a splintering crash and, without a word, gathered up the pieces.

He could have been a soft-footed Indian kneeling before his fire as he concentrated. After several attempts, the match rasped, the flame caught the dry wood and sputtered, sending millions of sparks racing and hissing up the chimney.

The stench of the old wet flue gradually gave way to a clean, burning wood scent. Barbara studied the glow cast on the ceiling by the pale illumination, conjuring an old-time, domestic image of kerosene lamps and candles, hooked rugs, books on the table, a tea kettle whistling happily on the stove, Mother and Father cozily together on a cold wintry night.

Rising, he braced his arm along the length of the mantel. She smiled to herself. He looked like a lord of the realm surveying his domain, or a field marshal watching his troops on maneuvers. It was in the genes, she figured, and liked him more than she expected to.

He nudged a piece of wood farther into the flames with a booted toe. "Come dry out," he invited her, squinting into the darkness.

She wasn't sure she trusted him, or herself, enough to do that. She sought for some suitably aloof remark and settled for, "I'm okay."

His silence was its own mocking commentary.

"Really," she insisted, flushing and grateful for the shadows. "I can feel the heat over here."

She hadn't really said that, had she? Oh, mercy, protect her from herself!

He chuckled. "I've got it. I'll come over there and lean against the wall and shiver, and you can come over here and get warm. Is that safe enough for you?"

With a reproof of pursed lips, Barbara put herself through a series of contortions, heaved to her feet and squished and padded her way to the fire. "Don't be ridiculous. I'm not a child." Turning down the corners of her mouth in a smirk, she added, "There's no need to behave like a . . . a . . ."

"Jerk?"

"Close enough."

When he threw back his head and laughed, letting the merriment ripple from deep in his belly, Barbara was mesmerized and outraged at the same time. Oh, she might have known he would laugh like that—making a person feel like the most important thing in the whole world, as if he'd never laughed quite that way with anyone else. And those lines at his eyes crinkling so fascinatingly and the path of the scar tightening and creasing a hair-thin valley across his jaw, his dimples making another crease alongside the smile.

"Ed Harris," she murmured.

Hesitating, he quizzed her with a half grin. "What?"

She shrugged. "It's a habit of mine. A hobby, I suppose. Movies and score composers."

"And you think I'm Ed Harris?"

"*The Last Innocent Man*. Composer, Brad Fiedel. You've got his mouth."

And she, Lewis thought with an irrational compulsion to forget all the lessons life had taught him and grab her in his arms, had the mouth of a woman he would like very much to kiss.

The room was suddenly too warm, and the heaviness in his groin swelled into a full-fledged ache. "You're an authority on Ed Harris's mouth?" he mumbled, when what he wanted to say was, *This isn't happening. I don't care why you're here or what you've done or what was done to you. I don't want this moment to end. I don't want you to leave my life.*

He expected her to read the subliminal messages buried in his reply, but she didn't. She waited uncertainly in the nexus of her own thoughts and rubbed flecks of dried mud from her wrists.

"No," she said presently, turning slightly away, as if lost, "I'm no authority."

"Then check it out," he mumbled as primeval heat rose high in his throat. "I like to be sure about these things."

Barbara didn't hear his last words. It didn't matter because what he was saying wasn't what he was thinking; he wanted her, and she didn't think she could just brush that aside. Next he would be dragging away all the debris at the door of her heart and making her want to rid herself of it forever, making her want to talk and talk and talk and . . .

She sought sanctuary in the fire, staring blindly and bracing a hand upon the mantel as he had done, but gradually the heat generated steam from her dripping clothes until she was compelled to step back. Slipping off her long jacket, she shook it free of mud and draped it as neatly as possible on the remaining rickety chair.

She considered her wrecked skirt, then impulsively untied the waist, stepped out of it, shook it out and hung it to dry with the jacket. She tucked her blouse modestly beneath her petticoat and, pressing her palms to her breasts, sighed.

At her back, his presence in the room was like the pressure of the storm. When the silence became too much, she slid a furtive glance over her shoulder. In open-mouthed fascination she saw that he had eased himself to the floor

and was removing a boot. That done, he removed the other
and, with typical male absorption, inspected their misery
and set them neatly aside.

Bewitched, she studied his profile as he peeled off his
wet socks and laid them across the tops of his boots. He
shrugged out of his jacket and tugged the tails of his shirt
free of his pants and stripped it off.

Smooth, tanned muscles bunched and played across his
chest in the firelight. A light smattering of curly black hair
shadowed its center. Not a hint of paunchiness existed
where his waist disappeared into the top of his jeans, and
when he twisted from his waist, she saw the rest of the scar.

It hadn't stopped at his neck as she'd first assumed. It
had hacked a path over his shoulder and onto his back.
What terrible thing had caused such a wound? The war?
A mortar? A car wreck?

Empathy caught her about the knees, like a tackler
coming from behind. What horror he must have felt when
he realized what had happened. And what strange meld-
ing of minds made her wish that she could have protected
him from such pain?

His head rose unexpectedly and twisted around. "You
can ask," he said bluntly. "Everyone does."

She jerked away. "I'm sorry. I—"

The fire made its own hissing comment on the awkward
silence spinning out between them. Rising, he walked toward her with light steps, and Barbara didn't dare turn.
Her pulse was a drumroll that went on and on, louder and
louder. When he positioned himself alongside her and
hooked his hands upon the mantel, studying the fire with
the same dreadful urgency as she, she wondered how he
could help but hear it.

"Usually I don't undress before a woman unless I know her name," he said, his voice low and sandpapery.

Barbara knew exactly what he was asking. "And I make a point of never telling my name to someone I don't know."

"Your circle of friends must be very small."

She stared witlessly at his bare feet. She could have reminded him that he hadn't exactly put out his hand and introduced himself. Besides, whose commandment would she break if she didn't tell?

She cleared her throat of an imaginary obstacle. "How did you get the scar?"

He drew in a long, slow breath. "You're not going to ask me my name?"

Tell me your name first.

No. Tell me your name first.

He didn't.

And she didn't. Barbara wished desperately that she'd had experience with someone a bit more sophisticated than John Woodward, and she prepared herself to unleash a vigorous self-defense.

He disarmed her before she even got started. "You're not on the Ten Most Wanted list, are you?"

Barbara couldn't prevent her own bitter laughter. "Not many people want me these days, I'm afraid." She closed her eyes, not having meant to expose so much of herself.

"It was a boating accident," he said without preamble. "I accidentally got in the way of a big cabin cruiser backing out of a slip."

Abashed, Barbara exclaimed, "Were you underwater? Didn't you see it?"

A sort of sodden regret passed across his features, and he lifted his hand to the ragged line. "Someone else was in the water. She had...they..." He sighed. "She'd been drinking too much, and she stumbled, fell into the water. Somehow she got under the pier, and I was afraid she'd drown. I dove in and found her and pulled her out, but just as I was surfacing—"

Without being told, Barbara knew the woman had been his wife. She didn't know whether to be relieved that he was married, or saddened. She considered the patch of white hair at his temple.

"Does she hate you for it?" she softly inquired.

No one had ever asked Lewis the question before. No one had ever realized that the inevitable resentment of such an incident was almost always on the side of the cause, not the effect. He wanted badly to be closer, to absorb her sensitivity like the sun.

He smiled sadly. "Maybe she does, at that."

Barbara looked away. She had enough pain of her own. "I'm sure I can't say any words to you that haven't been said many times before," she said, and moved across the room to stand before the mist of the open window.

Too late, she heard the whisper of his feet behind her. Before she could guess his intentions, he had stepped so close that he all but molded to her back.

"You are one mean lady," he said, mockery gentle in his voice. "Why, I try to keep you in out of the rain, and what d'you do? Thank me? No, you ask me to take your money. And now you won't tell me your name. I'm hurt, really hurt."

Don't do this! she wanted to shriek. *Don't be exactly what I need. Don't make me feel good.*

But with a ludicrous formality to match his irony she said, "I'm afraid the logic of that completely escapes me, sir."

"Sir?" He laughed and experimented with the word, as if trying it on for size. "*Sir*? She insults me, then calls me sir?"

Barbara's nerves burst into flame. She was too tired for this, too ready for his kind of agreeable cynicism. Twisting quickly around, thinking that in the end he would see she couldn't handle it and would back off, would allow her to pass, she immediately discovered that his nerves were much stronger than her own. Not only did he not step away, but he leaned so near that her eyelashes would have tangled with his had she dared blink.

She had no choice but to play by the rules he had declared. She jutted her chin. "The last I heard, 'sir' was a term of respect."

He was enjoying himself. "You don't call it an insult when you refuse to sympathize with my scar. Now that's a first, I have to tell you. This scar's my ace in the hole, you know. One hundred percent guaranteed to conjure up all kinds of maternal instincts and offers to mend my socks."

"I refuse to mend your socks."

Leaning even nearer, until the end of his nose was a hairbreadth from hers, he added with comical solemnity, "Are you sure? There are one hundred and six stitches in this scar. You know, if you had one hundred and six stitches in *your* face, I'd sympathize. I'd sympathize like crazy, but—" here, a deeply aggrieved and wounded sigh "—that's the difference between you and me, I guess."

It took all Barbara's self-control to keep from exploding with laughter. She swallowed and compressed her lips until she could take a long, deep breath. Letting it out, she narrowed her eyes until he was little more than a shadow above her.

"You're quite a flirt, aren't you?" she accused.

"Me?" He laughed. "Hell, no."

"And I've noticed another thing." She heaped his crimes into a pile. "You lie a lot. I don't think I like you very much."

He started first to laugh and return the tease, but abruptly he sobered. His features altered, and his breathing changed; his whole body stiffened. His eyes were so dark that they glistened like wet coals.

Barbara supposed that deep down in her most honest self, she knew what was coming. Her heartbeat throbbed until the whole room seemed to pulse as, without touching her body at all, he leaned forward and with a long, wondering sigh lowered his mouth to hers.

The room waited. His breath was a whisper. Barbara's own breath exchanged places with it, and a rush of warmth and energy flowed through her. She found his hesitation unbearably sensuous, and she wanted to pull away, but nothing had prepared her for the irresistible magnetism of all the male textures that comprised him, the hypnotic smells of his presence, the heat of his nearness.

She guessed he expected to be rebuffed. Each of their thoughts was circling the other, concentrating on the next move, and she knew, as he did, that something had to stop it.

Whimpering, she turned her head slightly away. "I—"

With a faint, infinitesimal murmur of protest, his mouth followed the path of her own. "Just one, just . . ."

His lips tested hers again. Then again, in a chain-linked series of feathery inquiries. Barbara didn't know how to reply. She didn't dare. Ever so slightly he touched the tip of his tongue to her lip, and she drew in a quick, helpless breath until gradually, in a time-stopped suspension that seemed to be from another lifetime, his lips parted and

Barbara heard her own moan coming from far away. Slowly, oh, so slowly, his mouth fastened to hers.

And then it was too late. Barbara struggled to open her eyes and focus them, but they were drugged, and through the haze she saw that his own eyes were closing, his lashes coming to rest thickly against the planes of his cheeks. His own breaths were being dragged into his lungs from a great, difficult place as the kiss deepened and blossomed into kiss after kiss, breath after moaning breath, each more shattering than the first.

Presently he stepped back, releasing her. Barbara stumbled. She hardly knew where she was. She hardly knew *who* she was. Did he regret it? Did she?

He cleared his throat finally, and wiped his hand over his mouth and looked away until his breathing grew normal and he could speak again. "You're wrong, you know," he said in a slow, experimental way, and turned back to see her breasts rising and falling, rising and falling. "You don't want to like me, but you do."

She gasped. "I never said—"

"And now you're wondering if I'm worth the risk of making love."

He was serious! Stunned—it was not true, not true at all!—all Barbara could do was gasp again.

"Okay." He grimaced his endearing, self-effacing grimace. "Making love's the wrong word. Making... whatever. You've never done that before, have you, mystery lady? Well, let me tell you something, neither have I. They say it can kill you, you know, this thing of casual sex, and I don't have any reason to doubt them. Until this moment I never imagined it mattering."

Looking away, he laughed without a shred of amusement. "But now it does matter—God, it matters." He returned to her by way of his feet, his hands, his eyes finally. "So, now you tell me, Miss Cinderella-Come-Lately-To-The-Ball, what happens when the clock strikes twelve?"

Chapter Five

"Secrets are like maidens: the closer they are kept locked up, the more certain they are to escape." Balzac

Barbara didn't know the answer. But then, she suspected they could have looked at each other until the world turned to dust and she still wouldn't have known.

Over their heads she could hear the steady tattoo of the rain upon the metal roof and the occasional afterthought of thunder. She could see, around them, the intermittent blue flashes of the lightning far away. But her other senses were too full of him to think straight—his largeness, his toughness, his powerful intensity, and her own softer symmetry that was the opposite side of his coin. Was he right? Did she hear, beneath all that, the peals of a clock striking the hour?

Nonsense. The return to reality was like a drop in a fast elevator. Her stomach gave a noisy growl and, startled, she grabbed it.

"Oh, dear." More than a little embarrassed—what a way to end a kiss!—she forgot about striking clocks and double-sided coins. Her stomach demanded food. She laughed. "My goodness."

He chuckled softly. "The weakness of the flesh."

Their laughter, once again, was a swelling tide, and for a moment they were like children whose only worry was to make themselves happy.

"Isn't life a bust?" Barbara laughed. "And here I was, working on my image and everything."

"What did you expect?" His seduction had a way of sneaking up on her. "To be Grace Kelly?"

She laid her hand upon his arm without thinking. "No, Emmett."

He started to touch her hand but didn't. "Stop clowning around."

"In this circus?"

They laughed until it was all used up. Presently, in stops and starts, they wiped the smiles from their faces. His eyes wandered from her face to the fire and back again.

He shrugged off his returning moodiness. "For your image, I think . . ." He touched her cheek, the crispness of a drying curl, the arch of an eyebrow. "I think, let's see...yes, a ring in your nose. Definitely. A diamond. For the finishing touch."

Barbara grasped her nose as if he might steal it, and murmured, "No remarks about the nose, please."

"But I love your nose."

"Of course you do."

"Mr. Durante."

She had no choice but to take a playful swipe at his chin for that insult, and he had no choice but to dodge and grip her hand: a point well made about the clock striking twelve. Everything spun around a hundred and eighty degrees again—laughter to an awareness even more stunning than before, smiles to wordless understandings that went so deeply they were almost subliminal.

Lewis imagined, for one twinkling moment, that he was strapped to a table beneath the cruelty of Poe's murderous pendulum. Holding her stare for a moment longer, he stepped back to invite her from the window with a buccaneer's flourish.

"I don't suppose," he asked as he indicated they should return to the fire, "that you have anything to eat in that bag of yours, along with all the money you're so generous with?"

"It's your party."

He searched the pockets of his jeans, and Barbara smiled at the intriguing male acrobatics of getting his hand between his groin and wet denim. What was it about the man? He had little of the glamour of John, but she found him a hundred times more fascinating and infinitely more appealing.

"Voilà!" he said, snapping his bare heels together as he held up a piece of chewing gum. Facetiously, he stepped closer and waved it back and forth before her nose.

"If madame pleases, tonight's entrée is fricassee of spearmint, featuring our famous, sugar-free house sauce. Would madame like the large portion or the small?"

Sniffing at the gum, Barbara coyly cut her eyes to the side and pretended to debate the matter. "I'm afraid I'm suffering a slight financial embarrassment at the moment. I shall be forced to ask the price."

"Perhaps some credit is in order?"

"Actually, I'm a cash person myself."

"Really?" With a wink, he peeled the paper off the stick of gum. "Ah, tell you what I'm gonna do. I'm gonna give you this half," he pretended to tediously measure the halves, having torn the stick in two, "and you tell me what you're doing out here in the woods. I'll write *paid* across your bill, and everyone will live happily ever after."

Barbara hesitated. If she hadn't been so emotionally attracted to him, it would have been nothing. Yet if he really were in trouble, running from the law or something like that, she didn't think she could bear to hear it.

A bit of pride, too, Barbara? A bit of shame that you, Miss Social Conscience herself, could be so sexually attracted to someone at the other end of the spectrum?

"I think I'll pass, if you don't mind," she said nervously, and turned to stare blindly at the fire.

He moved beside her and waited for some moments for her to lower the barrier she had just erected. When she didn't, he pried loose the fingers of her hand where she gripped the shabby mantel. Into her palm he placed the chewing gum.

His voice was now as wary as her own. "Well, I wouldn't have made a good collection agency, would I? Here, chew it in good health, mystery lady. Courtesy of Bumper O'Banyon."

Despising herself, Barbara managed a thin, final smile before putting the chewing gum between her teeth. "This doesn't mean we're engaged, does it?"

Only by a hairbreadth did Lewis keep from lapsing into the drugged stupor of his fantasies again, for everything she did, every small smile, every unwitting gesture, enflamed him.

"Shut up and chew your gum," he said.

Together they stood relishing the spearmint and listening to the rain and the cozy, crackling fire. "Do you think it will rain much longer?" she asked when the silence became a too-accurate barometer of her mood.

"Probably all night."

"You think so?"

"Maybe."

"Oh."

Two waterlogged foot soldiers entrenched in the same war zone. Two fragile wild things islanded from a forest fire. Two cell mates.

Passing a palm across his face and finding it damp with tension, Lewis braced his hips back against the stone of the fireplace, wriggling to find a comfortable slouch. "If it's not asking too much, Ms. Mystery Woman—" he elongated his words to the fine balance between sarcasm and self-ridicule "—are you married?"

Barbara's first impulse was to refuse to answer. He'd made enough entries into her personal life. But what would be wrong with talking to him? Just a little? About the safe things? She would never see him again.

She lifted her shoulder in an honest shrug. "I almost married. Once. Are you?"

"Married?" He tugged at his nose and sighed. "I was. For sixteen years." He huffed a short laugh. "I've been married all my life."

"I'm sorry. It was a divorce."

"With three kids. Boys. Yeah, I've got the boys. And a dog—oh, yes, we mustn't forget the dog. The boys are soccer freaks. The truth is, they secretly believe they're going to wake up one morning and be Pelé. She...well, leaving the boys wasn't all Sunny's fault. At least I have them. Does that surprise you?"

Yes, it did surprise her. Sunny? Why would Sunny, or any woman in her right mind, leave a man like him? And why *was* he here? Really?

The meager inches between his bare shoulder and her own thinly clothed one seemed to evolve into a magnet. She wouldn't have been surprised to look down and see little blue sparks arcing between them. She became absorbed with the slight amount of movement it would take to accidentally bump him.

"I guess it doesn't really surprise me," she mumbled. "Everyone wants what they don't have."

Removing the chewing gum and tossing it into the fire, Lewis let out his breath in a long, wondering stream. "I, uh..."

She prompted him to continue with a lift of her eyebrows.

He stared at his bare feet, not understanding why he wanted to tell her. But the place, the storm, the cozy safety inside was like a confessional.

"Sunny was pregnant when I married her," he said, and waited for a reaction.

None came. He shrugged. "At first I thought Steven was mine, but then later I knew he wasn't. I didn't ask. I don't know—because I was the one who'd pushed so hard to get married, maybe. She was the beauty queen, you see, and every man wanted her. I thought if I could just marry Sunny...well..."

Baffled at why he was confessing such a thing—he had never told anyone, not even his parents—Lewis studied her troubled profile. He wondered if she'd heard what he said.

Nodding, she gave him a look that didn't question his motives for marrying a woman for such reasons. Bless her.

He said, "You know, I've never told anyone that."

She smiled briefly. "Does your son know? About...?"

Lewis was bombarded with memories: Steven's bitterness to his mother, the awkward boyish frustration of wanting his real father to be Lewis, yet knowing he wasn't.

He sighed. "I don't know why she told him. I don't think it was meant to hurt either of us. Maybe it was an attempt to purge herself of guilt. We had another son by that time, and then she wanted another baby—to assuage something else. When she first told me about Steven, I wanted to kill her. I'm not kidding. It was as if all the pride I'd taken in being the best . . ."

"The death of pride is probably worse than the death of the body."

"You sound as if you know firsthand."

She brushed the question aside.

"Who called off the wedding?" he asked. "Him?"

A beat of time.

"I once did a very dumb, stupid thing, too," she woodenly admitted, and shook her head.

Lewis grimaced. "The dues of this club are expensive."

"I've never talked about it to anyone."

"Maybe you should."

She removed the chewing gum and threw it into the fire. The flames greedily devoured it. Perhaps he was right. She lowered her lashes. "You have to understand how it was. Maybe you can. John was the golden boy, kind of like Sunny was the queen. The high school quarterback and so-oo popular." She laughed bitterly. "He still is. Back then he was the boy every mother prayed on her knees would propose to her daughter. Except mine. Mother never was very impressed with John."

He laughed. "I like your mother."

Flushing, she said, "My mother's the kind of woman the word *gentlewoman* was made for. She wanted me to go to college before I got married."

"And you did."

"I had to. Believe it or not, I was a good girl. I never gave her a moment's trouble. Not her, not John."

She threw him such an embarrassed, sidelong look that Lewis heaved from the stones and pretended to step away and let his back cool.

"You're telling me that you never cheated on this John character," he said. "Right?"

"I was a virgin when I fell in love with him, and there were no others, if that's what you mean."

When he turned to look, she quickly glanced down and said, "That sounds so naive, I can't believe it."

"Why? I never played around on Sunny, either. And not because I was afraid I'd catch something. They didn't even have all the bad stuff then. I was faithful because it was the right thing to do. Maybe you find *that* naive."

Barbara found it unbelievable in this day and age, but she had no reason to doubt him. Why would he lie?

He said with a tad more lightness, "So, what terrible thing did you do? Have an abortion?"

"I did not have an abortion," she said with sudden sharpness, lifting her head. "Will you let me tell this my own way?"

Grinning, he placed his fist upon the end of the mantel and rested his chin there. "Sorry, Madame X. Continue."

Barbara couldn't keep the rancor from her voice. "I let John take some photographs of me, all right? I admit to having had a few reservations about it but, my goodness, is nudity a crime these days? He was a professional photographer, and he was good at his job. And anyway, in a matter of days we would've been married."

"I'm not blaming you for anything. Why're you so angry?"

Shaking her head, she nervously rubbed her bare arms, keeping her head bent like a guilty child. "The truth is, I got tired of being…" Spinning around, she all but lunged at him. "Well, look at this face, and you tell me."

"What's wrong with your face?"

"Oh, come on. You were married to a beautiful woman. You know how it is."

Lewis knew, but he didn't agree.

But she was hurrying on, as if desperate to exorcise her demons. "But I had hair then, you see. Boy, did I have hair! And John made me look so beautiful. Can you understand that? On that black-and-white glossy paper, I was—"

She clapped her hand over her mouth and slumped beneath the weight of her self-imposed penance. Then, in a tight, constricted voice, she said, "On that paper I was beautiful. I looked at those photographs, and for the first time in my life I thought I could hold up my head with any woman. I cried because I could believe in myself without wondering whether I was a fool."

She scrubbed her cheeks with the backs of her hands. Such compassion washed over Lewis, his breath left as if some great fist had plowed into his middle. He wanted, with a passion he had not felt in years, to take this woman into his arms and hold her until all the strength he possessed had drained from him into her.

But he jammed his hands into his pockets. "That's it? You're grieving because you let your fiancé take some nudes? I hate to inform you of this, my dear, but society has outgrown that taboo. It's my understanding that Charles is even planning to have some made of lovely Di."

The one thing Barbara hadn't expected from him was belittlement. He had no idea what it was like to live in Finley, Arkansas, and be blackmailed because of a few pieces of Kodak paper in the hands of an amoral rat!

Hot tears of disappointment sprang to her eyes. All the agony of the past several weeks built in her like volcanic pressure, and, whirling around so that her petticoat was a flashing swirl of silk, she literally hurled the words at him.

"Do you have any idea of what it's like to be betrayed and blackmailed?"

With a lift of his hands, he swore he was innocent. "Betrayed?" he said, hoarse urgency growing in his chest. "I don't know anything about betrayal."

"Obviously." She was a bundle of shivering outrage.

"You're not saying the quarterback showed someone your photographs without letting you know."

The obscenity of Simon Bodine's taunts rang in Barbara's ears. Though she had not yet wept over it—not truly, for the tears had refused to seep through the iron of her rage—now they rose in her throat and banked behind her eyes, pressing, pressing, and she knew her face was ugly and contorted.

Raising her arms, she covered her head. "He got drunk," she groaned as the misery came rushing back. "He got drunk, and now someone's got the damn things. He, this man, he calls me on the phone and says things, awful things. He makes demands. Oh, God." Bending at her waist, hugging herself, she weaved back and forth. "I don't know what to do anymore. I asked for it, I know, I know, but I swear I never dreamed...and I can't take it anymore."

Lewis wondered at the fragile nature of life. What if Simon Bodine hadn't pushed him over the top of his own temper? Or if he hadn't sent Bumper back to town with the car? If he hadn't gotten caught in the storm? And if Sunny hadn't left him?

Barbara was suffocating in her own self-condemnation, and when he took her by the shoulders, she struck out at him. When he forced her, as he would force one of his own sons when they didn't want the medicine that would make them well, she flailed wildly at his chest.

"I'm okay," she choked, unable to swallow down the sobs.

He closed his arms tightly and crushed her until she stopped wriggling. "I know," he crooned into her sweet, spiky hair. "Believe me, I know."

"You don't know." Her weeping left a stream of hot tears upon his chest. "You don't even know who I am."

Lewis chuckled. She felt so right in his arms. "And I don't want to know, either." He placed his mouth against her ear. "So don't try to tell me. If you do, I'll put my hands over my ears and refuse to listen."

It was difficult for Barbara to hate someone who was doing and saying all the most absolutely perfect things in the world. But it wasn't right for life to get so mixed up, she thought, putting John in her path instead of someone like this man.

She clung to him with a strange need to be closer, to drain every ounce of comfort he had to give, even if she had to climb inside his skin. "Oh, please," she heard herself saying over and over. "Please, please."

"It's okay."

"It's not fair."

"I know." He buried his face in the curve of her neck. "No, it's not fair, but very little in this life is fair."

He held her tightly, and, in her own mind, Barbara wasn't quite sure when his embrace passed the bounds of fatherly comfort and entered the domain of the lover. She guessed he didn't know, either, for he grew quite still, and she grew equally still. Dropping their arms, they stepped back from each other and stared for long, stunned moments.

The sound of rain and fire was everywhere about them. Barbara felt the return of her despair, but it was worse this time, much worse because now she knew what life had cheated her of. His magnetism was pulling at her like a lodestone of unquenchable power. Her thighs seemed to come alive from the inside, pooling with hot, silky life.

He was looking at her breasts where the damp blouse revealed the valley there; then his gaze moved hungrily over her face and her shorn hair.

"I don't know how to do this," he said softly, and shook his head, whether at himself or her, she had no idea.

Barbara couldn't move away when he started slowly toward her again. As if their moves had been choreographed long before this terrible night, he drew her carefully to him until his bare chest grazed her own stirring breasts. His head lowered with infinite caution. His parted lips moved toward hers, and Barbara, rising onto her toes as if she were coming home, lifted her face to his.

The electricity of his mouth was not to be believed. It triggered shock after rippling shock, and before Barbara could capture the sensations, she found herself lifted stunningly off her feet—floating there, balanced by his hands beneath her hips and his fingers that were curved between her soft inner thighs.

She tried to protest. "This is . . ." But his lips had swept to her neck, and her head went back with a sigh. "Oh!"

It wasn't a thing she would have done. Lucy might have let a stranger's lips find the slope of her breast and close upon it through the thin, frail silk of a blouse. But she, Barbara Regent, would never experiment with sex or become part of the one-night stand merry-go-round.

She groaned. He must stop. But he mustn't stop. How could she bear it if he stopped? He was doing all the right things. He was lowering her to the floor and pushing her deep into the shadowed corner. With breaths that struggled and sounds that made them the only two people left in the world, in the universe, he drew her bones into the angles of his own.

She moved against the fiery energy trapped there. Quickly he reached beneath the petticoat and stripped off her panties, and she, unable to make her hands work swiftly enough, tore off her blouse with her own two hands and left it an appalling stain upon the floor.

But she had, after all, stumbled upon him in a storm. Hadn't she? She put her hands on his shoulders and pushed. "I . . . I can't do this."

He did not release her. His voice was a wire when he spoke. "Why not?"

She hardly recognized her own voice. "I'm . . . afraid. I don't know you. I have no way of protecting myself."

The rain drowned out the sounds of their breathy dilemma. His mouth whispered secrets into her ear. "After Sunny left, I was . . . macho. Independent. Vengeful. All the things I'd missed, I don't know. I bought a condom, carried it for weeks. Every time I saw a woman . . ."

"Did you?" Barbara whimpered breathlessly through the film of her drugged desire.

He coaxed her lips apart with starving baby kisses and whispered into her mouth. "It's still there. What do you think?"

Kisses kept them connected—kisses that missed and kisses that landed anywhere, everywhere. While their hands and bodies engaged in activities perfectly natural to lovers, Barbara, protesting with moans and sounds of impatience, wrestled with his belt while he fumbled at his back pocket and groped inside his wallet.

Their busyness seemed only to heighten their impatience to an unbearable pitch until neither of them could wait. With his breathing an agony, he didn't bother taking off his pants. He braced her against the wall and reached beneath the silk that spilled over his thighs.

Barbara thought the heat would burn her to a cinder. The moment of searching was so intense—hers for his urgency and his for the proof that this was what she wanted—she didn't think she could possibly survive. As he pushed her more powerfully to the wall, he bent his knees and, drawing her hand between them to help, came up into her with one sundering stroke.

"Ohhh!" Her sigh was a combination of emotions: fear, alarm, ecstasy.

He moved very little, so deeply buried was he. Barbara's thighs trembled, and she braced a foot upon the ramshackle chair, and when, in her wonderful anguish of yielding, she placed her hands inside his jeans and held him closer than she thought a man could be, he tried to stop the sudden onslaught of the end.

He gritted white-hot words against her hear. "I'm sorry. God—"

His head dipped into the curve of her shoulder, and when he pressed his lips to her ear, catching the tiny lobe in his teeth, the release that had been pent up inside Barbara for weeks, possibly forever, burst upon her from out of nowhere. After that she hardly knew what he did or didn't do. She knew only the incredible moment of suspension when she wrapped her arms about his back, and when, from the depths of a brutal eternity, she experienced the inevitable, shuddering free-fall from a height so great that she must hold tightly to him or be crushed to death upon the treacherous rocks below.

Chapter Six

"Truth, like the juice of a poppy, in small quantities, calms men; in large, heats and irritates them."
C. C. Colton

Over here, over here!"

"Kick the dumb ball!"

"Catch, Charlie!"

"Hey!"

Outside Barbara's bedroom window, newly budded elm leaves danced in the spring sunshine and drew miniature shadow pictures upon the curtain of Barbara's eyelids.

She roused slowly from her dreams, half asleep, half awake in that downy limbo where truth is hard to hide and the mind cannot throw up its barricades. She had made love with a stranger. She was a different person now. She couldn't call it love because it was an interlude—an interlude, a canceled possibility, a brush with love that had left residual desire still banked inside her like coals only awaiting a breath to fan them into flame.

"Get out of the way, Rick."

"You missed! Ha, ha, missed me, missed me."

"Jerk."

"I'm gonna tell Dad."

From downstairs came a collage of familiar Saturday morning sounds: the collapse of water pressure in the old plumbing, Emma's low voice drifting sweetly up the stairs and Mr. Katt's fond reply, the slam of the back screen door. Alice Pruellyn, the housekeeper, was making breakfast. Jack, Alice's husband, who did the gardening and had taken Barbara under his wing when her father died, was rattling garbage cans at the end of the driveway.

Barbara opened one gritty eye. Groaning, she closed it again. How? How had it ended so badly? They had both known it had to end; only a fool would have pretended that they weren't caught out of time and that life had to go on.

But did it have to end that way? She hadn't said a word when it was over. He hadn't spoken, either.

Detaching herself from his arms, she straightened her clothes and moved slowly to the fire and, sitting there, wrapped her arms about her knees and leaned her cheek upon them.

In silence, he saw to his own clothes and fetched his socks and boots. When he was dressed, he walked to the front door and opened it: the cold-eyed reproach of reality, she thought.

Returning, he stooped at her feet. The funny part was, he excited her even then.

"The rain's stopped," he said.

"Yes."

The firelight defined his features, one side bright, one side in shadow, emphasizing the hollow beneath his cheekbone, the fascinating line of the scar. With tears glistening, she wanted to explain that no man besides John had ever touched her as he had. She didn't know if John had *ever* touched her so deeply—inside, where her soul was huddled in a frightened knot, shivering.

Rising, she walked to the door and stepped onto the porch. The wind was blowing the storm westward. Rain still dripped off the edges of the metal roof and spattered into the eroded gully beneath, but its fury was worn out. As was their own.

"It's nearly midnight," he told her as he braced himself against the post opposite hers. The timber groaned.

"It's over," she said.

"Yes."

A vast gulf lay between the terseness of his voice and the yearning of his eyes. Barbara wondered if they were still talking about the storm. A part of her didn't want it to be over.

Sighing, she glanced back inside at the dying fire. She opened her bag without thinking. The rustling and rattling of its contents sounded like a cannon.

"Shall we see about getting your car out of the ditch?" he asked.

With a nod she indicated yes, that would be a good idea. If she'd been like the women she read about in magazines and saw on movie screens, she would've pressed herself against him and kissed him. She would have climbed his legs and locked her own about his waist and whispered promises to make it all work out so they could live happily ever after.

But he was preparing to leave her life as suddenly as he had stepped into it. Definite hurry was in the shift of his shoulders. He buttoned his shirt and tucked it into his jeans.

Just passing through? she wanted to accuse him.

"I'll show you where it is," she told him with a taut, small smile.

After seeing how deeply she'd buried the car, he said, "Unless you relish getting down and digging with your fingernails, mystery lady, you don't have a hope in hell."

"What?" Her tone charged him with making more of the matter than it warranted.

"You're in deep. It's going to take a machine to pull this car out."

Yes, she was in deep. Like a lost child who comes to the alarming moment of truth, realizing that she is indeed lost, she turned full circle. Her lips were pinched and her features so tightly shuttered, she feared they would crack.

She sighed. "Well, what do we do now?"

He let his eyes close briefly. "We can walk out to the highway. Maybe someone will pick us up."

As they walked along the wet asphalt, talk seemed far too dangerous. She sensed something cruel in him that she hadn't seen before. He had to know that she was having second thoughts about keeping their identities a secret, yet he stubbornly refused to take the first step. He had to know that she would have jumped at an invitation to see him again.

Well, I don't need to know who you are. I don't need you. I don't need any man.

But what if she caught one of his fingers in the tiny crook of her own? What if she told him she had changed her mind?

Almost immediately a car came by and stopped. A craggy head poked out of the window. "Looks like you two got caught in the storm," it called back.

Barbara was grateful she didn't know its owner. "Sure did," her lover said.

"Could you use a lift?" the head asked.

"Sure could," her *ex*-lover said.

The worst blow of all was that with bucket seats, she couldn't even sit beside him. Climbing glumly into the back, she hugged her knees and listened in smoldering bitterness as the two men made nonsensical small talk. All too soon they were driving along the dark, rain-washed streets of Finley.

She sulked; if he wanted to keep track of her, he would have found a way, even to the point of turning around and discussing it openly in front of the driver. *What a putz you are, Barbara, tossing your heart into the ring without being able to retrieve it.*

When the driver drew up to the courthouse square, he looked across at the man sharing the front seat. "Is this all right with you, mister?"

She forced herself to look at the floor. Surely he would turn now and make some belated inquiry of her with his eyes.

"This is fine," he said.

Quickly she added as a useless subterfuge, "If you'd take me to the bus station, I'd appreciate it."

"Sure thing," the driver said.

For one fleeting moment as he climbed out she thought, she hoped, she prayed that he would reach into the back seat and take hold of her. But he was a granite monument standing beside the car. Then, to her agony, he reached through the window and shook the man's hand and thanked him.

She'd been tricked! Heaven had dangled a prize before her nose but had then meted out punishment instead. Because she had been a bad girl, she must now return to the wasteland of her life.

Breaking her heart, he walked down the wet street, his hands jammed deeply into his pockets, his rough boots slashing through the silvery reflections of the streetlights in the puddles.

As the driver put the car in gear and moved slowly away, she twisted in her seat and memorized, with despair, the sight of him leaving her. So now she had to live with it, right? She'd had sex with a stranger. Safe sex, yes, but morally, emotionally, what were her prices to pay?

She didn't know yet. She was still hurting.

This morning, lying on her own bed in her own bedroom, her body still tender from the power of him, she knew more punishment would be forthcoming for such a mistake.

"Have no doubts about that, Barbara Regent, great-great-granddaughter of Thaddeus T. Finley," she whispered in self-mockery. "Punishment will be dealt out slowly and with exquisite care. The gods will be pleased."

She closed her eyes.

"You cheated, Steve. I saw you touch the ball."

"What do you know, runt?"

"I know you cheated, that's what. Didn't he cheat, Charlie?"

"Steve is Steve."

"What does that mean?"

"Figure it out."

Forcing her eyes open again, Barbara angled a groggy look at her alarm clock. Twenty past nine. *Twenty past nine!* She never slept this late!

With a vigorous kick, she sent sheet and blanket billowing to the foot of the bed, then suddenly hugged her knees to her chest and waited for pain to subside in places she hadn't known could cause pain.

"Oh, Lord."

She eased her legs cautiously over the side of the bed and found the floor by painful degrees. Every muscle that had been abused yesterday was in rebellion today. Beneath the hems of her pajamas stretched sore, scratched legs and ankles. A bruise marred her left foot and hurt when she arched it. Her right knee throbbed when she bent it, and her hands, her nails, were hopelessly ruined.

"One must do these things gra-du-al-ly," she moaned, and hobbled toward the French doors that opened onto the sun deck.

"Play by yourself, then."

"Okay, I will."

"The grass is too long, anyway."

"Cripes, we're supposed to be mowing it. Get the gasoline."

"Not me."

"Yes, or Dad'll kill you."

"No."

"Then *I'll* kill you."

Barbara frowned and discovered that even *that* hurt. But boys' voices shouldn't have been outside her bedroom window. What was going on here?

Pushing open the doors, she stepped into a splash of sunshine that seemed bent on regaining all the time it had lost the day before. She was about to lean over the rail to find the boys when Tabor, the family cat, streaked up the elm tree in a flash of sooty black while below him, skidding to a stop, was a perfectly hideous monster.

A Saint Bernard, Barbara thought, and immediately dismissed every nice thing she'd ever read about the rescue animals; this one's jaws were drooling for a delicious bite of cat, and his barking literally shook the panes of the French doors.

Laughing, she scooped up the bristling feline and gazed down at the dog. It was then that she became aware of other extraordinary changes.

"Wha-at?" she murmured, squinting in wonder and dropping the cat ungraciously onto the deck.

For decades Castle Park Road had been the Gramercy Park of Finley, Arkansas. Here the homes were very old and in an almost constant, though elegant, state of disarray—not unlike an elite society whose days of peaceful senility are numbered.

Most of the houses had been structured out of limestone and brick and were three or four stories high. Many were under the guardianship of the local heritage society that preserved such old homes. Set far back from the street, they were approached by long, stately drives beneath trees as gracious and aging as the buildings they shaded. Yet they were enclosed by forbidding iron fences or great old hedges of privet and arborvitae arranged for privacy, designed to keep the world out and them in.

The hedge between the Finley property and the Hempstead estate next door was over twelve feet tall and impenetrable, except for the iron gate in its center that had grown rusty after Josephine Hempstead had turned her property over to her great-grandson and then had the bad taste to die. After that the house had grown up in rose brambles and creepers and greedy honeysuckle: a gardener's nightmare that even Jack would have been loath to tackle.

For nearly two years Julia Regent's real-estate company had tried to dump the Hempstead house onto a depressed market. The place might have been a historical landmark, but it was much more economical to build a new house across town than restore a relic that had degenerated into something out of an old Dracula movie.

Now Barbara realized that a moving van was backed up to the front steps. An Arkansas Power and Light truck was parked in the driveway. A telephone truck had pulled up at the front curb. The big oak door was thrown wide, creating a cavern beneath the half-moon of ruby, emerald and yellow-orange glass over the top.

Clay Wiley, the telephone man, was hovering in a cat seat at the top of the utility pole at the curb where Mr. Katt always parked his county sheriff's car. He was grinning at her.

"Heard you got yourself stuck down at the river, Barbara," he called from his perch.

With a rueful glance at her pajamas, Barbara leaned over the rail to see Julia's For Sale sign lying flat in the shin-high Bermuda grass. "You could save yourself a lot of work, Clay."

"How's that?"

"The grapevine is much faster than that phone line you're connecting." She flashed him a smile. "And a darn site cheaper."

Laughing, Clay returned to his task, and when Barbara looked for the boys and their dog, they had all disappeared. She started to go inside but hesitated to watch coveralled workmen laboriously unloading a huge grand piano from the van.

"Easy, now," one called. "Be careful."

"Do me a favor," another complained. "Get the darn roller off my foot."

From around the corner of the south walkway the three boys wandered, kicking a soccer ball from railing to railing until it sailed over the workmen and bounced into a jungle of grass.

They skittered down the front steps after it. The youngest boy teasingly lifted the lid of the grand piano and played a "chopsticks" pattern on the treblemost keys.

"Hey!" one of the movers hollered, waving the youngster out of the way. "Clear out before I 'chop' you."

Giggling mischievously, the boy minced his way across the veranda. The oldest boy, having located the ball, attempted to execute a kick from the grass, and they all lunged to retrieve it, even the dog.

Déjà vu played hide-and-seek with Barbara's mind: three sets of warm, wondering eyes, two brown-haired heads and one blond, all with faces of fresh, clear skin, all wearing jeans and scruffy variations of sneakers, their red T-shirts all bearing a peeling insignia of a soccer ball on the front.

The oldest spied her gazing down. With a swipe of his arm, he shushed his brothers and indicated that they were being observed.

"Hi," the smallest of the trio said uncertainly.

"Hi, yourself." Something familiar about them continued to trouble Barbara. "Are you my new neighbors?"

"Are you a schoolteacher?"

Laughing, she plucked the pink sleeve of her pajamas. "Tell me the truth, would a schoolteacher wear pink pajamas?"

They proffered shy smiles and visually quizzed each other to be sure it was all right to make friends. "We don't know anyone here yet," the middle one volunteered.

"You know me."

They didn't appear overly elated by that fact, but they were too courteous to make a point of it.

The youngest, stepping back to grasp the dog's collar, said, "My name's Richard, but everyone calls me Rick because I'm still a child. This is Max."

Barbara raised her brows at the Saint Bernard, who seemed to be interested in her only as a means of learning what had happened to the cat. "Well, Rick," she called down, "do you have another name?"

"Paccachio," he said. "Rick Paccachio."

Forgetting was a perfectly human trait. Everyone forgot. In fact, if people hadn't been blessed with the ability to forget, what a sorry state the world would be in.

But a chill and Simon Bodine's memory returned to Barbara with a vengeance. *That* was why she'd gone tearing out to the river—to find Lewis Paccachio, not to waste time falling in love with some scuz who'd stolen her heart, then walked away with it jammed in his pocket.

Love? Uncool, Barbara. Very uncool.

"He's Charlie," Rick Paccachio was brightly explaining. "My older brother's Steven. Steve's fifteen, but he don't have a driver's license or nothin'."

Charlie, the second in line, screwed up a pleasant boyish face to reveal a set of twinkling braces. He jabbed a thumb at his older brother. "Steve gets to practice drivin' in the Suburban, though. All I get to practice is the piano."

"I'm glad to meet you guys," she said, and shook her head to clear it of the troubling cobwebs. She smiled uneasily. "Actually, I've been looking for your father."

Three pairs of eyes narrowed. "You have?" Steven said, an edge of disenchantment underscoring his expression, his words, his manner.

"What for?" Rick quizzed.

Charlie took hold of Max's collar as if he needed the moral support.

Waving away her apprehensions and theirs, Barbara guessed that if the father was anywhere near as charming as the sons, they would all wind up stealing her heart.

Welcome to the neighborhood, Mr. Paccachio. I wanted to knock your head off, but since you have great kids, I'll spare you. Now, what's this about Simon Bodine....

She pulled a face. "I think I'll tell him that you're not boys at all. You're all grown men in disguises, and your dog is a pony in costume. You don't work for the government, do you?"

They giggled, but Steve recovered quickly. "Do you play soccer?"

"I used to play basketball until my teammates paid me not to. Does that tell you anything?"

They laughed.

Barbara felt a prickling at the back of her neck. A mocking part of her brain envisioned a long, winding network of dominoes whose pattern stretched intricately around her and behind, in front and between so that she couldn't discern where it began or ended.

"Soccer." The first domino toppled. *Click.* "Three boys," the stranger had said. Another domino fell. *Click, click.* "And we mustn't forget the dog." *Click, click, click.* "At first I thought Steven was mine." *Click, click, click, click.*

Barbara knew, deep in her heart, what the truth was, and that she could not escape; she knew it the way a driver who hears the scream of brakes and looks up too late knows the collision is coming from behind. May God have mercy upon her, they were one and the same—her stranger and Lewis Paccachio!

Damn the fates! Damn the geography that had placed Paccachio here, in this town that could not keep its secrets, with only a hedge between them!

Had he known who she was? Surely no man could have been clever enough to have kept that from her. Still, she had to know. She had to look into Paccachio's eyes in the full light of day and see the truth for herself. Oh, God, what a fool she'd been. What a fool!

With an abrupt turn that left the boys staring after her in bafflement, Barbara jerked around and ran through the French doors and across the old carpet to her closet. She tore off the pajama bottoms and dragged on a wraparound skirt. Her hands were so sore, she could hardly manage to tie it about her pajama top.

Searching through her closet, she located a pair of ratty sneakers and jerked them on. Deflecting a glance to the mirror, she could hardly believe the damage framed there—her hair that looked like a Brillo pad, her skin that looked as pale as a cadaver's stretched out in Mr. Montrose's morgue.

On her way down the stairs she wondered which caused the most pain—her sore, aching muscles, or her poor heart that had been so stupid she wanted to die.

By the time she reached the landing, she was shaking all over. "But I love March," Emma Parker was saying from the dining room. "I always look forward to spring cleaning."

Alice, with her usual crusty bossiness, was refilling coffee cups.

"Thank you, no," Granna said, and covered her cup with her hand, smiling up at the maid she had hired when she married Thaddeus's son over fifty years before. Alice had been seventeen years old then.

"You know I'm cutting down on caffeine, Alice," Granna added. "Doctor's orders."

Alice rolled her eyes. "Pah, what do doctors know? My father drank dozens of cups every day of his life."

"And he died," Granna saucily retorted.

"Yes. At ninety-two."

Granna cackled with glee. "Only half a cup, then."

"Drink a whole one, Granna," Mr. Katt solemnly advised. "Live forever."

Everything about the Charlatan County sheriff was slow: his gangling walk, his gestures, his temper, his condemnation of his fellow men, all of which had made him a carefully methodical sheriff for most of his adult life. He was working today, and he was dressed in his gray uniform.

"I like March, too, Miss Emma," he said with a fond smile. "But April—now, there's a month."

Emma's gasp interrupted them all. "Barbara," she said, her frail features widening as Barbara walked into the room, "what in heaven's name happened to you?"

Alice folded her arms like the genie out of the lamp, and Granna dropped her starched napkin. "Oh, dear."

Barbara wanted nothing more than to fly out of the house and charge through the hedge and pounce upon Lewis Paccachio, but instead she said mildly, "Last night I got my car stuck down at the river."

"What were you doing out there?" Edward Wheeler inquired as he looked up from his fastidiously folded newspaper.

"I was trying to find the engineer and got caught in the storm. Where's Mother?"

From the vicinity of the kitchen, the telephone was ringing. In the middle of the third ring, the receiver was lifted.

"Answering the telephone, I imagine, dear," Granna said, and rose carefully to her feet. "She's been up since dawn. Would you like some cereal for breakfast?"

With a brief kiss for her grandmother, Barbara shook her head. "But I'd take two Alka Seltzers if you had them."

"Oh, dear," Granna repeated, and stole a fearful look at Alice, who snorted.

"What's all the commotion next door?" Barbara asked innocently.

"Your mother sold the house, dear." Emma briskly passed the sugar bowl to Mr. Katt. "Isn't it wonderful? I think she got a handsome commission, too." She hesitated, worrying the brooch at her high collar. "Don't let me forget, Alice, I must remind Julia to take the ad out of the classifieds. That'll save her a whole week."

"A penny saved is a penny earned," Granna seriously observed, as if she were the one who'd thought of it.

The back door slammed.

"Who bought it?" Barbara asked casually.

Mr. Katt was holding a lighter to his pipe, and he drew vigorously, causing a wreath of white smoke to curl about his gray head until he looked like Santa Claus. "Someone out of state," he said around the stem clamped in his teeth. "Germany."

"West Germany, actually," Edward lisped. "A foreigner."

"That's what I said." Mr. Katt scowled darkly at the accountant as he removed the pipe and cupped its bowl in a palm. "From out of state."

Leaving them to rattle their own skeletons, Barbara swept out of the room. Their mouths were shaped in circles of speculation, and she let the back door slam shut with an emphatic this-doesn't-concern-you. But she knew they would follow; without a word, they would exchange a nod and rise in unison and tiptoe through the back door and along the walk to eavesdrop.

Her sneakers squished quietly through the dew, but her heart was thrashing in her chest, and her legs were quivering so badly she could have crumpled in her tracks. Had she been made a total fool of? Could she have been that stupid?

From behind the glistening privet hedge, she heard her mother's beautiful, low murmur. The gate shrieked rudely as she opened it, and her palm came away rusty. Muttering an oath, she started to wipe the rust on her skirt but stopped just in time.

"It'll take a few days for the deed to be recorded, Mr. Paccachio," Julia was saying. "In the meantime, if there's anything we can do to help you get moved in, please let us know."

"The famous hospitality of the South."

The man's familiar voice made Barbara stop dead in her tracks. "You don't know how good it sounds," he said. "The movers are cramming everything into two rooms. I think we'll just camp out till winter and be done with it."

Julia laughed. "There's a good foundation in this house. You'll be surprised what the renovators can do."

"Well, if you know a good carpenter."

"As a matter of fact, I do. But he's a bear."

Barbara wanted to rush to her mother and take her by the shoulders. *Don't you know who this man is?* she wanted to shriek. *Don't you know that I told him secrets that you don't know? That even Lucy doesn't know? Don't you know I offered my body and my love to him? That he took my body and turned down the love?*

"I find I can get along with most anybody and anything," he said, chuckling.

"It's the travel. They say it broadens you."

"What it does is tire you out so badly, you have no choice."

More pleasant, infectious laughter. Barbara ground her teeth. She didn't know what she disliked in Paccachio more: the fact that he could sway Julia with such perfect ease or the fact that his presence in Finley, which was supposed to have changed life for the better, had, in fact, made everything intolerably worse.

And the other, of course.

Like a general jerking down his field jacket in preparation for battle, Barbara smoothed her skirt and strode heatedly through the hedge. Julia was extending a folded paper. Like a victim suddenly spotting the fuse hissing its path to a keg of dynamite, Barbara followed the length of her mother's arm.

The sun was Lewis Paccachio's friend. The white-feathered wing at his temple that in the darkness had aroused her maternal instincts was now strikingly arresting. And the scar? In the darkness it had given him the air of a criminal, but in the brilliance of day it made him a bold, dashing pirate whose wicked brown eyes and white smile could steal your heart as easily as your jewels.

His hair, freshly washed and wavy, was caught close with a red headband. He was wearing loose, button-fly, cotton pants that moved with him, and the sleeves of his gray sweatshirt were ripped out so that the worn, frayed fabric capped the swells of his shoulders. He'd been helping the movers, and the underarms were marked with oval stains of sweat.

Their recognition was like two broken ends of the same live wire coming together—ragged, raw, swinging toward each other, then away, and glitching images upon both their minds.

He was in the process of slipping the folded paper into the hip pocket of his pants when he saw her. He missed. The gesture was so endearing that Barbara's anger slipped a notch. She wanted, foolishly—she never learned—to go to him and place her cheek upon his chest.

The man walked away, you idiot!

So, his smile said, *it's you.*

You knew all along, her eyes accused.

I did not.

Barbara didn't know if she could believe the message he was sending or not. *How much are you going to tell?*

How much do you want me to tell?

I want you to pretend you've never seen me before.

Ah, you really are the keeper of secrets.

People here care about me.

They also think you're Snow White. We wouldn't want to disillusion them, would we?

Color rose hotly from Barbara's neck and settled high on her cheeks.

Julia was gaping at her. Barbara touched her mother's outstretched hand in greeting. "Hello, Mother. I see you sold the Hempstead house."

Unaccustomed to such bristling antagonism from Barbara toward a perfect stranger, Julia raised her eyebrows in surprise. "Darling—" the endearment was the mildest of mild reproaches "—I didn't know you were awake. I was just returning some papers to Mr. Paccachio, our new neighbor."

"How nice."

Behind her, Barbara sensed the arrival of Emma and Mr. Katt and Edward Wheeler, with Granna bringing up the rear.

With her usual gracious hospitality, Julia motioned to them. "Things are such a family affair around here, Mr. Paccachio," she explained. "Everyone, I want you to meet Mr. Paccachio. He's in charge of building the new mill, and now he and his three sons have bought the Hempstead house."

An earnest chorus of "ahhs" ensued, and Julia obligingly called the roll of her household, each of whom stepped forward to present himself, along with a hand-shake and laughter and an eager welcome that included the three boyish heads that were by now peeping around the live oak tree.

Another man Barbara had never seen before, a giant with hands like baseball gloves, lumbered down the Hempstead steps and plowed through the jungle of grass, ordering Max to stay.

Lewis introduced him as Bumper O'Banyon, his house-guest. The gum chewer, Barbara thought lamely. Sweet heaven, did Bumper O'Banyon know what she and Lewis had done?

Motioning his sons to come stand beside him, Lewis introduced them. In the space of two minutes, the Pacca-chios were all invited to dinner by Emma, and Lewis was told that he was welcome to leave the boys with her any time. He was included in a fishing trip planned by Mr. Katt. He was questioned about the German economy by Edward Wheeler and promised free tax advice whenever it was needed. He was also informed that he must tell absolutely everything about his work all over the world and about all his plans for restoring the Hempstead house and whether or not he planned to join the Lions' club and take the open spot of shortstop on the baseball team.

How messy life was, Barbara thought. How sprawling and unpredictable. From behind the slash of sunlight that separated them, Lewis was dissecting her inch by inch, and she had the uncanny suspicion that he saw more of her fully dressed than he had half-naked.

"The First State Tigers," Emma was saying, comically cheering the team on with her fists. "They've already started practicing."

A true man of occasion, Mr. Katt hovered over Emma. "The wet ground will slow them up, I expect," he said.

Realizing that he was expected to respond, Lewis tore his eyes from her and blinked. A winglike shadow passed over Barbara at his tiny departure.

"That's a good idea," he told them, and awkwardly cleared his throat as he looked at Barbara, then back to them again. "My team won a pennant in Manila."

"My goodness," Julia said. Then, with a healthy laugh at herself as she discerned the real object of his interest, she added, "Silly me. Why, I forgot to introduce my very own daughter. This is Barbara, Mr. Paccachio. It's largely because of her that you're here."

Chapter Seven

"Uncertain in her temper as a morning in April."
Sam Slick

The charade was played marvelously, without a flaw. But then, the principals had acted together before, and Lewis guessed it was an easy matter for Barbara to fool her mother's boarders. Their love for her was unconditional and mutual, and he wondered if they could sense how incredibly easy it would be for him to feel the same way.

With a smile that said one thing and a grip that said quite another, he extended his hand and closed it upon Barbara's. The moment they touched he was back in the river shack, reliving those stolen moments when his body had been part of her own and she was as tight about him as any woman could be. In the summer blue of her eyes he saw his own truth: the storm was in their blood now, and he didn't think either of them could escape its gale force.

He managed an unconvincing smile. "We're very happy to be in Finley, Miss Regent."

The pupils of her eyes dilated. She could have been gazing into the muzzle of an M-16, he thought, and she attempted to retrieve her hand. When she discovered she couldn't, her brows snapped a warning.

Lewis released her. Not expecting that, she stumbled backward. Around the congealed edges of her smile, she said quite formally, "I've been looking forward to meeting you, Mr. Paccachio. Welcome to Finley."

Lewis considered the small brand of rust she left on his palm. Grinning, he worked it into his hands. "I only hope you're as happy to have us for neighbors as we are to have you."

"I was so sorry to have missed you yesterday."

"Well—" he inclined his head "—sometimes more important things come up."

"Not more important." She hesitated and flicked her tongue over her lips. "What I mean is, I was looking for you but accidentally got involved with—"

She shut her mouth with a snap, and Lewis touched his tongue to the inside of his cheek. "You were saying?"

She glanced grimly at her mother. "Nothing."

Lewis thought he could die happy as long as he was in her arms. "What a strange coincidence," he said cheerfully. "So did I. Get involved, I mean. A very unexpected matter, as it turned out."

The summer blue of her eyes had turned to winter ice. Drawing herself quite tall, she mimed the word "bastard," and Julia Regent, who was no one's fool, studied him with the same unsettling X-ray vision he thought his own mother had mastered.

With exaggerated innocence, Lewis smiled. Julia Regent was one person he wanted as an ally, not an enemy. Presently she began talking to Steven, and soon everyone was chatting.

"So," he drawled when he had Barbara's attention all to himself, "now that we've finally met, what was it you wanted to see me about, Miss Regent? Oh, I'm sorry, I assume it is *miss*."

"It's *miss*." A bee sting was in her reply.

"Ah. I thought so. Well, now, what can I do for you, *Miss* Regent?"

"Nothing," she mumbled acidly. "I'll talk to you later about it."

"Later?" murmured Lewis beneath the hum of other voices. "Perhaps we should make an appointment."

Her thinned nostrils and jutted jaw accused him of being a sadist. "I don't think that's necessary, Mr. Paccachio."

"Whatever you say, Miss Regent. I'm at your command."

Time missed an awkward beat between them, and Barbara, reeling from his impact, thought she could have heard a pin drop, so silent did everyone become. Lewis Paccachio was a terrible person!

She raised a hand to the nape of her neck, expecting to find long tresses of hair perfect for fidgeting with. Emma, bless her heart, tried to relieve the strange tension she felt but could not fathom.

"We're so proud of our Barbara, Mr. Paccachio," she said with enthusiasm. "You can't imagine how hard she worked to lure you here."

Groaning inwardly, Barbara rolled her eyes heavenward. *Oh, Emma.*

Lewis smothered his laughter with an expression that Barbara thought deserved brimstone and ashes. "How wonderful." He added, as if it were a matter of grave concern just between Emma and himself, "You know, Miss Parker, my mother always said that dedication would tell.

I'm afraid I find dedication sadly lacking these days, don't you?"

Emma's tiny head nodded raptly, and she clung to Lewis's words with a reverence that made Barbara want to take the woman by the shoulders and shake her.

"How very true," Emma purred. "I certainly agree, Mr. Paccachio, I certainly do."

"That's why it's so refreshing to run into someone as self-sacrificing as Miss Regent." Lewis smiled broadly.

"She's a jewel, our Barbara," Emma agreed, and beamed.

Barbara swore she wouldn't have been surprised had the woman stooped to kiss his hand. *Stop while you're ahead, Paccachio!* she wanted to snarl through gritted teeth.

If Edward Wheeler hadn't stepped to the fore, she might have done just that, but the small man, having found an immediate friend in shy Charles, looked up and spoke to Gene Katt with the most adamant independence Barbara had ever heard him use. Even his lisp seemed to have improved.

"If no one has any objections—" he leveled a look at Gene Katt's uniform and the revolver buckled about his waist "—I'm going to show Charles the duck pond."

The sheriff scowled so that deeply engrained lines made his visage almost terrifying. He loomed over the accountant and growled, "Why should anyone object?"

The little man pursed his mouth. "I'm sure I wouldn't know," he said with a huffy sigh, "but then, around here, one never knows."

As Charlie and Edward Wheeler trudged away, their heads bent in serious conversation, Julia laughed and Emma said, "Mercy me, would you look at Mr. Wheeler?"

Not to be outdone, Emma turned to Rick and announced with a proud smile, "Late next month our Granna will be seventy-five years old. Every year we have a gigantic party in the city park. Everyone comes. Even if they're not invited, they come, and there's lots to eat and games. Doesn't that sound like fun? Then at night we have a wiener roast and fireworks. You, especially, must come, Richard."

"Me?" Rick's brown eyes danced with anticipation. "Hey, Dad, can I go?"

"Of course. What do you tell Miss Parker?"

"Thanks, Miss Parker." Rick scrunched into a mass of wriggling shyness.

"You're very welcome," the woman said. "And you know what, I've got an idea that you're a vanilla man."

Over his shoulder, Rick giggled at his father in anticipation of good times. "Well—" he spoke behind his hand to Emma "—chocolate's really my best favorite."

"Aren't you in luck!" Emma crowed, throwing back her hands. "That's exactly what I was going to bake!"

While Mr. Katt drew Steven aside and described his boat and dangled the irresistible bait of inquiring if Steven knew how to steer, Lewis scratched his jaw and said for the benefit of the few who remained, "Well, well, I think I've just been orphaned."

Bumper laughed his earthquake laugh, but Julia laid the back of her hand upon Barbara's cheek. "Are you all right, dear?"

No, I am not all right! Barbara wanted to shriek. *My whole life is rolling around like mercury, and there's nothing I can do about it!*

She smiled thinly. "Mother, if you've ever tried to jack up a car by yourself in the middle of the night in pouring rain, you wouldn't ask such a question."

Momentarily satisfied, Julia extended her hand to Lewis. "Mr. Paccachio, I'm afraid you're going to have to excuse me. There are some houses, unfortunately, that can't be shown except on weekends."

Smoothly, graciously, Julia moved among her people like unassuming royalty, kissing her mother's wrinkled cheek. "Granna, don't expect me home until late. Murray and I are having dinner in town. Oh, by the way, Barbara," she added, turning, "Polly Bodine called for you last night. Have you checked the messages?"

Barbara guessed there must have been a red alert button in her brain with the name Bodine engraved on it. Even without having shared her guilty secret with Lewis, she would have been alarmed. Of course, she knew what he did not know, that he must give Simon a job or her secret wouldn't be a secret any longer.

She looked at Lewis but spoke to Julia. "Did she say where she was?"

"The hospital, I believe. I asked her what was wrong, but she didn't want to tell me. You know how shy Polly is."

"The hospital!"

Barbara's exclamation was like some final punctuation mark that Lewis guessed was about to end the currents swirling between them. In the instant when she turned from him, something was in her eyes—not easily seen, but there—some touch of dread, of fear.

She spun around, mumbling that she had to go immediately, and started for the hedge. There was about her motion—the tilt of her head, perhaps, or the unintentional swing of her hips—that made Lewis disregard what anyone thought. Following, he grasped her arm and hauled her up short.

"This Bodine woman," he said earnestly. "She wouldn't be related to Simon Bodine, would she?"

Though Simon Bodine had already unwittingly been the liaison between them before she and Lewis had ever met, Barbara knew that to reveal any more was risk-taking in its purest form. "It's a rather complicated matter, Mr. Paccachio," she said with deadly honesty. "One you might find a bit more difficult to walk away from."

Slap!

Lewis took the force of her open-handed blow on the chin, and his first impulse was to serve her back in kind. She didn't know what the hell she was talking about! He hadn't wanted to walk away from anything. *She'd* been the one to insist on keeping everything such a damned mystery. After getting out of the car without a peep that might have endangered her precious reputation, he had walked straight to the bus station. There he'd found a sleepy-eyed, overweight woman reading a tattered copy of an old Harold Robbins. No bus had come and gone, she told him, nor was one scheduled to do so. No woman in a muddy skirt and jacket had come inside.

Under his breath, he said to her in a voice just as low and just as hurt, "Put away your guillotine, my darling Barbara. Isn't it enough that you have my heart? Must you have my head, as well?"

Before he could read her response, she twisted away. She dodged Steven and Mr. Katt and slipped through the hedge. He caught up with her as the gate was screeching shut and stopped it with his knee.

"Barbara." His command was stripped clean of pretension as his hand encircled her wrist. "Listen to me, damn it."

She stopped walking, but she refused, mutinously, to lift her head. The color had drained from her cheeks.

"Simon Bodine is Polly's older brother," she said huskily. "The family has serious problems. Leave this alone, Mr. Paccachio. It can only get worse. Now, if you'll excuse me, I have to go to the hospital."

"Don't call me that. I'll drive you there."

"I can drive myself."

"You're going like that?"

She glanced down at her pajama top and, finally, up at him. "Your car's at the river, axle-deep," he reminded her. "Along with . . . other things."

The misty sparkle of her lashes acted with surprising violence upon Lewis's heart. Oh, yes, she was in his blood—too soon, too irrevocably, too hopelessly. He'd known it when he returned to the motel and had lain there, staring at the flash of neon on the ceiling until dawn.

How had it happened? How was it that in less than twenty-four hours she had him searching for ways to find her, get her alone and make her want him desperately? He wasn't that kind of man. He waited on others to come to him. But now his breath was shallow in his chest, and he felt like a kid walking up to the front door on his very first date.

She crossed her arms as if his look had made her feel naked. She whispered, "What do you want?"

He didn't answer immediately because he knew she wouldn't believe him. God help him, he wasn't sure he believed it himself, that he wanted her, all of her, forever.

Only a moment did she hesitate, and then her head rose and her slim shoulders squared. He smiled helplessly, which meant, *Please understand, I'm in over my head.*

Did she read him right? Or was her sudden pivot a statement that she could not have cared less? "I'll meet you at the curb in front of your house in five minutes," he called after her.

* * *

At the Shell station at the intersection of Main and Fourth streets, Simon Bodine was stuffing quarters into the soft drink machine while his cronies, Chino and Dale, were putting five dollars' worth of gasoline into the tank of Chino's pickup.

The machine promptly gobbled his quarters and waited smugly for more. Swearing the vilest oath he knew, Simon gave the box a vicious kick that placed a dent in it and sent a stab of pain racing up his leg. He reached beneath his flapping shirttail to search for more quarters, but he'd used his last two.

"Hey, Jake!" he bellowed to the station attendant. "This damn thing ate my money again."

As a car pulled away from the full-service island, Jake Penny approached him, wiping his hands on a grimy towel. Simon saw him looking, not at the thieving machine, but at a point somewhere over Simon's own shoulder.

A man at the self-service pump whistled shrilly through his teeth and yelled, "Bring it on, baby!"

From behind him Simon heard a husky feminine voice say, "Give me the quarters, Jake. I need 'em more than this louse does."

Jake rolled his eyes comically.

Simon let his lashes lower in dismay at the sight of May Lamont. May was a senior at Finley High School, and her reputation, even before he'd started going out with her, was that of being the hottest skirt in Charlatan County.

Not that hot, in his opinion, but then, he'd been watching other skirts of late, one of which belonged to John Woodward's sexy little ex-fiancée.

Removing two quarters from his pocket, Jake laid them atop the soda machine and wisely stepped back. With a come-hither wiggle of her hips, May laughed and stood on tiptoe to pluck the quarters. With two fingers, she shoved them into the pocket of a pair of jeans whose seams could not have withstood the stress of anything larger.

"Thanks, Simon," she purred from deep in her throat. "I'm savin' for my hope chest."

"What kind of chest, May?" yelled the man at the pump.

Laughing, May threw her arms into the air in the sign of victory. "Community chest. Return to go, collect two hundred dollars and give it to me."

"Give it to me," Simon parroted, and made a vulgar sign at the man. To May, he growled, "Keep your voice down. Didn't I warn you about that kind of stuff?"

Looking even younger than her seventeen years, May pouted prettily as Simon pried a cigarette from his shirt pocket and lit it. She threw her body into the shape of an S and tapped her toe until he placed the white cylinder to her lips.

Her lips remained slightly parted, and smoke drizzled through them into her half-lidded eyes. "What good will it do to keep my voice down?" she declared, and finger-combed her long red hair. "In another couple of months, everyone'll know."

"Shut up."

"And everyone knows I'm not seein' anyone but you, Sexy Simon."

A thin line of sweat formed on Simon's upper lip. He felt anything but sexy and even less like a father-to-be. He'd been counting on the construction job to pay for May to get herself fixed, but lately she'd been talking about moving in and having the baby. There were already enough babies around his grandmother's house, where he and his brothers and Polly lived.

He could feel Jake's eyes drilling into his back. He turned to look at Chino and Dale. Without a word, Dale climbed out of the truck and got into the back. Taking May by the arm, Simon steered her toward the truck.

Calling over his shoulder, he told Jake, "Hey, I'll catch you the next time around, Jake."

Jake was ambling out to wash a windshield of a car beneath the full-service canopy. "Hang loose, Bodine."

"Gotcha, man."

Simon gritted his teeth as he yanked open the truck door. Placing his hand on the curve of May's buttocks, he gave her a shove upward.

"Watch out!" she yelped. She fell across the seat, catching herself on Chino's thigh and smiling up at him with a twangy, "Hi, Chino."

"What's goin' on, May?" the man said, leering down the front of her top.

A pretty pout formed on her face. "Nothin' that lover boy here couldn't fix if he ever had any money."

Glowering, Simon shut the door and slid low on his spine beside her. Chino jerked his head aside and turned the key in the ignition, and before the truck was out of the lot, Simon had dragged May into his arms and was kissing her roughly.

Chino burned rubber from the gasp pump to the curb and halfway down the street, and May giggled. "What's the matter, lover boy?" she purred, and reached up to bite Simon on the chin. "You got troubles?"

An image of Lewis Paccachio materialized upon the screen of Simon's bitter memory, and he absently slid his hand beneath May's tight tank top and sneaked beneath her bra.

"Nothin' I can't handle, sweetheart," he growled.

"Yeah," Chino threw in, keeping his eyes straight ahead. "Simon's got a plan."

"Well, it better pay good," May said as her nipples, sensitive with pregnancy, grew hard and taut. She gripped Simon's wrist and pulled his hand lower to the skintight seam of her jeans below the zipper.

As she snuggled around so that she could lift her head and lick his jaw, she added sultrily, "The doctor says he won't deliver the baby unless the bill's paid up-front, Simon. And 'fore I'll be a charity case, I'll tell my daddy what you did. He'll call the law on you, Simon." She laughed. "And you know how nasty old Sheriff Katt can get."

Simon was hard as a rock beneath the relentless bone of May's pelvis. He could have cared less about Sheriff Katt and the delinquency of minors. He settled himself more comfortably on the seat.

"Drive out along the docks, Chino," he muttered thickly as he unhooked May's bra. "And keep your eyes on the road."

As Barbara had hurried through the old hedge on Castle Park Road after having watched Lewis Paccachio fit neatly into her life like the missing piece of a puzzle that she'd searched high and low for, she didn't think that five *hours* would have been time enough to prepare herself for him. Who was she kidding? Five *years* wouldn't have been time enough.

By the time she returned to her own house and reached the bottom of the stairs, she truly panicked. All the muscles and bones that were she seemed to disconnect, and she draped over the banister like a rag.

Where, she wondered with a groan, had all that serious, civic-minded, down-to-earth, Thaddeus T. Finley blood gone that was supposed to make her immune to foolishness such as this? She was a fool to think about Lewis Paccachio in any kind of terms, much less as a permanent part of her life. She was, after all, on the rebound, which was temporary insanity in anyone's books. And Lewis? How realistic a candidate for a relationship was he after sixteen years of marriage?

She let her breath out slowly. So, could she do what must be done? Yes. She would calmly change clothes and get a grip on herself. Then, with a rigorous rein on her senses, she would go down to meet this man who had walked into her life with heavy-duty boots. Only this time she would let Lewis Paccachio know in a kind, mature way that just because they had stumbled into each other's lives at a weak moment didn't mean she wasn't intending to put it behind her and get on with life. If he wished to be part of that life—in a sensible, adult way, of course—they could behave like normal people and become friends, neighbors. Then, after a reasonable time, if—and she stressed the word *if*—they still wanted to think about . . . well, falling in love or . . . whatever, they could.

Barbara gazed blankly at herself in the mirror. "If Simon Bodine isn't the death of you first," she whispered.

Deliberately ignoring the tendency of her fingers to become thumbs and her stomach to flutter with winged creatures, she walked briskly to the bathroom sink and scrubbed her face and quickly brushed her teeth. She dragged a pair of soft khaki jodhpurs from her closet and her best polo boots and a lightweight, powder-blue sweater. After a quick blast of perfume, a flurry of blush and a careful thirty seconds to mascara her lashes, she snatched up her jewelry box and dumped the entire contents upon the unmade bed. Porcelain? Plastic? Wood? What?

Deciding upon the tiny pearls Granna had given her, she peered into the mirror and was disappointed to find her usual average self staring back.

"What did you think?" she demanded, scowling. "That you'd turn into a princess after a night in the arms of a prince?"

To heck with it!

She sprayed mousse into her palm and rubbed it between her hands. She ruffled it through her short hair until she looked like something out of *The Legend of Billie Jean*. Score by Craig Safan. *Stop that!*

She distractedly shoved her glasses onto her face and dabbed her mouth with lip gloss.

Alice had cleared away the breakfast dishes by the time she got downstairs, and everyone had returned to the front of the house to talk over the excitement and drain every last, luscious drop from the morning's goings-on.

Barbara winced as Emma anchored her needle in her hooped embroidery and said, "How nice you look, dear."

Car keys jingled as Mr. Katt prepared to drive uptown to check on the county jail. He pinned his badge over his pocket and checked the mirror to see that it was straight. Edward Wheeler had just come in from the duck pond and was preparing to fret over the newspaper again.

"Thank you, Emma," Barbara politely replied.

Granna chose that particular moment to emerge from one of the bedrooms on her way to the laundry. "Why, don't you look lovely, Barbara, dear," she said.

Barbara rolled her eyes.

"Going out, are you?"

Laughing and sighing at the same time, Barbara placed an obliging kiss upon her grandmother's cheek. The rascals—they all knew exactly where she was going and with whom.

She would be all right if she could just make it to the front door. "Yes, Granna. I'm going out."

"Don't forget, you're going to help address the invitations to your grandmother's birthday party, dear." Emma's reminder followed Barbara out into the hall.

"You get them into the envelopes, and I'll address them," Barbara called back.

"Oh, pooh," Granna protested to Emma. "I'm too old for birthdays. I told you, Emma—"

Mr. Katt casually called, "And don't forget your car's still stuck out at the river."

"I'll get Jake to tow it in."

"Jake'll charge you thirty-five dollars."

With mounting nervousness, Barbara peeped through the panel of beveled glass beside the front door. A shiny black Suburban was parked at the end of the sidewalk. Its windows were tinted so darkly she couldn't see inside, but she knew he was there. Oh, yes, he knew her secret, and he was waiting.

Don't walk out the door, her good sense warned. *You can't resist this man, and you know it.*

Like blazes! She was furious at him, and she jolly well could resist him. To prove it, she walked out the door and down the sidewalk. She would do the Finley name proud and show Paccachio a thing or two. She would be as tough as old Thaddeus himself.

The motor was running. As if by magic the door of the car swung open, and Lewis leaned across the passenger seat. Barbara expected one of his famous dimpled grins, but he wasn't smiling. The headband was gone now. He had replaced his sneakers with loafers and slipped on a jacket. She had no idea why he should look as dangerous behind the wheel of a car as he had coming in out of the thunderstorm, but even his hand draped casually over the gearshift was a threat. What his brown eyes missed would have fit on the head of a pin.

Her nerves snapped like rubber bands. She stuffed her hands into the pockets of her jodhpurs.

He followed the path of her stare to the wind-ruffled puddle trapped between the curb and the car. "You mean you can't walk on it?" he quipped.

It was Barbara's intention to scowl straight into his face, but, fearing he might look into her head and see just how full of him her thoughts really were, she straightened, drawing on her aloofness like a reliable old coat.

Lewis figured he was as uncomfortable as she was. Realizing now that he'd hoped five minutes would bring her to the point of throwing her arms around his neck and whispering, "Yes, yes, I'm mad about you and want to marry you and be the mother of your children," he felt silly for having grabbed his poplin jacket simply because burgundy was his best color. He'd also taken time to run a razor over his jaw, though he'd shaved early in the morning.

"So now you want me to throw my body across the water," he said with a weary sigh, "so you can stomp over me and grind your heel into my throat because you think I walked out on you last night."

She stooped low to bring her eyes to his level. "You did walk out."

"Come on, now. I couldn't even wheedle an initial out of you."

"You weren't overeager to hand out your own, I noticed."

"I was merely following suit, darling. Besides, I—" Lewis felt himself flushing. "Oh, hell, would you get into the car?"

Rising, she pretended interest in something down the street.

"Someday," she said softly, "when you've got a few years, I have one or two bones to pick with you, Attila."

His arm was still stretched across the back of the passenger seat, his fingers drumming impatiently on the top of the cushion.

"They say he was a dwarf, you know," he drawled. "Do you plan to go to the hospital today or next week?"

"Who says that?" She swiveled around to put a snappish look with her question.

"I read it."

"Well—" she combined a halfhearted grimace and a shrug "—I never heard of such a thing."

His laughter ricocheted off the windshield. "I hate to disillusion you, sweetie, but there may be more than a few things you haven't heard."

"You know, Paccachio—" abruptly she slammed a fist emphatically on her hip, then pointed a finger of the same fist at him "—you lied to this town. We made it very clear to your company what Finley needed in the way of employment opportunities, and your company agreed that the town could be involved in construction. If they hadn't done that, we would have shopped elsewhere."

"Wait a minute, Barbara—" Lewis's own forefinger came up.

"And then you come in and just railroad your way through, making up your own rules as you go along, not honoring anyone else's commitments."

So swiftly was he out of the car that Barbara leaned back, aghast. She wondered if her original impression of him as eminently dangerous wasn't closer to the mark, after all.

"I don't know who told you what—" his tone was that of a machine gun "—but you were sold a bill of goods. I've been with Abrams and Bean for fifteen years, and they have a standing arrangement with the construction unions. They make this very clear on every contract. Up-front."

A buzzer sounded inside Barbara's head. That wasn't possible. She couldn't have made a mistake like that.

She focused stupidly upon a stray wisp of hair at the base of his throat. "I think, Lewis," she assured him with totally false coolness, "that Mr. Abrams himself assured the mayor that our town would get special consideration. I remember Murray saying those exact words. Which would mean..."

"You don't know Reuben Abrams. He wouldn't give special consideration to his own mother unless there was something in it for him."

"I know Murray Levitt!" she cried. "I've known him all my life."

"Then maybe you should talk to Mr. Levitt. Maybe *he's* the one who got 'special consideration' in return for a favor."

Barbara wanted to hit Lewis. She wanted to pound some sense into him. She slammed her boot to the sidewalk and felt the impact clear to her spine. "We're talking about the most respected man in this town, Lewis Paccachio. My mother once considered marrying Murray Levitt."

"Does the saying 'ladies love outlaws' mean anything to you?" He leaned toward her until their noses nearly touched.

"You know, Lewis," Barbara enunciated with needle-sharp nastiness, "I don't like you one bit better in the daylight. You're the most stubborn, weaselly man—"

"Weaselly?"

Barbara planted her feet firmly apart and glared furiously.

"Weaselly?" he repeated.

His laughter bathed her in rich warmth, and though she tried to keep from laughing, a smile tipped the corners of her lips and refused to go away. She concentrated on maintaining her scowl.

"Barbara," he said around his chuckles, "if you don't get into the car, you're going to upset me." Suddenly he, too, scowled, but with mock ferocity. "Do you know what I do when I get upset? I cause scenes, Barbara. You can't even imagine the scenes I can cause." He threw out a hand. "People will forget all about your canceled wedding—and anything else that's ever happened in this town—by the time I'm through. The scandal in front of Julia Regent's house will be so bad, you'll probably end up losing your job, which means that you'll go on welfare and end up life broken, destitute and alone. Now is that what you want for your life? I'll tell you what I think. I think you ought to get into the car."

He was nodding as he finished his speech, as if he were agreeing with himself, and though Barbara pressed her lips as tightly together as possible, she couldn't prevent the laughter from escaping around the edges.

"Are you finished?" she gasped.

His pleasure continued to wrap around her with silken arms. "It won't do any good to resist," he said with lazy fatalism.

Barbara couldn't have spoken if her life had been at stake.

He scratched his head boyishly. "You know all those chains of DNA they taught us about in high school?"

Choking, she nodded.

"Somewhere inside you, maybe right about here..." He brazenly poked a finger below her bottom rib, making Barbara catch her breath. "Right here is a microscopic link that has my name on it. It's programmed: 'Fall in love with Lewis Paccachio. He'll make you very happy.'"

Barbara giggled, and he chuckled. As the joke ended, however, and her laughter died, she found his brown eyes glistening like smooth, wet stones—taking her apart, searching out secrets, touching the untouchable.

"And right here," he said solemnly, fastening his look to hers as he laid a finger upon his own heart, "is one that says, 'Treasure this woman, you fool, or you'll regret it for the rest of your life.'"

Oh, he was lethal! *Make up a lie, any excuse,* Barbara told herself, *then turn around and walk—no, run!—back into the house and hide under your bed.*

"Oh, Lewis..." She lifted a hand uncertainly to her cheek and lowered it again. "I shouldn't have agreed to this. I knew before I came out here that I—"

Lewis glimpsed the window curtain of the living room move a furtive amount as Barbara turned and started walking away. He chewed his lip. When Sunny had walked out of his life, except for the sake of the boys and a certain masculine pride, he'd been almost relieved. But to see Barbara do it, when she'd been there only long enough to set the hook in his mouth, was intolerable.

Lunging after her, he closed his hands over her shoulders, pulling her to a halt and spinning her around to face him.

She was a reed before the sway of his determination. "They're watching us," she whispered.

His frustration was a growl deep in his throat. "Then let them watch."

Barbara strained against the powerful bands of his hands. She could feel the boarders inside, watching, wondering, waiting. She didn't think she could explain her world to Lewis, about the tendencies of small towns to devour their own.

"It's too soon," she mumbled.

"Compared to what?"

"You know things about me that no one else knows, Lewis. Can you imagine how that makes me feel? I told you things, I admitted things...."

Spinning around so she no longer had to bear the stripping honesty of his eyes, she bent her head. She felt, upon the nape of her neck, the warm caress of his breath.

He said gently, "You admitted things that made me certain of what I'd already figured out for myself, Barbara—that you're a lady, in the finest sense of the word."

Barbara belatedly glimpsed someone move at the edge of the front window. "They really are watching us."

"The whole town can watch, for all I care. Look, Barbara, I know all your arguments before you can make them. Do you think I didn't say them all to myself in the time it took me to back this car out of the driveway and wait for you here? Do you think because of what I told you that I'm a man on the make for any woman who'll climb into bed with me and make me forget Sunny?"

"Lewis, please—" She wanted to face him now, but he stopped her with a heavy hand on her back.

"I don't need anyone to make me forget Sunny," he stated. "I've been in the process of doing that for the last five years, and just because you and I crossed paths at an unfortunate time in our lives doesn't mean that I'm going to bury my head in the sand. You can't walk away from this any more than I can."

"Last night you did," she reminded him bitterly.

His hands were suddenly gone from her arms, and before she could turn, his steps were clicking over the sidewalk. Stunned to realize that he could be hurt as easily as she, Barbara forgot the people watching and hurried after him.

"Lewis," she called to his back, more desperate than she meant to be, "even if I wanted to agree with you, don't you see what you're asking? Only three weeks ago, I stopped a wedding in a town of seven thousand people. And here you are, so newly divorced that you still have the ink on your hands. And your sons—just what do you think they would say?"

When he turned, Lewis didn't ask for the kiss—he took it. Stepping toward her with no warning whatsoever and clasping her head hungrily between his hands, he crushed her lips hard with his own. Her hands were splayed wide upon his chest, and when she tried to push herself free, throwing her head back, he pinned her hands there by trapping her forcibly to his length.

Barbara fought. "Wait—"

But his hands seemed everywhere at once, on her waist, at the base of her spine, the side of her hip. One of them buried itself in the short furls of her hair, insisting.

"They might as well know now as later," he argued, his lips poised above hers, his eyes already plundering what they wanted, his breath hot, his heart a trip-hammer. "Let it happen, Barbara. Get it out in the open so they can say their words and forget about it. Let them know."

"Know what?" she whispered.

"That I'm in your life."

Was that what she wanted? Him in her life and all the mountains of problems, small town and otherwise, that came with him?

His breath seared her skin as he strewed branding kisses along her throat, and Barbara's own fingertips unwillingly skimmed the expanse of his shoulders. She honestly did want him in her life. It wouldn't work—never in a thousand years would it work—but for the space of this moment, as his mouth drank thirstily of hers, there was no town, no cruel gossip, no troubled sons, nothing but his needs sliding into her own until neither could be distinguished from the other.

His mouth finally gentled its assault, easing to featherlight brushes of her cheeks, challenging her to deny her own response. "Coward," he said, and smiled down at her.

Barbara ruefully dropped her head to his shoulder. "Lewis Paccachio," she said, "you do have your moments, I'll give you that."

Laughing, he smoothed down her sweater where it had gotten pulled up. Without looking to see if four sets of shocked, adult eyes still gaped, to say nothing of three young pairs that wouldn't be above spying on their father from behind the hedge, he let his arm graze the swell of her bosom.

"I understand one thing—that you're still not in the car." His narrowed eyes clashed laughably with his smile. "If you tell me no this time, madam, it will be at your peril."

Too dazed to do more than to smile, Barbara disengaged herself and walked to the open door of the Suburban. Over her shoulder, she said, "I guess you know that Emma believes women get pregnant by kissing."

A devilish warning appeared in Lewis's winged brows. "Barbara—"

Disdaining his help, she stepped over the puddle without getting a drop on her boots. Lewis hesitated as she settled herself in with easy grace. She didn't even give him the satisfaction of shutting her door but, like a perfectly seasoned wife, closed it neatly and emphatically in his face.

Chapter Eight

"Cling around the soul, as the sky clings round the mute earth forever beautiful." Anonymous

Polly Bodine was on the women's ward at Charlatan County General.

When Barbara walked down the hospital corridor with Lewis at her side, her steps automatically falling into sync with his as if they had walked down a thousand halls a thousand times before, people turned to watch.

It was the scar, she thought with an unexpected thrill, the pirate in Lewis, the sexy flair of his stroll that she knew was completely beyond his conscious thought.

"I'd like to see Polly Bodine, please," she told the pink lady at Reception, smiling for no good reason.

The older woman looked from one to the other, considering Lewis, the way he stood at Barbara's shoulder with the air of a smugly contented proprietor. She, too, smiled, as if she had just remembered other days and other smiles.

"Room two-twelve, Miss Regent," she said with quaint, old-fashioned approval. "Third door on your left past the elevator."

With eyebrows raised in puzzlement, Barbara smiled. "Why, thank you."

"Who's she?" Lewis asked as they waited for the elevator to open its doors with a hiss.

Glancing up to find herself caught in a visual embrace, Barbara stepped quickly beneath his arm when he held the door. "I never met the woman before in my life."

Grinning, he followed her. He slouched against the wall as the doors whispered shut. "And here I thought you knew everyone in this county."

"You're confusing me with God, I believe."

He chuckled. "I've been getting the weird feeling that we're something of an item already."

"In this town it's weird if you're not an item. Perhaps you should reconsider, Paccachio. Don't you think you'd best change your mind?"

He dipped his head to his fingers and pretended to give the matter grave consideration. "Not on your life," he said.

The elevator rocked gently to a stop, and the doors opened. With a flaunt she knew would unsettle him, she swept out and said over her shoulder, "Don't say I didn't warn you if it comes to that."

Lewis grinned as he studied the inside of her jodhpurs where smart leather insets reached halfway to her knees. He felt like a hunter who'd been captured by the fox, and he wasn't altogether certain she was joking. He imagined making love to her again.

"Tell me about the Bodines," he said hoarsely as they approached the women's ward.

She had reached the entrance and craned to see the beds. From here, the odors of illness and medication and suffering reached them. She seemed undisturbed by it, as if she had been here many times before.

To his surprise—and Barbara's too, Lewis thought—at the far end of the ward Gene Katt stepped from behind a curtained enclosure. He made some parting remark, unconsciously fondled his holster and shook his craggy gray head.

"How did *he* get over here so fast?" Barbara wondered aloud.

Lewis retucked the front of his shirt into his pants and said, "Maybe he's following us. Are you sure, darling, that you're not on the Ten Most Wanted list after all?"

Her expression would have felled a less determined man, Lewis thought. "For murder one, too," she murmured. "Be forewarned. Don't get on my bad list, Paccachio."

Some of the women were watching the tall, slow-moving lawman as he walked out, and Barbara drifted into her own private worries. Though she spoke, she continued to watch Katt. "It's a very unhealthy situation over there, Lewis. At the Bodine house, I mean. Allamay owns the place—the grandmother—but she's on welfare. The children—Simon and two other brothers, plus Polly—were dumped on her by their mother, who finally wound up on the streets of New Orleans, I understand. Allamay's done the best she could, but she's beaten into the ground. The boys have dealt her nothing but grief."

Lewis wryly reminded her, "I've met Simon."

"Well, Polly now has an illegitimate daughter she can't support. It's all quite sad."

Though he didn't consider himself the best father in the world, and he certainly wasn't the best mother, Lewis had always possessed a savage sense of pride in providing for his children.

Gene Katt had reached them now, and he extended his hand to Lewis but answered the question Barbara was already posing. "Yes, it's Polly."

"What's the matter? What happened?"

"You'll see for yourself. She's not talkin' to me, but maybe she'll open up to you. If she does, I want you to convince her that she's got to do something about it this time." Sighing, he glanced back into the ward and shook his head. "Don't ever let them put me in one of these."

A mist of affection clouded Barbara's eyes, and she laid a hand gently upon the sleeve of his uniform. "Now, Mr. Katt..."

Katt's old-school look at Lewis informed him that it was now his responsibility to take care of Barbara, that he would be held accountable if he failed to do it well. He awkwardly patted Barbara's hand and gave Lewis a respectful nod.

"I'll be goin' now," he said. "Nice seein' you again, Mr. Paccachio. Take care of yourself."

"Same to you," Lewis said to the man's back as Katt walked out into the hall.

A frail feminine voice called, "Miz Regent, over here."

Quietly, Barbara said, "Well, well, chalk one up for you, Paccachio."

Searching for a face to go with the voice that had called out, Lewis grinned. "Why, whatever do you mean?"

"I could count on the fingers of one hand the men Gene Katt would trust with me. How did you manage that?"

"The man is one of the all-time great judges of character."

"He's a chauvinist, and you know it."

Lewis was foolishly, irrationally happy, and the only regrettable thing about his life at this moment was that it had taken him so long to reach this point.

Turning, Barbara waved to the figure in the bed at the farthest end of the ward. She seemed, Lewis thought as he followed her through the ward, to know everyone.

She took a moment to speak when they raised their hands or spoke her name. "How's that grandbaby of yours?" she would say. Or, "We missed you at church last week. Hurry up and get well." Or, "Buddy says if you don't get back behind the cash register, the whole business will go down the tubes."

Chords of respect deep inside Lewis responded. These people, he sensed, needed Barbara, depended upon her steady sweetness in some old and patterned way. And if Barbara were ever cut off from that dependence, he suspected she would be like a mother who had lost her children.

Oh, he hadn't made a mistake by wanting her in his life. She would be good for his sons, good for himself.

"Miz Regent, over here," the small voice insisted.

Lewis wasn't prepared for what he found sitting in the hospital bed. Beneath the distortion of her contusions, Polly Bodine hardly seemed older than Steven. Bandages swathed the top of her head, and a brace supported her neck. Her face was a mass of purple bruises, and her lip was split. One of her eyes shone purple, and her left cheek had several stitches in it. When she bravely tried to smile, great crystal tears spilled from her lashes and streaked over the discolored skin.

With a whimper of anguish, Barbara went to the girl. Leaning over the bed, she opened her arms, and Polly fell into them as if she were an orphaned waif finding her

mother at last. Back and forth Barbara rocked her, stroking and crooning comforting words.

Barbara flashed him a look over her shoulder. Moving
behind her, Lewis drew the curtain around the bed, remaining at its foot, however, his gaze fixed discreetly upon
the corner of the sheet.

"My poor, poor Polly," Barbara murmured. "This is all
my fault."

"No, it ain't," wept the girl.

"But it is, Polly. I knew it could happen, and I put it
right out of my head." She held the girl at arm's length and
bent to look into her eyes so that Polly could not avoid the
truth. "You have to tell this time, Polly. You can't do like
you did before. You have to tell me who did this. Otherwise, I can't help you."

Thunderstruck, Lewis realized this wasn't the first time
the girl had been beaten.

Polly tremblingly covered her head with her arms and
wailed softly. "He'll kill me if I tell, Miz Regent. I got
Chrissie to think about. What would happen to her? I can't
tell. I just . . . *can't*!"

Barbara gripped the frail arms and drew them down.
Tipping up the battered face, she kissed it and said, "Polly,
I'll go over to Allamay's and get Chrissie. Mr. Paccachio...I'm sorry, Polly, this is Lewis Paccachio. He's going
to build us the new paper mill."

Lewis extended his hand, and Polly, shrinking, gazed at
it as if it were a snake prepared to strike. "I know about
you," she said coldly.

Confused, Lewis consulted Barbara with a telepathy that
came quite easily now.

Barbara shook her head for him to pay no mind. "I'll
have Mr. Paccachio drive me over to Allamay's, and I'll
take Chrissie home with me." She laughed thinly. "You

know Emma and Mr. Katt—they'll think they've gone to heaven, having a baby to play with. Chrissie'll be just fine."

"I don't want *him* to take her."

Lewis felt like a total criminal. Starting to fumble his way out of the curtained enclosure, he was stopped by Barbara's hand circling his wrist.

Don't go, she begged. *I need you.*

Seemingly drained of anger, Polly sank back to her pillows, her features pinched and white.

Barbara brushed the damp tendrils of hair back from Polly's face. "Polly, you haven't seen Chrissie's father lately, have you?"

"He didn't do it, Miz Regent." The girl shook her head from side to side.

"Who, then? You have to tell me who did this, sweetie. I'll get you a lawyer. We'll get a restraining order on this man. I'll go with you to court, Polly. I'll do everything. All you have to do is tell the truth."

Polly suddenly sat straight up in bed and said, "He can't go with you to get Chrissie."

"Why, darling?" Not understanding, Barbara cocked her head. "What're you talking about?"

The girl shrugged. "Nothin'. I just don't want anyone else gettin' hurt, that's all."

Bafflement engraved a furrow in Barbara's brow. She was smoothing the frail hand, outlining the thin fingers and shaping the gnawed, ragged nails. She shook the hand earnestly. "Polly—"

"Simon done it."

Until that moment Barbara supposed she hadn't actually coupled physical danger with Simon's threats. Mischief perhaps, bullheadedness, drunken meanness, maybe. But not evil.

What kind of trouble had she stumbled into here? Sweet mercy, if she helped Polly, she could very well be endangering herself—if not her person, then certainly her reputation. Simon would slaughter her! But if she didn't help, she could conceivably be endangering Polly's life. She couldn't live with that.

Afraid to look at Lewis now—he was far too prone to read her mind—she laid Polly's hand carefully upon the sheet and smoothed the fold of the blanket. Reaching across the bed, she drew the blanket tightly until not a single crease was left. She tucked a corner, then another corner, then became aware that Polly was gaping at her.

Abruptly realizing what she was doing, Barbara jerked her hands to her sides.

The old feeling of protectiveness drenched Lewis as she stood, rigid and vague, her eyes burning sightlessly into space. Polly unwittingly broke the spell.

"He come home last night drunk as a skunk. He couldn't get work at the mill, he said. Grandma tried to calm him down, but he was throwin' things around, bouncin' 'em off the wall. Then he started to go at Chrissie. When he started yellin' at her, I just walked up and punched him, Miz Regent. Right in the stomach."

Polly looked from one to the other, as if needing confirmation that she'd done the right thing. Since she'd included him, Lewis braced his foot on the frame of the bed.

"You did right, Polly," he said quietly.

Relieved, she nodded. "Yeah. Simon needed to be punched. Boy, that was when he let me have it. Clear across the room. I don't remember too much after that, but Grandma was cryin', and Simon, he had me down on the floor, kickin' me. I don't know, Miz Regent, he's my brother. If I sic the law on him, he's gonna be plenty mad. You know how he is."

Until three weeks ago Barbara wouldn't have hesitated about hauling someone who'd behaved the way Simon Bodine had off to jail. But that was before she and Bodine had become embroiled in her own guilty secret, wasn't it?

Lewis was looking at her as if he were turning pages inside his head. She should never have told him about the photographs. Now he could be hurt. He would go out, glove in hand, and slap Simon Bodine across the face and challenge him to a duel.

Arranging a smile, she cleared her throat. "Well, Polly, no one's above the law, not even your brother. I'll tell you what, I'll see Simon myself, talk to him, warn him about what could happen. Maybe—"

Lewis closed his hand upon her arm, silently urging the professional restraint her job demanded. "What in God's name are you saying, Barbara?"

For the first time in her career, Barbara let her emotions take precedence over the realities of one of her cases. Shivering, desperate, she added sin to sin, getting more and more personally involved; making promises she might not be able to keep. "Polly, I'll take all this to Mel. We'll arrange some legal counsel for you. I'll find somewhere you can stay so you won't have to go back to Allamay's. Leave Simon to me."

Polly was no fool. She knew Simon, she knew life, and she knew what welfare workers and "human resources" folks could—and, more likely, couldn't—do. "You do that, Miz Regent," she mumbled, and lay back on the pillow, hardly seeming to care now.

The last thing Barbara wanted to do was look into Lewis's eyes. Keeping her head down, she gripped Polly's fingers tightly. "I'll see you, Polly," she said hastily. "Now, you just get well. Okay?"

"I don't have no money," Polly whispered miserably.

Before Barbara could reply, Lewis said, "Money isn't the problem, Miss Bodine. Is it, Barbara?"

Barbara couldn't escape quickly enough. Holding herself stiffly, she stepped quickly through the curtain and walked rapidly off the ward.

His steps lengthened to keep up with her. "Barbara?"

She was rushing beyond him, raking her fingers distraughtly through her hair, the heels of her boots clicking over the waxed tile. "Lewis, please, just go away. Leave me alone."

"No."

All but running now, she dodged nurses and visitors and an orderly pushing a cart. Lewis watched her dart into a niche at the end of the hall, and when he caught up she was holding a paper cup beneath a spout, and ice was grumbling and grinding as it filled.

Glancing over his shoulder to make sure they weren't overheard, he draped an arm over the top of the machine. "That was some performance, *Miz* Regent. Congratulations."

Her eyes flashed fire when she jerked the cup from the spout and glared at him. "Don't start with me, Lewis."

Grinning, he stared pointedly at the cola now pouring through the stainless-steel grate. In exasperation, she stared at her cup and dumped the ice into the trash can. Still holding the cup, she squeezed her eyes tightly shut and crushed it.

"Damn, damn, damn," she whispered hoarsely. "Damn Simon, and damn the foundry for closing, and damn—"

As he stepped into her, lifting the wadded cup from her fingers and tossing it into the can, Lewis was suddenly lost in the fragrance of her hair. Not caring at this point if someone did walk in, he drew Barbara into the hollow of his side.

With a gesture of impatience at herself, she threw back her head, and he cupped her chin. When he bent and touched her lips with his own—lightly, briefly, lovingly— she blinked back the frustration.

"It's Simon Bodine, isn't it?" he asked. "The man who called you is the same man who just beat up his own sister?"

If she cared anything about Lewis Paccachio, Barbara told herself, she would keep him from becoming embroiled in the trouble that was about to erupt in flames around her. She had to lie to him.

"You're wrong," she said, with a shake of her head.

The tenderness fell away from his hands, leaving only the disbelief. "Look at me, Barbara."

She couldn't bring herself to do it. *Just leave me alone now,* she wanted to rail at him. *Don't make me love you.*

He didn't berate her. He didn't shake her. Though he knew she was lying, he didn't drill her with accusations. A sad little curve appeared briefly at the side of his mouth, and he shook his head. "When you're ready to tell me," he whispered, "I'll be ready to listen."

As they walked back to the car neither of them said a word. They both seemed lost in the vast chasm of differences between them. Barbara gave him quiet directions to Allamay Bodine's house.

Lewis turned left and drove down a street so narrow that one car was barely able to pass between those parked at the sides. No sidewalks existed here, and the tiny frame houses had settled unevenly like two rows of crooked teeth in need of braces.

"There," she said finally, the life gone from her voice. "The one with the motorcycle on the porch."

* * *

Lewis hated the way the Bodines lived.

Not that the house was dirty; on the contrary, it was

quite clean. Allamay Bodine tended the children of her grandchildren the best she could. Their pictures were placed neatly in a row on top of the television set—three snaggletoothed toddlers sitting on bright crib blankets and holding balls with chubby fists. In the corner of the living room, baby strollers were neatly folded. A playpen was set up near the window. Lunch was bubbling on the stove.

But a sense of futility filled the house, as if a time bomb had been set long before and no one knew how to defuse it. In the playpen, a baby was screaming at the top of its lungs. A blond-haired child, Lewis noted. Was it Simon's?

Allamay gave no appearance that the crying affected her one way or another. "This is my friend," Barbara explained over the sound of the dreadful crying, "Mr. Paccachio. We've been to the hospital to see Polly."

Mrs. Bodine accepted that. "You come for the baby."

It wasn't a question. Turning, Barbara looked at Lewis.

"Do you want me to wait in the car?" he softly asked.

Her reply was to close her hand upon his own reaching fingers.

Allamay shuffled lifelessly across the floor, and Lewis could see the discoloration of her legs beneath the heavy cotton stockings. Without a shred of emotion, she indicated a door and said, "She's in there."

Moving forward, Barbara gently touched the woman's shoulder. "Allamay, I want you to talk to Mr. Hinchet at the welfare office."

The woman shook her head. "There ain't nothin' he can do. You said things would change, Miss Regent. You said that the men would go to work. It would all get better, you said."

Barbara angled a look that made Lewis wince. *See what the mill means to these people? And you tell me to keep my nose out of the construction business?*

To Allamay, she said, "I'm sure things will improve soon. Try to be patient. I know it's hard."

Allamay's look would have depressed Pollyanna. "Patient?"

"I wouldn't accept it, either," Barbara answered, sighing.

The woman silently opened another door, and the creaking set up a second wail that drowned out the first.

Lewis couldn't help smiling at the look of dismay on Barbara's face as she moved into the room. Dropping her bag to the floor, she rushed to the crib against the wall and reached for the infant.

In the most endearing of ways, it was apparent to Lewis that Barbara, while she was expert in devising ways to help people, didn't know a fig's worth about babies. As she attempted to comfort poor, screeching Chrissie, Chrissie fought like a cougar cub.

Looking back, Barbara said through her teeth, "If you laugh at me now, Lewis Paccachio, I'll never speak to you again for the rest of my life."

Lewis made his expression one of wronged innocence. "How your false accusations pain me, Barbara."

"Good."

"I'm only glad poor Polly isn't here to see how the mighty are fallen."

Chrissie would never be serious competition for the Gerber baby food label. In the throes of her fury, her nose looked like Rudolph's; her nightie had literally mopped the floor. Her fists had rubbed her eyes so angrily, they were puffy little slits. Her poor hair was the worst: three-inch-long peach fuzz standing straight out all over her head.

"Great hair," Lewis murmured, reminding Barbara of her own shorn locks.

Not to be outdone by someone barely two feet tall, Barbara doggedly went through her mothering routine. She attempted to hold Chrissie with one hand while she fished a tissue from her pocket to wipe the babe's drippy nose with the other.

As far as Chrissie was concerned, nose-wiping was grounds for war. With a strength that Lewis knew, first-hand, could be surprisingly great for a package so tiny, she threw back her head and stiffened her body to the consistency of a small two-by-four. She shrieked until there was not a breath left in her small body, and then she refused to let any more come in.

Her face turned a perfect shade of blue. Horrified, Barbara whirled around, her mouth open and her wide eyes colliding with Lewis's own and pleading for help, *any* help.

Lewis guessed he would have fallen in love with Barbara that very moment if he hadn't already. "Problems, little mother?" he teased. "When we have a baby daughter, I swear you're going to need a crash course."

She missed the whole point. "You don't mean you *want* one of these wretched things!"

"I think it would be delightful. Are you offering?"

Her jaw set murderously. "Will you shut up and do something? She's going to die, Lewis. Do something!"

Steven had been the true tantrum-thrower of the Paccachio family, but his small fits had ended over a decade earlier. Lewis had a fleeting worry that he might be out of touch with the new generation.

But babies had to be like bicycles. Or swimming. Once you got the hang of them, the skill never really went away. Lifting the baby out of Barbara's arms, he swung Chrissie out and up until her screwed-up little face was on a level with his own. Drawing in his breath, he blew it in a steady stream directly into her eyes and nose.

Chrissie jerked, attempting to twist away, but he only blew again.

"Lewis!" Barbara protested, grasping his arm in an attempt to stop him. "That's cruel. Stop that."

"You think it's not cruel to let her go through life doing this?"

Lewis elbowed Barbara out of the way. Just as Chrissie sucked in a fresh breath and was gearing up to let them feel the full force of her wrath, Lewis blew in her face again. Chrissie gasped and tried to cry. Again he blew, and again she tried. After several repetitions of this tiresome routine, Chrissie attempted one halfhearted squawk.

Lewis waited her out. When she screwed up her face, he shook his head. "Uh-uh-uh. I'm bigger than you are, puddin' pie, and I'm a lot more stubborn than you could ever be."

"You'd do well to listen to him, Chrissie," Barbara ruefully advised, turning down the sides of her mouth in a clownish pout.

Chrissie's retort was a long, self-pitying snuffle, followed by several sullen hiccups.

"That's better," Lewis said, and threw back his head in one of those delicious, wonder-inspiring laughs that made Barbara's resistance melt like ice in the sun.

"I think I ought to tell you, Lewis," she said with disdain, "obnoxious winners have never been very high on my list of favorite people."

Lewis wondered if he shouldn't be holding Barbara instead of the baby. "It's not how you play the game, darling."

"Intimidating an infant. Some game."

"Was that who I intimidated?"

Flooding with color, Barbara spun around and ducked her head. If ever there was a natural father, Lewis Paccachio was one. His hands were phenomenally gentle, and they didn't make mistakes.

His lack of awkwardness turned a key in her mind, unlocking memories of her own childhood and family that were the best part of herself: the sweetness of the sun rising over her deck, Lucy's friendship, the unquestioning love of her mother and Alice and Jack and Emma and Mr. Katt, the hopes of growing up and falling in love herself.

"Why don't we see what's going on outside?" Lewis kept up a low, husky level of talk that lured Barbara into the net along with Chrissie. "We can tell the lovely Miss Regent what a great guy I am, and maybe we can get on her good side, hmm?"

Barbara smiled. The wily con artist!

"She's thinks she's so tough," he went blithely on. "It's all an act, you know."

"Don't listen to him, Chrissie," Barbara said on a fluttery rush of breath.

"And the trouble she's in? Um, um, um. Letting herself be blackmailed. I don't know, Chrissie, I just don't know."

He brushed back a strand of Chrissie's rebellious hair, and Barbara thought how very stupid it was—or was it very clever?—for two adults to communicate through an innocent baby who couldn't understand a word.

"She can take care of herself, Chrissie," she dourly said.

"Take my advice, Chris-girl, don't ever let a man psyche you out. Once they do... like, wow."

"Like, wow," Barbara imitated. "And Barbara did *not* let a man psyche her out."

"Did she do anything wrong?"

"She didn't think so at the time."

"Case closed. She let the man psyche her out, Chrissie. And now she turns away from the one person who could help her, the man who wants to help her very much."

Shifting toward her, the teasing gone now, Lewis's eyes were as dark as the depths of an unknown night as they moved over her. A slow fire began to burn in the ashes of Barbara's memories. She wanted to feel anger, to hate Lewis for knowing her faults and her failings. But she found herself remembering the way her hands had pressed the strong planes of his back and the unspeakable happiness she'd known when he moaned, so very softly.

She pulled away in quick retreat—not from him but from her own dangerous thoughts. He had seen the very worst of her, and he hadn't preached sermons, he hadn't made lists; he accepted her the way she was.

"Barbara, darling," he said quietly as he continued to strip her down to bare bones, "would you hand us a tissue, please?"

With studied nonchalance, Barbara forced herself to walk across the room and flick a tissue from the box. Returning, she slapped it into Lewis's outstretched hand like a nurse delivering a scalpel to the surgeon.

But she wasn't quick enough to prevent his fingers from grabbing at hers. He missed, and his nails engraved a small scratch across her forearm. He gripped her for real and leaned over the baby until his breath was warm upon the side of her face.

"Did I hurt you?"

"Not where it shows, Dr. Spock," she whispered.

Chrissie lost the battle of the tissue, but she won the war; her diaper simply refused to absorb one more drop, and Lewis, lifting her out and away from the wet stain on his jacket, groaned, "Agh, Chrissie. Is that any way to treat a friend?"

If not for the shadow of a movement outside, Barbara guessed, she probably would have become totally enamored with Lewis's fascinating domesticity. He was placing Chrissie on her back in her crib and was going through the powdering and diapering bit. Chrissie, if she didn't actually like him, certainly respected him, and she rewarded him with a seductive giggle.

At first Barbara thought she must have imagined the shadow, the way you might think you see a mouse darting past when you turn your head too quickly. Yet when Lewis handed her the wet diaper and she absently searched for a wastebasket, she heard voices murmuring outside the bedroom door. Lewis, picking Chrissie up again and smoothing her nightie into place, sensed Barbara's uneasiness and moved to her side.

"What's the mat—"

When the door was thrown open with a crash, Simon Bodine filled the space like a wicked and beautiful fallen angel. "Well, well, well," he drawled, his eye lowering in a lascivious wink, "as I live an' breathe, if it ain't Mr. Pacatcho and Miss Pin-up Princess herself."

His remark was met with shocked silence.

"I hate to end this touchin' little scene," he said, smirking, "but I'm afraid I'm gonna have to put a stop to it. We have the neighborhood to think of, ya know."

As a blurred procession of imagined horrors marched through her mind, Barbara thought that the repercussions of this one moment could be with them all for the rest of their lives.

She looked distraughtly from one man to the other. The groundwork had been laid well, hadn't it? When Lewis placed Chrissie into her arms, she didn't want to free his hands.

"Lewis, please," she whispered. "For me. Please, no scenes."

"Hey you, Mr. Big Shot!" Simon barked at Lewis's back, "this is my house. I'm talkin' to you."

Turning, Lewis stared into the blond man's eyes with eloquent disgust. Barbara held her breath. Was it only this morning that she had lain in her bed, dreaming?

From the side of his mouth, Lewis was murmuring sardonically, "Show a little finesse, Bodine. Gently, gently."

Chrissie whimpered, and Barbara realized she'd been squeezing the baby nearly in two. "Sorry, Chris," she breathed, trembling.

Simon recoiled in a parody of fright, and laughed. "Well, I can't argue with that, can I? Hey, Miz Regent, you dig finesse, don't ya? And you did good, too. Pacatcho, he's more of a man than Woodward. Tell me now, when you were wearin' Woodward's ring, were—"

"That—" Lewis's word cracked like the sudden report of a rifle, causing everyone to flinch "—is an area I think you'd be wise to stay out of, Mr. Bodine."

Barbara guessed her cheeks were scarlet now. As Lewis turned, more to scorn Bodine than to actually look at her, he did a double take, and the telepathy that had served her in such good stead before now betrayed her. All his doubts were washed away, instantly. He knew now that Simon was the man.

Dread clotted in Barbara's throat. She stepped past Simon into the kitchen, where Allamay was waiting beside the sink.

"Chrissie will need some bottles, Mrs. Bodine," she said quietly.

Allamay pointed speechlessly at some, and Barbara gathered several and placed them in the bag.

"Hold on now," snarled Simon.

"They're takin' the baby," Allamay said dully.

"On whose say-so?"

"Hers." Allamay indicated Barbara.

"And you listened to the bitch?" sneered Simon.

Barbara would have accepted the insult, knowing she was only the pawn in a much larger game. Simon wanted to push Lewis past the limit, and he had. Like a darting moth, she stepped between them. Lewis's lips were drawn back over his teeth now, so that they were a slash of white across his murderous fury. His eyes glistened like wet coals. The scar, drawn tight, could have been a thread of steel stitching the taut skin.

"Lewis!" she cried. "No!"

She didn't think he even heard. Still crushing the baby in her arms, she faced Lewis. She winced as he moved his arm, meaning to sweep her aside. Whirling, weak with fear, she faced Simon Bodine with a courage she could never have summoned had she been defending herself.

"Not him, Simon," she said on a rough, low breath. "Me. It's me you want. Come on, hit me. See? I'll even get rid of Chrissie so you can do it right."

Twisting, she placed the baby on the floor before Chrissie could protest by so much as a whimper. Already inured to such scenes, Chrissie crawled mildly toward her great-grandmother.

"What's the matter, Simon?" Barbara taunted as her knees turned to water. "I thought you liked hitting women."

"Look, Miss Fancy—"

"No, you look. You want to break my face like you did Polly's? Go ahead."

Behind her, Lewis's voice was a machine gun. "That's enough, Barbara. Go to the car."

"No, Lewis." She shook her head, not daring to obey him. "This is between Simon and me. But I must warn you, Simon, I won't take it like Polly did. Gene Katt is my friend, and I'll have you in jail so fast, you won't know what hit you."

Simon looked as if he'd been dealt a felling blow by a butterfly, and he caught the inside of his cheek between his teeth and stood for some seconds with his weight thrown to one side. Then an ugly sneer turned down the corners of his mouth.

"Well, hell, princess," he drawled. "You just ain't worth it."

It was his way of saving face, and Barbara pleaded mutely with Lewis to let it go. Slowly, with great effort, he brought his fevered rage under control. He knew that in sparing Simon he would be sparing her, and in that momentary glimpse of his heart, Barbara saw a terrible, terrible strength.

With a single move, then, he swooped the baby up in his arms and placed the diaper bag into Barbara's hands. Without a word, he nudged her forward and out the front door.

Simon followed them onto the porch and bawled, "You ain't heard the last of me, Miz High and Mighty. Hey, Pacatcho, you better watch out. The next thing ya know, you might find your lady friend in a centerfold."

Lewis opened the door of the Suburban and helped her inside.

Feeling as if she had just escaped a war zone, Barbara hugged Chrissie close. Lewis didn't speak as he opened the door and slid into the driver's seat, but his hands were like vises upon the wheel, and his knuckles were white with violence. It wasn't over, Barbara knew. It was far from over.

Chapter Nine

"Love is like a charming romance which is read with avidity, and often with such impatience that many pages are skipped to reach the denouement sooner." Pierre S. Marechal

When Barbara and Lewis walked through the front door of Julia's house at lunchtime, Chrissie in Barbara's arms and Lewis, very fatherlike, burdened with small-person supplies, it was almost a relief when they were descended upon.

"Well, I declare, look who's here!" Emma exclaimed, and, rising, dropped her embroidery to clap her hands at the baby. "Look, Mr. Katt, did you ever? Well, come to Emma, poor darling. Tell Emma all about it."

Chrissie, Barbara decided, was a shameless little hussy. Scrambling to the floor, she not only went to Emma, but she also performed her clever walking trick as if the whole world had been holding its breath. But the boarders were not guiltless; they cheered her on until Chrissie, with the sweet taste of success in her mouth, went through her entire repertoire of coy hesitations and winsome giggles and most accomplished baby coos.

"A brilliant child," Granna decided on the spot, and set about to fetch a comb and brush, leaving Mr. Katt, who was on his lunch break, to be the first to indulge himself in grandparenting.

Barbara intoned to Lewis from the corner of her mouth, "Would you look at that? And in my own house, too."

"My, my," Lewis said from over the top of diapers, diaper bag, formula and sundry items from the drugstore, "I do believe you're jealous."

"Me?" Barbara slid him a reckless sidelong look. "Jealous of a tiny flirt like that?"

He laughed. "Take a few pointers. I think she's got it down to a science."

"You're hinting that I don't?"

"Hell, no."

"That's better."

"I never hint."

Barbara made her scowl vinegary and pretended to drill her fingernail into the side of his arm. "Monster."

"I hope you don't mean for me to go through life like this."

Barbara had forgotten about the diaper bag. Lifting it out of his arms, she swept across the room to drop it beside Emma's feet. Returning, she glided past him and motioned, "Follow me."

"With what?"

"Don't get ideas, Paccachio," she purred.

Lewis thought it was considerably late to talk about getting ideas, and he wondered, as he trailed along in her wake, if she knew how close she came to breaking the law in those jodhpurs. It also occurred to him to wonder if he'd thought of anything besides X-rated sex since the moment he'd first laid eyes on her.

She led him toward the kitchen, turned the corner and stepped into a niche beneath the stair, where she opened a small, solid door to a walk-in pantry. Stepping inside, she groped for the cord to an electric light, found it and pulled. The room was instantly flooded with brightness.

Grinning, Lewis ducked his head and entered the tiny enclosure. He looked around. "You'll go to any lengths to get me alone, won't you?"

"Lewis, Lewis, Lewis." She shook her head with pretended woe. "That's the trouble with you, you know. You're always jumping to conclusions. What am I going to do with you?"

The teasing that had twinkled in Lewis's gaze suddenly disappeared, and in its place swelled a connection even more direct and more intimate than the ones before. The tiny room shrank, and Barbara would have sworn it turned into an oven.

"Funny you should ask," he said with a soft, throaty challenge. "I was just coming to that."

With a puppet's stiff awkwardness, Barbara lifted the formula from his arms and, stepping onto a tiny stool, placed it upon one of the brightly papered shelves. He held her eyes prisoner as he handed her the extra box of diapers.

She placed it on the shelf with the canned peaches, and as he passed her the other drugstore items, she shelved them alongside Emma's store of Mozart *Sonatas and Fantasies* and Bach *Preludes and Fugues, Volume Two*.

But when she turned to step down, he was blocking her way. She poised where she was, not daring to move, hardly able to breathe. Finally, however, she had to, and one of

Emma's music books slipped to the floor in a clatter of pages.

Neither of them considered picking it up. Coming here had been a mistake, Barbara realized. They were too effectively shut off from the rest of the house. They had survived a crisis together, and now his nearness, his smell, the sound of his breathing, the virile force of his presence was too heady a potion.

With a catch in her throat, she carefully extended her hand for the light cord, thinking he would realize it was time to go. Before she could touch it, however, he flicked a finger, and the cord flew away like a lost sigh and landed upon the stack of Bach. With the same quickness, he reached behind him and shut the door.

Barbara stood rooted to the stool. Lewis thought, from the depths of the longing that engulfed him, that she looked like a person about to be swallowed by an avalanche. If he were a gentleman, he would say something. He would open the door he had just shut.

But discretion was the last thing on his mind. Heat, thick and viscous, was rushing into his throat and plunging into his groin. What woman had ever bewitched him half so quickly?

He stepped toward her, his desire written plainly on his face and body.

"Oh, Lewis," she whispered, reaching for balance but afraid to touch his shoulders. "Don't do this."

"Don't say don't."

"This is wrong."

"Don't say wrong."

"Lewis—"

From where he stood, looking up at her, he could see her pulse at the pointed neckline of her sweater. When he reached up to draw her glasses slowly off her face, placing them upon a shelf beside her head, she didn't say a word.

"And if you can't find enough things wrong," he challenged her, "you can always look under the rug for more, right?"

"Simon Bodine's not under a rug." This she said so softly that he could scarcely hear her.

"Simon Bodine is under a rock."

Lewis reached out to place his hands upon her waist and watched her eyes for clues. He saw a stirring in their sapphire depths, but she took a sharp breath and crossed her arms over her breasts.

"You move so fast."

"I don't move often," he admitted, wanting her more than he imagined possible, "but yes, when I do, it's fast."

Silence unspooled around them, silken threads of a soft cocoon. More than anything he could think of, Lewis wanted her fingers entwined in his hair. He wanted her scent in his nostrils, wanted the feel of her pliancy pressing against him.

Before she could rally her arguments, he swiftly placed her arms around his neck and, fitting one palm about her skull, brought her face down to his. "Don't shut your heart away from me," he pleaded against her quivering lips. "Let us happen."

Shivering, closing her arms about his neck, she took as much of his kiss as she gave, but Lewis wanted more from her, much more. His hands found their way beneath her sweater and sleeked over the smooth contours of her back. His fingers closed upon her hips as his kisses searched her mouth for a way across the past they had not shared.

"What happened before," she moaned, "in the storm. You mustn't think—"

He was tasting the tip of her nose, her silver-dipped lashes. "I don't think anything."

"Lewis..."

He wanted to draw into his mouth the sweet whiteness of her shoulder and her arm, her breast. When he lifted her sweater, her heart was a hammer. His own left a thunderous trail in his chest.

"I live by my own rules, Barbara," he said thickly. "I'm not a womanizer. I never was."

Barbara held her breath as he watched his own hands shaping the curves of her breasts. He was absorbed with the way they strained against the lace of her bra, the way her jaw was dropping when he glanced up to read what her words could not say.

"You want me, too, Barbara."

Her nipples belied any denial she could give, springing exuberantly to his touch, yet somewhere, far, far away, a voice was calling, *Be wise, Barbara. Don't play the fool again.*

"Want isn't love, Lewis. And love... Love is the most overused word in the English language."

"That's foolish talk."

Of course he didn't want to hear it. But that didn't make it any less true, and Barbara didn't understand how, simply by touching her, he could make time stop and all those history lessons disappear. He had her hands trembling. He had her tightening her fingers in his hair and pulling his head closer, closer, until it was the most natural thing in the world for him to hook his finger in the edge of her bra and draw it away and to take that small, quivering button of flesh between his teeth until her head lolled back in the sheerest ecstasy she had ever known.

She closed her arms about his head and trapped his mouth there, yet she said the same word over and over, "No, no, no, no."

He didn't believe her. "Meet me tonight," he begged as his mouth found hers and his kisses deepened and his frustration grew. "I haven't been able to think of anything else. No storms tonight, no hospitals, Barbara, no battered women or blackmailing men, just you and me."

"I can't."

In her delirium, she had loosened one of the buttons on his shirt and tried to slip her hand inside. Her clumsiness brought him pleasure, and he had to help her. He greedily placed her hands upon his chest. Barbara thrilled to find the hard contours she'd lain in her bed and dreamed about.

But one sterling truth was unavoidable: Lewis Paccachio wasn't the kind of man for open-ended relationships; he was made for loving, not petting, for wedding rings and visits to his parents' house for holidays. He was made for parenting and commitments and life over the long haul.

Her life wasn't in order for that. She was too much a mass of loose ends. It wasn't fair.

She twisted her mouth free of his hunger. "Don't make me be the one to be sensible," she pleaded as she leaned upon his chest and struggled for sanity. "Don't make me do this alone. Help me. Please."

He was too near the perimeter of his control. He was too intent upon seducing her with his breaths and his raspy whispers. He was unzipping her, making it all too easy. Through the glaze of her vision, Barbara knew she had to stop him.

She pushed weakly at his head, but his breath was a torch against the film of cotton, and pleasure raced through her center. He knew too well how to find her and that silky wetness that put the lie to all her words. Perhaps if she hadn't been so near the edge of arousal all day, having dreamed about him from her first waking moment, perhaps if she had had more warning, it wouldn't have happened.

But through the fabric, as he stroked her, fire seemed to suffuse her, making the sensations more keen than they would have been had he been buried deep inside her. He would not stop, and she could not make him stop. When his mouth claimed hers anew, she cried into the kiss, delirious to end the pagan torture that now seemed unbearable.

Their lips were crushed together. His taste filled her, and she strained against him. His mouth found her ear, and his whispers were hot and guttural. "I want you to," he groaned. "For me, for me."

"No," she said on a torn, raspy sigh. "No, Lewis..."

Yet she closed her hand about his. Her head snapped back, and she held him there until it was over.

He did not stop until she was drained of it and was slowly, whimperingly, crumbling into a bundle of shaking, sweat-moistened femininity that had no strength left to even stay on her feet. Lifting her off the stool, for some moments he held her in his arms.

When Barbara could breathe again she said, her voice small and rusty and muffled, "I guess you're proud of yourself."

"I'm happy," he whispered into her hair. "I'm sorry. I'm happy."

Was it self-protection that made her say the words? Was it a need to hold her world intact? Or was she thinking of him? The future?

"It doesn't change anything, Lewis," she muttered. "Just because you know how to do that doesn't change anything."

He didn't stiffen all at once, but by degrees. Presently he stopped holding her. "That's not a very nice thing to say, dear."

Feeling like a guilty child and so embarrassed she could hardly face him, Barbara jerked her jodhpurs into place. When he tried to tip up her head and force her to look at him, she pulled away. "I've wanted to tell you, Lewis. I've been trying all day to tell you."

"Tell me what?"

"But then you can sneak up on me and make this happen..."

"I hardly sneaked up on you, Barbara," he said dryly.

Anger licked at Barbara's skin. When she made the connection with his eyes, she saw that he had already constructed fortresses, battle stations.

"It's that very thing!" she cried. "That very look, that air you have about you. You know, Lewis, there are people in this town who're just holding their breath for me to make another mistake." She gave him her profile. "They were right. I just made another one."

"Thanks, Barbara."

Slowly, not understanding how something that felt so right between two human beings couldn't simply fit into the overall scheme of things, she narrowed her gaze upon him. "Can't you please come out from behind that black-and-white complacency of yours for just one minute and see what it's like for me?"

He pursed his lips, and the scar stretched tightly across his jaw, threatening her defenses.

She balled her hands into fists. "You think I'm contriving it? Blowing it out of proportion? Do you think I'm looking under the rug?"

A muscle in his jaw clenched viciously. "You said it; I didn't."

Barbara felt as if the wind had just been knocked out of her. She gave him a furious profile. "Well, why don't you think about your own sons then, Lewis? On the other side of that hedge are three sweet, wonderful boys who aren't necessarily in the market for some woman to take their mother's place. They're too busy surviving a divorce. What will you tell them about me? With their mother just gone?"

Lewis had given considerable thought to that, and he was furious at her for reminding him of what he already knew: that it was a problem, a serious one.

"You know, I never realized it before," he drawled. "You're a real saint, Barbara."

"Oh, shut up, Lewis."

"The mistake, darling, was not yours but mine. I should have let you simmer awhile longer, shouldn't I? Whet your appetite a little?"

Before either of them guessed she was capable of it, she swung at his head with a fist. The blow glanced harmlessly off his arm, and with reflexes just as quick and just as harmless, he grasped her hand. Their looks did the real damage, striking with bright, cruel blows, bruising, battering.

"Then this is it?"

His question was a cat-o'-nine-tails, and Barbara felt blood trickling from her heart. "This is what?"

"The bottom line. Knowing what we know, we walk away and call what's happened between us one of those free-sex encounters that everyone's so fond of? We just—what do they say?—live and learn? Ciao, baby?''

Fearing him, adoring him, hating him, loving him, Barbara slumped back against the shelves and turned her head away. Lewis raked his hands through his hair, wishing he were anywhere else, doing anything else besides fighting with a woman he knew he didn't want to live without.

"We..." She hesitated, shrugged, then pressed her thumb and forefinger into the bridge of her nose.

"We what?" he demanded raspily.

Barbara shook her head and wished she'd never said anything. "Maybe..." Her voice hacked at the words like a dull machete. "Maybe we could pretend." She raised a shoulder. "A little. Maybe we could..." Sighing, she closed her eyes. "You know, keep things—"

To hope, after sixteen years of a disastrous marriage, that he might find a bit of romance left in the world, made him deserve the insult she was inflicting, Lewis knew. "A secret? Have a secret love affair?" He chuckled bitterly. "And just how do you propose we conduct this affair?"

"Forget it, Lewis." Barbara turned to face the canned peaches and the baby formula.

"Would we pretend to be friends?" he demanded. "Or would you have us—just for the sake of Simon Bodine and his kind, you understand—not speak even in public?"

"Lewis..." His words were battering her, flaying her.

"Maybe that's the best thing, after all. Maybe then Bodine wouldn't rock the boat and give away your secret. Hmm? And how many years would you propose to conduct this affair, my love? Until Simon dies? Until my children are grown and we don't have to worry about scarring their young lives?"

Oh, the pleasure he took in putting her words in the worst possible light, Barbara thought. In a small voice she yielded him the victory without a fight, knowing that later, much later when she was alone, she would curse herself.

"You're right, Lewis," she said woodenly. "It would never do for us to be hypocrites."

The stone of his silence settled heavily. He pushed open the door and stood in its too-small enclosure, the light of the house at his back like violence. Every muscle in him was quivering. His face, a sun-browned shell, had the wary, listening expression of someone waiting for a twig to break, a guillotine to fall.

He was waiting for her to say the words she had not uttered, *Please don't go.*

But she was hobbled with too much fear and uncertainty. She could not, would not beg him to stay.

"I'll see you around, Barbara," he said, his voice sodden with disappointment and regret. "If you need to borrow a cup of sugar or anything, you know where I am."

The word was out. Around the square the old-timers were talking. In the unemployment office the lines were abuzz with gossip. At the *Finley Crier*, the editor began receiving disgruntled letters demanding to know more about the strange Yankee company that had stuck its toe below the Mason-Dixon line into Rebel territory and then had not delivered.

The *Crier*'s first interview was with Murray Levitt, the mayor.

"No problem," Lucy's widowed father said with a grand smile, and he encouraged the people of Charlatan County to be patient. "These big companies, well, you know how slowly things move. Soon there'll be more jobs around here than you can shake a stick at.'' A smile more grand than the first. "Trust me."

Women, when they came to Barbara's office in despair, asked just how competent the industrial committee had really been. Who had selected Abrams and Bean, anyway? Surely lots of other industries would have liked free land and free taxes and the great Arkansas River. Companies that might have put their husbands to work immediately.

Barbara found her own name coming up as that of the culprit.

"Let's have dinner and talk," Lucy said when she called on Tuesday.

"You think I need to talk?" For Barbara, hearing Lucy's voice made Lewis's memory worse, tangling all those furious kisses with memories of garbage bags filled with roses and broken candles.

"Daddy's real upset, Barb," Lucy said.

Wasn't everyone? Still, Barbara found herself unable to confide in Lucy. Not about how she had left John because he'd betrayed her to Simon Bodine, or about how she had then fallen in love with another man in a matter of weeks, or about how that same man had raised the question of whether Lucy's own father might be playing fast and loose with Finley.

Barbara stopped eating. In the next weeks she lost five pounds. She stopped sleeping. She couldn't read; she couldn't watch television. Everything was gray. The world was gray; she was gray. Gray, gray, gray, when only yards away, on the other side of the hedge, the sun was shining and the laughter of children rang out on the dusky evening air.

Often, after the dinner things were cleared away, she would slink into the shadows of her deck and watch, like some despicable voyeur, as Lewis spent precious leisure moments with his sons. Knowing him as she did, she knew that learning to be both father and mother wasn't easy. Sometimes Steven would spend the time between dusk and dark in sullen solitude, mauling a soccer ball and carrying his own troubled world upon his shoulders. There were times when Lewis would sit on the front steps with Charlie imprisoned in the hollow of his legs and would rest his chin upon the tousled brown curls. More than once Rick darted out into the yard and roughly rubbed his eyes, and Lewis followed to crush the boy tightly to his chest and kiss the weeping head.

It was the times when Lewis was alone that broke Barbara's heart. In the soft glow of inside lights he would sometimes sit on the steps and gaze across the hedge. Then she would cringe against the wall of her deck and slip inside to wrestle with a solution that refused to come.

She was too much of a coward to brave the gossip of the Mary and Catherine Woodwards of the world. That was what it was: she was a coward. They were only people. They could only say words. They could not kill her.

Life became almost unbearable, and she stopped going onto the deck at all. Instead she climbed into the Mustang and drove through the grim, tight-fisted streets across town.

At dusk, bleak-faced boys collected their dreams and climbed into pickup trucks and drove across the county line to lie about their ages and buy whiskey. By day, their fathers would get into the same trucks and sit in Barbara's seminars with their wives to hear how to cope with financial disaster. Or they would drive to the market and dig into little brown workers' compensation envelopes at the checkout lane.

The town's resentment spread like a virus. On Thursday the television station brought a crew to Barbara's office and asked if she would talk about the mill. "Yes," she told Pete Callahan of Channel Three, "I did work very hard on the committee to bring the mill here."

"When you signed the contract with Abrams and Bean," Pete asked from behind the camera as he gave hand signals to the operator, "was it your understanding that the town would be asked to wait so long for employment opportunities?"

Barbara began to get the feeling that she was caught in a giant spiderweb. It wasn't possible that she was going to be made the human sacrifice in all this, was it?

"Pete, Finley is lucky to have any hope at all. Look at the towns around us, all the empty houses for sale. And by the way, *I* didn't sign any contracts with Abrams and Bean."

"Are you aware of the remarks floating around town?"

"I don't follow you."

"The term, Miss Regent's paper mill? The idea of special consideration, secret arrangements, and supposed compensation for some unknown party?"

Fury grabbed Barbara by the ankles. "No," she told the camera as if it were the barrel of a cannon, "I have not heard any such remarks. And furthermore, I only served on a committee, Pete. There were five other people on it besides myself."

"Do you feel that the mill's hiring policy could be more accommodating if Abrams and Bean wanted to be?"

As Pete had instructed, Barbara was sitting behind her desk, her hands resting lightly upon her blotter. Her hair was lightly fluffed, and her lips were glistening with fresh gloss. Her nails were buffed, and the collar of her suit lay perfectly flat.

She waved both hands before the running camera. "Forget it, Pete!" she exclaimed. "I can't do this. Get out of here. Go interview someone else."

Dixie Crowley popped up from behind the camera and glanced at Pete. "Now just wait a minute, Barbara," Pete protested. "There's no need—"

"No!" Barbara brought her palms down hard on her desk. "*You* just wait a minute. You come in here and ask me—Dixie, will you turn that darn thing off?"

With his mouth curled, Peter shrugged blandly. "Cut it off, Dix." Then, to Barbara, he said, "This is your last chance, Barbara. I don't want you telling me later that I didn't give you an opportunity to state your case."

Case? Drearily Barbara wanted to remind Pete of the time when he'd broken the window in the gym and had cried on her nine-year-old shoulder all day.

Rising, she walked around her desk and threw open the door. "Pete, you're all heart. No, I did not know about the corporation's hiring policy when I worked so hard. And yes, I think they could bend a little. Maybe there has been some special arrangement made, I don't know, but I know where you're going with this interview, and to blame Lewis Paccachio for the situation is like blaming Little Rock when the river floods. You won't get me to say a single word about the engineer, and that's final."

Pete gave her a curious look. "Just whose side are you on, Barbara?"

"Whose side?" Barbara snapped her mouth shut. "Excuse me, Pete..."

That evening, just to make sure Pete didn't betray her and run a clip of the argument, Barbara went downstairs when Emma turned on the local news. Uncomfortable around the boarders now—they missed Chrissie, who had gone back to her mother, who had gone back to her brothers, who had gone back to the same old ways—she skulked around the edges of the room.

When the brisk musical theme announced the news and the day's headlines were shown, Pete came onto the screen, followed by a trailer and the face of Lewis Paccachio.

"Some of the residents of Charlatan County," Pete was saying as he stood in front of the mill's skeletal frame with the equipment laboring in the background, "have raised the question of whether the contract between Abrams and Bean and the city of Finley has been breached." He transferred the microphone from himself to Lewis. "Do you have any comment on that, Mr. Paccachio?"

With a hand covering her mouth, Barbara watched Lewis gaze out across the acres of land that were so drastically changing their appearance. Calm, unruffled, dressed in rough cotton trousers and a shirt with the sleeves rolled to his elbows, his work boots spaced apart and his scar catching the light, his on-screen presence was formidable.

Barbara wondered how many times she had held his face in her mind as she was falling asleep and how many times his name was on her tongue when she awakened. As if he were looking straight at her, he gave the question some thought before he smiled.

"Actually, I'm just a hired gun, Mr. Callahan. I suggest you contact the head office of the corporation for the answer to that question."

"Would you be willing to meet with the city's industrial committee to discuss the matter, Mr. Paccachio?"

Lewis grinned, and Barbara's longing made her unwittingly move closer to the set. "I did sort of discuss it with one member of the committee, yes."

"And?" Pete prompted.

"It was enlightening. We . . . agreed to disagree."

Swiftly, Barbara glanced around to see if anyone had noticed how her cheeks had begun to burn. Folding her arms, she furtively hunched behind her hands.

"Would you care to reveal whom you talked to?" asked Pete.

Lewis stared straight into the camera, giving the impression that he could project his vision through it and see the faces staring at him.

"I've heard the rumor," he said with careful precision, "that the company had a special arrangement with this town. Why don't you tell me who the arrangement was with, and I'll tell you who I talked to."

"I have no idea, Mr. Paccachio."

Lewis shook his head. "Then the answer is no. I would not care to reveal who I talked to."

Dixie's camera had captured the tension between the two men, and the comparison made Lewis look like the intelligent, considerate person he was. Sensing that he was losing to the man he wanted to crack open like a nut, Pete returned to the viewing audience.

Lewis's face disappeared, and Pete raised the question of whether or not there really was a 'special arrangement' with Finley. Was there something that someone wasn't saying? Something that someone was covering up?

"When questioned today, one of the primary liaisons between Finley and the corporate heads, Barbara Regent, had this to say...." In shock, Barbara saw her own picture flash onto the screen.

Everyone in the room gasped. "Barbara?" her mother murmured. "You never said—"

"Shh!" hissed Granna. "Listen."

She was sitting at her desk, Barbara saw. She looked very nervous and distracted, and her hands, which she had thought were resting serenely upon her blotter, were fidgeting. Once they rose to push her glasses higher on her nose.

"Maybe there has been some special arrangement," she heard herself say. "And yes, I think they could bend a little."

Pete's image materialized. "As to whether or not the contract between Finley and Abrams and Bean, Incorporated, has indeed been breached is something only an investigation will prove," he said, and gave the usual pregnant pause. "One thing is certain: the mood around the county is one of despair, not hope. This is Peter Callahan, Channel Three, on the Arkansas River."

It's not right, Barbara, the spot they're putting Lewis in. It's not fair.

His spot? What about my spot? Did you see how everyone looked at me after the broadcast?

You can take care of yourself. These are your people. They want to hate him.

Well, what difference does it make now? I've ended it. And if I hadn't, once he saw that newsclip, he would have.

Because you love him, stupid.

I do not love him. I thought I could, but I don't want to love him.

He loves you.

He doesn't.

He would take care of you if you were in his place.

Maybe.

Then why don't you take care of him?

Because I'm . . .

You're what?

Afraid.

Everyone's afraid.

*But I'm on the rebound. Look, maybe any man who
said a kind word would have looked good to me.*

Maybe.

*Lewis is on the rebound. Maybe the same is true for him.
Everyone says . . .*

Everyone says something about everything.

*Maybe he subconsciously needs a mother for his chil-
dren more than he needs a wife.*

You really do look under the rug, Barbara.

*But the boys might hate me. Being a stepmother is
tough.*

*And you're a dumb, insipid woman. I don't want to
hear any more about all the courage you have and about
how much you care about this town.*

Shut up.

*You're a coward, Barbara Lee Regent—a disgrace to the
great-great-grandfather you're always going on about.*

Shut up, shut up.

When Barbara climbed the stairs and moved heavily
through her bedroom to the deck, the air was so quiet it
ached. She anchored herself on the railing and looked
down into Lewis's yard, where Max lay upon the front veranda, his great nose tucked between his mammoth paws.

How near and yet how far away, eh, Barbara? From the
living room of the Hempstead house came the glow of the
television set, where Bumper and the boys were watching.
Lewis, too, probably. Had he seen himself on Channel
Three?

In the soft, velvety light, oak leaves in Lewis's yard were
a dusty green color. The night was beginning to fill with
sounds. The breeze was a slow, sad susurration on her
deck, and from down the street came the purr of a car

turning the corner. The pale amber parking lights grew closer.

When that same car pulled up to the curb before Lewis's sidewalk, Barbara drew back against the wall. Who had come to see Lewis? Whoever it was, he had company, for another car pulled up behind the first and parked, then another, until there were three.

Amazed, she watched as Bucky James climbed out of his station wagon, followed by Seth Irwin, John MacMurphy and Tiny and Robert Thiebaud. The men waited until everyone was together, and they conferred briefly before beginning to move up the walk to the house.

Roused, Max came to his feet and barked, and Barbara shuddered but wasn't sure why. Something was wrong. She wondered if she should telephone Lewis and warn him. Warn him of what?

Evidently Lewis already knew about his visitors, for the big oak door opened, and he stepped across the veranda—looking so dear in his cotton trousers and no shirt, bare-footed.

"Stay, Max." His quiet, deep order reached her ears.

"Mr. Paccachio?" Bucky James called, a tremor of recklessness making his voice quiver.

Barbara didn't hear everything that was said. The men were decent men, family men. They wouldn't cause trouble. But she could tell that they'd seen the newsclip, and she guessed they'd come to the horse's mouth to check out the rumors.

If she had not known before just how deeply she'd fallen in love with Lewis, to watch him meet the frustration of the men with kindness and tact and dignity cinched it. She had probably wrecked whatever chance she'd had for winning his love, but she wouldn't have a moment's peace for the rest of her life if she didn't do something to help him.

She turned. The moment she did, from far below her, Lewis raised his head and looked straight at her. As if he'd known all along she was there. Love, inside her like a jessed bird, fluttered its wings to escape, to soar.

Then he returned to the men. Quickly, before he could glance back, Barbara slipped through the glass door and walked briskly to the telephone, checked her personal directory and dialed.

When Reuben Abrams answered, she told him who she was. For one terrible moment, she feared he wouldn't remember her. Impatience was in his voice at being called at home.

She asked him if he'd heard about the trouble with the townspeople over the contract.

"It brings me great distress," he said. "There's no excuse for it. I don't understand why everyone's going on so."

A fine, thin wire uncoiled between Barbara's temples and stretched tight.

"Going on so? Mr. Abrams, the people feel betrayed."

"That's their problem. We arranged everything up front when we were first approached on the matter. You know, our own labor—"

"Up front? What up front?"

"Where have you been, Miss Regent? What do you think I'm trying to tell you? Surely your committee knew. I, myself, explained the arrangement with your mayor, What's-his-name. He was quite adamant about wanting to use some of your people which we clearly couldn't do, so we set aside a hefty escrow account to help compensate the city. I suggest you get your facts together, Miss Regent, or let someone else do the job. I would hate to think that I must come down there myself."

Stung to the quick, humiliated and feeling like every kind of a fool, Barbara, also, hoped he wouldn't come. She never wanted to lay eyes on him again.

"Thank you very much, Mr. Abrams," she mumbled.

She hardly remembered replacing the receiver. Stumbling to the terrace, she felt the weight of her silly pride. Murray Levitt. How was it possible? Lucy's father. The man who had come within an inch of being her own stepfather.

But of course, it had always been there, hadn't it? Staring her in the face. There were a dozen places she could have learned about such an arrangement. Had everyone else known? The others on the committee? Had she been too immersed in her own self-importance, being the woman who could pull it off, that she had been blinded?

What now? What could she do? Murray Levitt was the father of her dearest friend. He was a close friend of her mother. He was Mr. Katt's superior. Murray Levitt was a man she had been taught all her life to respect. What now?

Chapter Ten

*"Her tears, like drops of molten lead, with tor-
rents burn the passage to my heart."* Edward Young

Somewhere on the lean side of midnight, Lewis trapped
his arm between himself and the mattress he'd dragged out
onto the back veranda. When the sting reached his brain
he groaned and rolled over to shake his arm awake.

At least something about him had gone to sleep, he
thought as he stared listlessly at the porch roof. Overhead, two stories up, the boys and Bumper lay sleeping to
the irritating screech of crickets and the drone of tree frogs
from over at Julia Regent's duck pond. But he, skivvies-
clad, depressed, lay with his legs tangled in a sheet, wide
awake.

The night was warm, too warm for midspring and too
warm for sleeping. The old house was restless, too, suffering a kind of late-evening fatigue that seemed to aggra-
vate the woodwork and set the floors to creaking.

Thinking of Julia Regent's duck pond made Lewis remember why he was so miserable. Muttering an oath, he flopped onto his stomach and forbade his brain to go off on the usual fantasy-riddled torture about Barbara again. But even devising tricks to keep from thinking about her made desire well between his legs.

Moaning, he prayed for release from his images of begrimed heroines on stormy nights.

Did he feel her presence? Or did she make some low, muffled sound, some soft whisper upon the floor? Lewis wasn't sure as he jerked around and snapped up to sit, nearly colliding with her as she was stooping to kneel beside him.

"Good God, you scared me!" he gasped.

Starting to laugh, at himself as much as at the fright she'd given him, he registered the pair of limp pink pajamas she was wearing. And the distorted planes of her face, the streaks of unhappiness and the jeweled tears trembling upon her lashes.

"Lewis," she whispered as she groped in the darkness for his arms, his hands.

Her clumsy efforts to find him sent a wave of overwhelming tenderness washing over Lewis. He leaned carefully toward her and touched her face with the tips of his fingers.

"Sweetheart? Darling, what is it?"

She could hardly speak. She dropped back to sit on her heels. Her fingers moved distraughtly up and down her throat, as if it were about to burst with some terrible pent-up pressure, and she muttered his name over and over.

Being needed so much was a powerful thrill, and Lewis, thanking heaven for her, pulled her into the nest of his body and cradled her head.

He pushed back her dampened hair. "Shh, shh, tell me now. What's happened?"

With an agony of effort, she clawed her way up his shoulders and searched fearfully for the truth in his shadowed eyes. "Can...you...still...love...me?"

Lewis felt as if all his prayers had been answered at one time. With a sound of his own pleading, he pulled her onto her knees so he could hold her close and touch his mouth to her cheeks and her lips, her dripping lashes.

"Barbara," he whispered against her hair, "I have so many different kinds of love. I love my sons, I love my parents. I love my friends and my job and my country. But I have never, never loved another human being in quite the same way as I'm learning to love you." He peered down at her. "I didn't want to love you this much, you know. I don't like to hurt. But it doesn't ask me, Barbara, it just keeps on growing. Yes, God help me, I do love you. And now you must tell me what's wrong. What's happened?"

She did not tell him that. She only draped her arms about his neck and climbed onto his lap. The hunger of her mouth when it fastened on his shook Lewis to his roots. He had known her feelings ran deep, much deeper than she had let him see. But the fiery urgency of her tongue and her fingers that savagely searched his neck and moved over his face, tracing the place where her lips clung to his, were more like his fantasies than reality.

"It's okay, it's okay," he crooned, and pulled her mouth from his long enough to turn her around and draw her down beside him. "It's okay, Barbara. I'm here, sweetheart, I'm here."

"Don't ever leave me," she begged.

"I won't leave you. I love you. How could I leave you?"

"Show me, Lewis," she pleaded, caught in one of Dante's hellish circles between love and purgatory. "I think I'm going to die."

Smiling at her confessions, Lewis knew better than to take them lightly. She was clawing at the buttons of her pajamas, tearing them free and throwing her top on the floor. Lewis suffered an uncomfortable vision of one of the boys awakening and stumbling out onto the veranda, but her mouth was starving as it moved over his face. He could feel a furnace inside her. When she found herself unable to wrest off his shorts, she whimpered and traced the outline of him, causing him such sweet agony.

"Now," she whispered. "Please, now."

Pushing her down upon the mattress, he threw a leg across her waist to keep her there. "Barbara," he mumbled hoarsely, "wait a minute."

Through the misty darkness, he studied her brimming, desire-glazed eyes. Swiftly he kissed them, and when she stirred, he shook his head. "No, Barbara. I told you that I love you, but you were right when you said that love doesn't solve everything."

"No." She shook her head. "I was wrong."

"I want to hear it from you—all of the truth. Do you want me because your heart's been broken? Is that what you're looking for? A patch job?"

"John broke my pride, Lewis, not my heart. I didn't know what heartache was until I met you."

"You saw the news tonight, didn't you?"

Shushing him with a hand upon his lips, she begged him not to search too deeply into her secrets.

But Lewis drew her hand aside. "You saw, and you know that it's out of control. You know that people are misjudging me and that it's unfair."

She clapped a hand briefly upon her mouth, then said, "I didn't know what to do, Lewis. I couldn't believe it. I didn't say those things."

With a disappointment she could not begin to fathom, Lewis hugged her until she could not breathe and buried his face in the curve of her neck.

Tears were close to his own surface as he groaned, "I don't want sympathy from you, Barbara. I don't want you to make up for some wrong that's been done me. I want you to love me. I want you to see something good that only the two of us can put together. I want you to build a new life with me."

"Lewis—"

"I tried to hold a woman once, out of pity. Pity isn't enough, my darling."

As he rolled over with her until she stretched along his warm, hard length, Barbara sought her own reflection in the mirror of his eyes. Not once in her life had she exposed herself as much as he was wanting. Always, even with John, she had been conscious of who she was supposed to be, what people wanted her to be. In her heart of hearts, she had never even made love without that awareness, that consciousness about what John would think: was she enough?

"Lewis?" Her whisper was ragged as her fingers stroked his hair back from his ears and forehead, over and over. "I'm not really a very good person. Oh, I know you think I am and all that, but—well . . ." Her lips trembled. "I'm not easy. I get worked up about things when I shouldn't. I worry a lot. I'm not like you; I'm insecure. I'm not a great beauty, and I'm certainly not a sophisticate. Please don't think I'm being facetious or anything, but do you really want to marry that? Are you sure?"

Not having dared hope for the manifestation of his most deeply secret dream—someone on God's green earth whom he didn't have to pretend with, someone who could simply be what she was without any of the head games—Lewis didn't think he would live long enough to rid himself of his shorts. Catching the waistband of her pajamas, he stripped them from her.

But in those moments of soul-baring, she had grown incongruously strong. "No." Now she placed her hand at his chest and pushed him back. "You started this honesty, Lewis, now let's finish it. Do you think your sons will accept me? I'm talking about all the things I read, all the stepparenting problems. Do you think we can do this without hurting anyone?"

Lewis forced himself to lie very still. She had come to him and with her need and her honesty and her hunger had aroused him until he was ablaze with readiness. And now she told him to wait. Did she have no idea that one more touch of her hand would surely push him over the brink?

His breaths came with great effort, but he willed them level. In a tightly strained voice, he said, "Charlie and Rick?" He closed his eyes and moistened his lips. "They'll be fine. I have to be honest about Steven. He's had so much laid at his young door, I'm not sure what he will or will not accept. But whatever it is, it won't be made easier by us staying apart."

The darkness was a wedge between them, though their faces were nearly touching. The silver of her hair captured all the available moonlight and turned her into a goddess. Or a witch, for she had drawn up her knee, and it pressed into his groin with unbearable urgency.

"Lewis?"

"What?"

"Could I have time? Would you give me time to get everyone used to the idea? I worry so much about that."

With trembling hands, Lewis drew his fingertip over the bridge of the nose that she hated and he adored. "I shouldn't have pushed you earlier, sweetheart. I'm sorry."

She smiled briefly. "I've been watching you," she whispered. "I've seen you with your sons."

"I know." Slowly, gently, Lewis reached around her hip and guided himself between her legs.

She pushed briefly at his chest. "What didn't you let me know? Why didn't—"

"I was hurt, Barbara." Lewis dropped his head back onto the mattress in despair. "God, my heart gets on my sleeve, too, sometimes."

The inferno inside Lewis had been stroked to an intolerable heat. But Barbara, now that her soul was satisfied, wanted to learn more leisurely about the man she was agreeing to spend the rest of her life with. With the age-less charms of a woman who loves and trusts her man, she began to weave what was to Lewis a most sublime and exquisite spell.

She was fascinated with the way his manliness lay trapped between them, pulsing in rhythm with his own heartbeat. And when she curved her fingers about him, her soft sigh like a spur in his flank, Lewis thought he had never known such pleasure-pain in all his life. Utterly at the mercy of her lack of expertise, he thought more than once that he could not bear it.

But time was misplaced, and soon everything else was misplaced except a white-hot coil deep in the center of his body. She was silk to his steel, and the muscles in his back tensed hard. He came up to meet her, and Barbara, when she felt him reaching the last boundary of human endurance, offered him the sweetest human sacrifice two people can offer each other.

"Say it," he growled as he pulled her on top of him and rose up into her like a sword in its own specially sculpted sheath. "Say the words again."

With the flex of a muscle, Barbara gripped him as fiercely as she could, and her breath was a soft, shuddering sigh. "I love you, Lewis."

"Now say, 'Yes, I'll marry you.'"

"Didn't I say that already?" She could hardly speak for the desire that choked her. She moved sensuously, her hips working in a fascinating rhythm.

"You must," he insisted, a winch about his throat. He squeezed his eyes tightly shut, then opened them.

"I will marry you."

Her head went back, and her eyes snapped closed.

"Say, 'I will be the mother of your children, Lewis,'" he grated.

She strained against him, wetly, hotly. "I will be the mother of your children."

"Until we die." Groaning, he grasped her, turned with her, rolled with her and in doing so poured out all the love that was his to give, body and spirit.

"Until we die," she whispered and, clutching him blindly to her heart, accepted.

Of the two things Lewis had on his mind to do, he decided to do the good one first and save the bad for later.

When the jeweler spread out his array of diamonds, he was forced to guess at Barbara's ring size. He wanted the ring to be a surprise, and not until it was tucked safely away in his bureau drawer did he return to the mill. That night he and Bumper put the boys in the movie theater and drove across the Charlatan County line.

"Seems like old times," Bumper said when they reached a string of warehouse-type buildings that made up the "hot" strip. "You know, I spent half my life in one of these dives."

Preoccupied and glad his friend was driving, Lewis was hard pressed to smile. "Down in Mobile?"

"Up in Kansas City." Bumper chuckled. "That's where my nose got broken the first time."

"But not your heart?"

"Aw, that, too, I guess." Bumper sighed.

Bumper had been the one who learned that Simon Bodine's hangout was The Green Frog, and as he veered the Suburban onto the wide expanse of the parking lot where George Jones's voice drifted out to blur with Kenny Rogers's from the next saloon, Lewis watched him cut the engine and sit drumming his large fingers upon the steering wheel.

He threw a sharp glance at Lewis. "Are you sure you want to do this?"

Lewis gazed out over the ocean of automobiles. His options weren't all that many, not if he wanted to retrieve Barbara's photographs. He'd already explained more about the situation than he'd wanted to, but one didn't ask a friend to spy without giving a good reason for it.

"You don't think he'd turn them over sober, do you?" he asked Bumper with a wry grimace.

"I don't particularly see Bodine sober period, if you want my opinion. There's something seriously wrong with that man."

"He does have a problem."

But then, who didn't? Lewis thought, and recalled unpleasant memories of hunting for Sunny in places such as this. "Well," he said with a slap of his knee, "sitting here isn't improving my love life."

Laughing, Bumper swung out of the Suburban. "Maybe it'll improve mine. Follow me."

Bumper O'Banyon knew his way around saloons, and Lewis gratefully allowed the ex-bouncer to shoulder a path for them once they were inside. After their eyes adjusted to the smoky dimness, Bumper pointed to a place near the disc jockey's booth.

"Wait here!" he yelled as he placed his mouth near Lewis's ear. "I'll be right back."

In five minutes he returned with two cold beers and Simon Bodine's whereabouts.

Lewis's first thought, as he weaved his way along the edges of the dance floor and spotted Bodine at the end of a long oaken bar, was that the man had probably been expecting some move from him. He also fancied he saw a flicker of satisfaction pass over the handsome, sullen face.

"Why, Mr. Pacatcho!" Simon exclaimed, pushing back the brim of his Western hat to a brash angle. "As I live and breathe."

Hardly able to hear for the throbbing decibels and hardly able to see for the haze, Lewis glanced blandly at Chino and another man who had been with Simon at the mill. He wasn't sorry Bumper was waiting a few paces behind, his muscles bulging reassuringly against his sport coat.

Bluntly to Bodine, Lewis said, "I want to talk to you."

"I kinda thought ya might." He flashed the usual Bodine smile. "What's on your mind, Pacatcho?"

"Not here," Lewis said, a steel edge to his voice. "Outside."

Simon hesitated, reluctant to go anywhere without his buddies. "Ah, I don't think so, man."

Tension built between them, bright and brittle. It was never going to work, Lewis thought, and heeled sharply, starting to walk away. "I made a mistake. Forget it."

Bodine's voice hit him in the back of the head. "Hey, don't be in such a hurry, okay?"

Slowly, Lewis stopped and turned. He didn't move a muscle as Bodine approached him lightly, like a boxer, on the balls of his feet.

Prancing, he said, "I know what ya want, man. I've known since th' day you and her come to my house."

Giving him a sour grimace, Lewis shrugged. "Now that you know, what's your price?"

"What're you offerin'?"

Lewis hesitated. What had he been hoping for? Honor among thieves? Deals such as this one were made all the time. Hell, he was almost certain now that deals such as this one had been made by his own company and Murray Levitt. Not that that made him feel any better. But for Barbara, he would have made a deal with the devil.

He lifted a shoulder and glanced back at Bumper. The big man was chatting pleasantly with a waitress, but Lewis knew he didn't miss a thing.

"Five hundred," he said to Bodine.

Bodine's pretty face fell. "Aw, man, that won't even get my attention."

"Sorry."

"Just a minute, just a minute. I didn't say I wasn't interested. What I thought was, you might offer me a job. That's all."

"You know I can't do that. Do you want to make a deal or not?"

When Simon didn't reply immediately, Lewis, fed up, turned away once more. Bodine caught him by the sleeve, and Lewis came within an inch of striking him.

Paling, Simon took a step backward. His lip curled. "Cool out, man."

A muscle in Lewis's jaw spasmed with anger. "Then don't waste my time, *man*."

The pretense fell away from Simon's face, and the hatred of years was visible, a hatred for the outsider who had come in with power, a hatred of the loser for the one who had refused to go down.

"How about a thousand?" he said, gritty sludge in his voice. "I got myself a kind of emergency on my hands."

If ever a remark had "woman trouble" written on it, Simon's did.

Grinning, the blond man took a large swallow of his beer and swiped the back of his hand over his mouth. "She's worth it, ain't she, man?"

"That kind of talk," Lewis said venomously, wanting badly to plant his fist in the man's mouth, "is the quickest way to send me out of here."

"Okay, okay."

"Where are they?"

Simon hesitated, then smiled. "In the truck, man."

So, Lewis thought, he had been expected, after all. With an ugly curl of his lip, he gestured to the space before him and said, "After you, Mr. Bodine."

Chapter Eleven

"A base deceiver, like a deep well whose mouth is covered with smiling plants." Kalidasa

For two days Barbara spent most of her waking hours trying to intercept Lewis. At first she was aglow with the aftermath of loving and being loved. The world took on a new look. The sky was stuffed full of mighty clouds sailing across its sea, their majestic whiteness as dazzling as fresh, clean sails. The air was full of wonderful, trembling smells.

So she didn't mind the promise of summer that turned Finley's streets into shimmering waves. Everything was glorious. In her generosity, she forgave Lewis for his tiny sin of being lost when she wanted him.

But the second day saw his halo listing slightly on the side of humanity. And if to forgive was divine, Barbara discovered that her canonization was a long way off. When she drove out to the mill, trying to recapture the beauty of life only twenty-four hours before, she found Lewis had gone home. When she returned home, her discouragement mounting, she called his house, only to find he had returned to the mill.

"There's a message for you on the machine," Edward Wheeler told her.

Downstairs, she found it. "Absence makes the heart grow fonder, my darling," his voice spoke out of the box. "How's yours doing these days? If I weren't such a macho hardhead, I'd say that mine was lovesick. I called my mother, told her about you. Her first words were, 'Can she cook?' I told her that Julia was a member of the family. By the way, Max dug through the hedge and ate your cat food. What can I say? He's such a dog."

"Such a dog," she mumbled testily, and jerked up her bag and made the stairs tremble with her stomping. "What can *I* say, Lewis Paccachio? We'll just *see* what I can say."

At the dinner table she snapped at Alice, and every head rose in shock. When her mother gave one of her injured looks, Barbara gathered up her miserable, foul mood and dragged it back up the stairs like an iron ball chained to her leg.

For two hours she stared mutinously at the telephone. Across the hedge, the house was the same as it had been for ten years: boring and empty. Even Max was nowhere to be seen. Out eating someone's cat, no doubt.

She took a serious shower. She tried to do something with her hair and saw, to her relief, that it was getting longer. She flipped idly through the *TV Guide* and saw that *Out of Africa* was showing on cable.

"John Barry, composer," she mumbled blandly to herself, then thought of the film's tragically romantic love affair between Karen Blixen and Denys Finch-Hatton.

"If I were Meryl Streep," she told herself, "I would have taken a rifle by now and gotten on my horse and ridden out into the bush."

She laughed, then frowned, then snatched off her clothes and turned out the light and went to bed. But every car that passed on the street made her pulse quicken and her body grow damp with longing. She touched her breasts beneath the old T-shirt she was wearing as a nightie and remembered Lewis's insatiable mouth.

It was too painful to love, she decided. She hadn't asked for this! Love made you too vulnerable. It made you wait all the time. *I hate you, Lewis Paccachio.* But she didn't. She loved him.

A rustle. A creak. Hushed crickets. A thump. A muttered curse.

A burglar! Barbara's eyes flew open, and she blinked away the rust and rose from the senseless chatter of her dream. Was it really a burglar, or had she imagined it?

Unfolding in excruciatingly slow motion, with her heart pounding, she took tiny, tiptoeing baby steps until she reached the wall, then positioned herself just beyond her glass doors. He stepped through her doors with no more sound than a sigh, and for some seconds she was so taken by surprise, she could not speak.

Spinning around, he found her as truly as an arrow seeking its target.

"Oh!" she gasped.

"Shh!" He grinned guiltily. "I've come to borrow a cup of sugar." He jauntily hooked his thumbs in the belt loops of his faded jeans as if he were a modern-day pirate. "Don't wake up the household."

With menacing eyes, Barbara stared at the jeans that were wet about the hems, the sneakers that left damp marks on the carpet. Above the waist, he was naked. A tiny trickle of blood flowed over the smooth plane of his right breast.

She attempted a smirk that wasn't very successful. "Is that a dueling scar or a bullet wound?"

"A vampire bite, actually," he said, and moved through the shadowy room to find the mirror above her bureau, where he inspected his injury.

Barbara padded along behind him. Reaching around, she flicked a tissue from the box and thrust it at him. "Please don't grow fangs in my bedroom."

Turning, he leaned forward and blew into her eyes. "Don't worry about anyone mistaking you for Florence Nightingale," he said dryly, and daubed the tiny wound. "And don't say I never shed blood for you."

"That little dribble was for me?" she taunted.

With a grievous sigh, he dropped the tissue to the top of her dresser and inspected her knee-length T-shirt with such thoroughness that Barbara flushed and took a step backward.

"Hmm, I see we're a tad miffed tonight," he drawled and made a point of licking his lips.

"We," Barbara said with exaggeration as she leaned over to give a curl on his chest a not-too-gentle tweak, "were looking for you. *We* have been looking for you for two days."

Grinning, he leaned back against the wall and crossed his legs at the ankles like a cat burglar satisfied with his booty. "Tsk-tsk-tsk." He shook his head. "Maybe I should wait until you're in a better mood. No need to waste a good surprise on a foul-tempered woman. Well, no matter. It can wait."

With a set of her jaw and a lowering of her head and a squint of her eyes, Barbara drilled him with a quelling frown. "Don't try to get on my good side, Lewis."

"I wouldn't even if I could find it." He coolly took time to inspect his wound, which was sealing over nicely.

Now Barbara wasn't sure if he was baiting her or not. "Lewis—" she planted a fist on her hip with a tad less rancor "—would you please be serious?"

An odd smile kept flirting with his lips. "Bitch, bitch, bitch. Tell me, what movie was that from?"

"*The Gauntlet*. Clint Eastwood and Sandra Locke."

"Correct. Score?"

"Ah..." She turned, cocked her head and rubbed the tip of her nose. "Well, I'll be, I don't know."

"Sorry, you don't win the surprise."

Now Barbara could hardly remember if her anger at him had been real or imagined. She was on the verge of stamping her foot but remembered the sleeping people beneath them. With a sense of purpose, she closed the small distance and rose up on her toes so that her face was mere inches from his.

Her smile was only half teasing when she said, "You know, Lewis, I was doing fairly well before I met you. I wasn't extraordinarily happy, but neither was I all that sad. I was content to take my licks and get through the days with a minimum of pain. So, tell me why it is that since I first laid eyes on you, my life has been nothing but sheer hell?"

The moment was time-trapped, caught in a box like a butterfly, hauled up short and held suspended in that fragile limbo between love and torment, fire and water, yin and yang.

"Just lucky, I guess," Lewis murmured, and with a sigh, lowered his head.

Smiling, forgiving him everything, Barbara angled her lips to be kissed. But he only wrapped his arms slowly about her and lifted her off the floor to keep her there, imprisoned between heaven and earth.

She felt the hard, knobby pressure in his pocket, and she thought, *The surprise! Why, he really has brought me a present, the wily fox.*

"I want my present," she demanded.

But the contents of his pocket seemed far removed from his thoughts. As a frown deepened between his brows and his breath mingled with hers, his words grew serious.

"But you have to promise me first," he said.

Not understanding, Barbara searched his eyes. "Promise you what?"

"That you're not going to change your mind if things get hard."

"Ah." Now she understood. "You're talking about the boys?"

The breath went out of him in a sigh, and he finally put her down. "I'm not sure what I'm talking about. I just have this fear, Barbara, of turning around and finding you gone."

With a tenderness she had never expected to feel, one that could have spanned oceans and lifetimes, Barbara dragged her arms from around his neck and cupped his hard, scarred face in her hands.

"You really, truly need me, don't you?" she whispered, awed.

"You had doubts about that?"

"The moment you turn your back, Lewis, I'm nothing but a mountain of doubts. I go to sleep with doubts. I wake up with doubts."

He placed his finger across her lips. "I brought you something."

Placing enough inches between them so that he could pry the tiny jeweler's box from his pocket, he opened it, removed the ring, snapped the box closed and tossed it to the carpet.

"I was in a hurry," he confessed with a grin, lifting her hand and slipping the ring upon her finger. "This is just between us, Barb. Wear it only when you're ready. However long that takes. Well, what do you think?"

Barbara hardly looked at the ring. It wouldn't have mattered if it had been made of tinfoil or chipped from the Queen's crown jewels. "I think that I'm a fool, Lewis Paccachio," she said with tears of emotion in her voice. "A silly fool."

His mouth possessed her with molten need. It ripped away her doubts and her fears and all her resistance. It opened her up to an even deeper exposure than before, but she didn't care. He would not think she was silly or foolish. He would not find her lacking. He would not find her plain.

Barbara let him linger at taking her, let him sate himself with long, savoring looks and tastes and smells and feels. Never in her life had she been so thoroughly touched, so adored. From texture to texture, top to bottom, they learned each other. Their passion grew unbearable, and they exhausted it.

For long moments afterward they talked. He lay between her legs with his head resting upon a pillow of bone, and he closed his eyes and dreamed. Rested, they began again, and Barbara grew brave with her torments. She tried things she had never dared before, and she drove him wild with desire. She depleted him, and she demanded more. In turn, he wearied her, then let her sleep only to awaken her and drag her to the brink of superlative bliss, with his mouth and his hands and his hard, driving strength.

When she awakened, he was gone, and the sunlight was creeping through the sheer panels spanning her doors. Sore from love but grateful, she pulled the sheet about her and moved slowly out onto the deck. She wanted to see his house and imagine the time when she would wake up in his bed, in that house. Or wherever he was.

Her foot scuffed against an unfamiliar crispness, and she glanced down to see the large brown envelope smudged with dirty fingerprints and no other outside markings. Puzzled, she picked it up, and as she did so her fingers began to tremble and her heart to thrash.

She didn't dare hope, did she? She ripped the envelope in her impatience and watched the pictures John had taken slip through her fingers to the floor until she was left with a small fold of paper. Blinking, feeling a knot the size of a fist rise in her throat, she opened it.

"I love you," was all it said. But Barbara knew that brash, bold scrawl. It was the first thing she'd ever known about Lewis Paccachio.

"Oh, Lewis," she said as her face crumpled and her legs buckled and she was forced to drop to her knees in the middle of the torn brown paper and glistening black-and-white reproductions of herself. "Thank you. Oh, Lewis."

And there, she wept until she couldn't weep anymore.

In an attempt to attract some of the tourist bonanza of the fifties, Finley had once undertaken a massive beautification program. They had installed picnic pavilions beneath their great pecan trees. They built a miniature train with its own tiny bridge crossing the Arkansas River into the next county. A new boat dock sprang up on the river. For one dollar and seventy-five cents, tour boats would take you leisurely upriver and back.

Now it cost five dollars, and two of the tours had gone out of business, but with the arrival of the new paper mill, there had been talk of things picking up. When Barbara parked her Mustang near the boat concession and the train station with its charming twenties decor, she spotted Jack Pruellyn—Alice's husband, the Regents' gardener and the Finley handyman.

She waved for him to help her unload the ice chests and washtubs that would be packed with canned soft drinks for the birthday picnic.

"Is Alice coming along?" Jack yelled. "Miss Emma and Mr. Katt just brought the salads and need more ice—a lot more ice."

"Mother's running behind." Walking toward him, Barbara scanned the grounds for sight of a beloved tall figure. "They won't be long. You haven't seen our new neighbors, have you, Jack?"

Jack wiped a bandanna over his face and grinned. "Nope. But then, I ain't been lookin'. I reckon you'll find 'em if you keep at it."

Barbara gave the man one of her fond scowls. "I'm not *at it*, Jack."

The old man cackled. "Look over at the train station. It's due to arrive in...let's see..." Pulling out a pocket-watch as if the train were the Rock Island Line and he was the man responsible for any and all delays, he gravely calculated. "In three minutes exactly, by my calculations."

Not hugging the man was out of the question. She playfully punched his chest.

"I won't be far, Jack," she said, and struck off toward the station.

"If I see the new neighbors," he called, "I'll tell him you're lookin'."

"Don't you dare." She laughed.

A number of people lounged about the train station, sipping soft drinks and iced tea from the concession stand but mainly chasing toddlers and coaxing their offspring to be patient until the train could return for another trip.

Barbara had known most of them all her life and had addressed their invitations personally. But even the strangers were welcome to Granna's party. Between the offerings of the River House Café and tons of goodies from the Finley house, there was always food to spare. And Granna's closest friends brought extra.

Everyone smiled and said "Hello, Barbara" when she walked past, remarking upon what a beautiful day it was for the party. It was true; no day could have been more perfect. But then, Barbara was looking at things through love-tinted glasses, she knew.

Did they know? Would they think her fickle if they did? Like a widow who remarries disgracefully soon?

When she couldn't find Lewis or the boys, Barbara waited until the *toot-toot* of the whistle brought the train chugging around the bend. The children squealed with delight as it pulled into the station and the conductor doffed his starched, striped cap and rang the bell.

"All passengers, please watch your step," he called. "You, too, Peggy Sue. Josh, stay with your mother, now."

When she saw Mary Woodward with her brother, Tom, John's father, Barbara wasn't really surprised; it was bound to happen sooner or later. Despite all their crankiness, Mary and Catherine knew that declining the party invitation would have given the impression that they were ungenerous. And generosity was a necessary commodity for moral guardians.

Refusing to cringe, Barbara smiled thinly as she stared straight into their eyes. But when John stepped into view from behind his father's shoulder, the small-town mentality seemed to slip a noose about Barbara's neck. She imagined phone lines glowing hot with scandalous talk. She envisioned reproductions of John's pictures being dropped from airplanes over the county and a scarlet letter *A* sewn to her white knit top.

The noose warned her with a jerk, and she decided that facing the Woodwards wasn't worth a hanging. Barbara prepared to leave them to their gossip. Lucy and her father ambled up to join everyone. Spying Barbara, Lucy hurried forward with a happy exclamation.

Barbara hugged her, and Lucy whispered from the corner of her mouth like Philip Marlowe, "Don't jump to conclusions about this."

"Why, I wouldn't think of it, Brutus," Barbara murmured.

"Would you believe Mary called this morning and asked if we would drive over with her? Of course, Daddy said yes, and guess who just happened to be in the car when we came out of the house."

"I haven't the foggiest," droned Barbara.

Lucy laughed.

Barbara frowned. "Did John say anything about me?"

"Do you think I would have let him? He knows better, the louse, but Daddy is so upset about this labor thing, he growls constantly. So your name did come up a couple of times, Barb. Look, I'll tell you all about it later."

A pang twitched in Barbara's chest, and she caught Lucy with an urgent grasp as her friend was turning away. "Tell me about it now, Luce."

With a shake of her head, Lucy made a fierce throttling gesture in Mary's direction. "Punch the old biddy in the nose."

"I can't." Barbara spoke through gritted teeth. "It's stuck in my back."

Lucy giggled.

Though Barbara returned the awkward smile, she didn't find anything truly funny about the situation, for behind the small Woodward-Levitt clique was another group of people waiting for the train to load up. Straggling around the edges of that group were others who had been attracted by the appearance of the mayor at the park and wanted to see what would happen. Everyone looked from face to face with visible expectancy.

Suddenly finding herself center stage, Barbara hesitated, uncertain of her role. Was she the heroine in this drama or the bitchy villainess everyone loved to hate?

With a helpless look, Lucy shrugged. "I know what John did, Barb," she muttered as she was leaving. "Mary told Daddy, and Daddy told me."

Barbara's brain was ticking furiously. She wasn't prepared for this; as many times as she'd constructed scenarios, she wasn't prepared.

Did others sense her dread? People were moving back like an outgoing wave, leaving only the lead characters onstage. Far beyond her, at the end of the park, she could see Lewis and his sons climbing out of the Suburban. She watched as he stopped to speak to Rick. The boy went scampering back to the car and appeared again bearing a large box tied with a red bow.

Lewis took the box from his son's arms, and a brief flurry occurred that ended with Lewis letting Rick carry the box and stagger beneath its weight.

Barbara threw a split-second look at the people who stared at her with curious faces. She saw Mary's pinched expression and the deep creases between her brows. She saw the dark circles beneath Murray Levitt's eyes and the defeat in Tom Woodward's jaw. She saw John's conceit as he glanced around to see if anyone was watching him. And she looked once more at the tall man walking toward her, saw the strength of character behind the scarred face.

It was very simple. These people who took such pleasure in maligning Lewis Paccachio—or her—weren't worth a flick of his finger, and they certainly weren't worth lines in her own face. Suddenly it didn't matter anymore that John was shallow, nor that his aunts were narrow-minded and his father a yes-man. It didn't matter that they all thought she was a disappointment.

Looking at Lucy, she laughed, and the sound of it floated out over their heads, rippling and vibrant.

Lucy looked at her with shock. *Are you out of your mind? These people intend to roast you alive!*

With a shake of her head, she said aloud to Lucy, "I don't care."

Lucy's mouth dropped open, and Barbara pressed her fingers upon the ring nestled on a chain beneath her knit top, its hard circular shape pressing into her breast.

As Rick placed Granna's gift on a picnic table, Lewis's smile reached across the distance and kissed her. Conscious of heads turning to see who she smiled at, Barbara reached deliberately into her cleavage and pulled out the chain. She heard Lucy's gasp, and she guessed that John was struggling with an ego-bruising awakening.

Once she dragged the chain over her short flurry of hair, she unlocked the clasp and slipped the ring free. Just as she placed the ring on her finger, Mary, who had not yet grasped the entirety of what was happening, said, "I suppose now would be as good a time as any. Tell her, Tom."

Mary's bait was thrown out with a strong line. From habit, Barbara started to take it. She turned from Lewis and focused upon the stout, bitter woman.

"Tell me what, Mary?" Her gaze moved from sister to brother. "What, Tom? What's going on?"

Tom Woodward smiled at her with such utter spinelessness that Barbara twisted the ring nervously about her finger.

"Nothing, Barbara," he said pathetically. "Mary shouldn't have said anything."

That certainly was not the consensus of the several dozen people who stood around listening; the conductor was even holding up the train's departure.

Mary squinted her small eyes and pointed a finger at Barbara. "If you don't have the courage, Tom, I certainly have," she said. "Nothing was ever gained by beating around the bush."

"Aunt Mary—" John broke in to protest, anguished.

Barbara slapped her ex-fiancé down with a glare. "Oh, shut up, John."

"The city council had a meeting, Barbara," Mary said. "It's their opinion, in light of everything that's happened—all the unrest, the failure of the mill to supply the town with work—that it would be better for the town if someone else headed up Human Resources. You understand that we have your best interests at heart, dear, but we must think of the town. I told Tom that you would be the first to understand."

A murmur rippled through the milling crowd, and Barbara, wrapped in the robes of her brave new freedom, shuffled values and weighed possible retributions. She felt herself sinking into the ground. It wasn't right. She might have done some foolish things, but she hadn't betrayed Finley.

She glared at Murray Levitt. He had blanched until he looked like a ghost. When he moved past Lucy to slip his arm around her shoulders, Barbara shoved him away.

"You're part of this, Murray?" she snapped, her voice like a taut wire.

"Barbara, dear . . ." Murray took out his handkerchief and mopped his sweating face.

"Don't 'dear' me, Murray."

"God knows none of us meant for you to learn this way, but since the matter has come up, yes, there are some people on the city council who would be greatly relieved if you would tender your resignation."

Pain, fresh and brightly red, seemed to be all around Barbara now. She was hardly aware of Lewis walking up behind John Woodward. When Lewis stepped in front of Murray, however, and lifted her hand and saw the diamond that he had given with such love, he threaded his fingers through hers very tightly and turned to rivet his look with that of Finley's mayor.

"Sorry to interrupt, Mr. Levitt," he said evenly.

Murray, a Southern gentleman to the very end, bowed politely and murmured, "Think nothing of it."

"Oh, but I do."

A sea of heads turned.

"What?"

"I do think something of it," Lewis repeated so quietly that the hush that befell the eavesdroppers let the sound of the riverboat's faraway horn drift through. "In fact, I think quite a lot about it."

Benumbed, Barbara leaned upon Lewis's arm and was grateful for his strength.

"What I don't understand," Lewis said icily, "is what these people think about it." With his free hand he gestured expansively to the crowd.

Murray seemed to grow smaller inside his clothes. Lucy made a small sound and stepped toward her father, but Murray was lost in Lewis's hard, laserlike gaze.

"Sir—" Murray gripped his tie.

"Ask them, Mr. Mayor." Lewis punched out his words. "Ask them if they mind that their mayor took a kickback from the people who hired me to come here. Ask them if they mind being used. Ask them if they mind that you took three percent while they went on food stamps."

Not until after Lewis had paid the skipper of the Arkansas Trawler the necessary dollars and extracted a sworn oath from the boys that they would not misbehave on the boat ride upriver did Barbara lay her head back on the seat of the Suburban and close her eyes.

"I can't believe you did that, Lewis Paccachio."

"What's to believe?" he growled as he stood in the wedge between the car and the door and waved goodbye to his sons. "The bastard was hurting something that belongs to me. I don't take that casually."

Loving him more than she thought she would ever love anyone, Barbara smiled contentedly at his hand resting upon the door. "Well, I think you may have caused a very casual lynching with that announcement. Murray will undoubtedly resign. Will you run for mayor in his place?"

Chuckling, eager to forget about small-town politics, Lewis got into the car and started the engine. "I'm running for husband of the year. How do you plan to vote?"

Barbara waited until they were out on the highway. Ten miles to the north they would meet the boat and drive the boys back in time for lunch at the pavilion. She smoothed her skirt over her knees.

Grinning, Lewis adjusted a wrinkle she had missed. "Come here," he said, reaching for her. "All that space depresses me."

"I'll bet lots of things depress you." Barbara let him cuddle her and draw her head onto his shoulder.

"Not this," he murmured into her ear, his breath warm on her hair.

She shivered at the pleasure of his words and the pressure of his hand as he held her pinned firmly against him. How easy it would be, she thought dreamily, to let her life fashion itself around him. How easy it would be to be a mother to his . . .

She stiffened slightly, and his puzzlement was in the arch of his eyebrows. Sliding onto her own side of the seat, she angled a look at him.

"What?" he said.

"Nothing."

"Liar."

"I was just wondering."

"If I love you?"

"If Steven could love me, Lewis."

"Give him time, Barbara. Give all of them time."

"They don't know me."

"They're learning."

"But will they want me when they learn? They're going to hear some pretty tough things about me, I expect."

"They've heard tough things before."

Then the tension passed, and for long, untroubled moments they let the silence have its way between them. How nice it was to be so comfortable with another human being that words weren't necessary.

"Turn here," she said presently and indicated a small, angling road off the main highway.

"To where?" he quizzed her.

"Don't be so nosy."

He made a pretense of tweaking her nose. "I thought that word wasn't in your vocabulary."

She giggled. "The first thing I'm going to do with your money is have a nose job."

"You do, and I'll divorce you."

Smiling, she directed him up a winding road that ended in a paved turnaround. Beyond it snaked a rutted trail the four-wheel-drives and motorcycles had blazed. It wound up and up and up the hill, peeping now and again between the thick stands of pine.

"If you think this Suburban can make it," she said, "there's a place up there where you can look down the river for miles."

Lewis made an appalled face. "You think this car can't get up that hill?"

"It's rough."

"I like it when it's rough," he growled suggestively.

Flushing, Barbara watched him handle the Suburban with a hard discipline. Ten minutes later he swung the car around with a spinning whine and came to a skidding stop at the crest of the hill.

As they got out of the car, there was nothing around them but the sun and the wind and the hill and the soft slopes of grass. The trees had succumbed to campers long before. Below them, the river was a thread of shimmering silver that stitched its way through the hills.

They sank to the ground, and Barbara dribbled handfuls of loose, sandy soil through her fingers. Stretching out, she spread her skirt in a great fan, and Lewis sprawled out and placed his head in her lap.

"Thank you, Lewis," she said softly and brushed off her hand to arrange the snowy patch of hair at his temple.

"For what?"

"I never could have done that to Murray. I couldn't have hurt him or Lucy. But it had to be. You saved me from all that."

"You saved me, too."

She smiled down at him. "How?"

Lifting her hand, he kissed the ring he had given her. Turning to prop himself on an elbow, he traced the soft indentation of her skirt over her lap. His glance up at her was quick and to the point.

"I said I wouldn't rush you," he muttered. "I spoke before I thought. I want to rush you until you can't breathe. I want to marry you today."

Barbara shaded her eyes and stared blindly at the river. So many things had to be resolved. So many people were woven into their lives.

The wind blew wisps of hair about her cheeks, and he swiveled around to fit his body about her back, his knees about her sides, his arms about her shoulders, his chin dropping down into the curve of her shoulder.

He kissed a curl. "Your hair's growing out."

"Have you talked to them?" she whispered, turning her head so that their mouths all but touched.

"I think they probably know already. Have you told your family?"

Barbara thought of how much pleasure it gave her to be able to take the smell of him deep into her lungs. She brushed his scar with her lips. "I think they've figured it out."

"Then all our problems are solved."

"Of course."

"Except one."

"What?" Barbara's breath caught in her throat.

"There's only one way to say it, and I'm not quite sure your small-town ears are ready for that, lady."

She laughed softly, and Lewis wanted his kiss to capture her there, in the center of her pleasure. When their tongues touched, it could have been the first time. He drew her down into the grass with him and felt her body become supple against his. He thought he could listen to her breathing and feel the warmth of her breasts and belly forever. He touched her cheeks with his hands, and the length of her throat.

When he grazed his teeth along the velvety curve, she moaned deep in her throat. Seeking her beneath her skirt, he found her ready for him. Sighing, he drew himself upon her.

Her eyes were glazed with desire, and she reached to loosen his belt. "Lewis," she whispered as she freed the zipper and helped him brave the awkwardness of their clothes, "did you really mean what you said before?"

"What, darling?" he asked in a voice that was thick and burdened with arousal.

"About wanting a daughter?"

He luxuriated in the silkiness of her. "Are you offering?"

"Are you asking?"

"Do you want me to ask?"

He was buried deep inside her, and she unconsciously began to move with him.

"Ask me, Lewis."

As he forced himself to hold back, wanting the world to stop turning for just a little while, wanting time to stop and history to roll back upon itself, Lewis braced himself on his hands until he could see the way they fit together so perfectly. He waited until she watched him watching, and when she looked up, he smiled at her. "Do you want to make a baby, Barbara?"

"Yes."

"Then you must marry me very quickly. It's a moral imperative."

"Please hurry, Lewis. Please hurry."

Chapter Twelve

"Fight as fiercely in defence of his mistress as Blandimar and Paridel, of romantic fame, are said to have fought for the lovely Florimel." Anonymous

That's all they said, Mr. Paccachio," Jack Pruellyn told Barbara and Lewis after lunch when everyone was sated and sleepy and mothers were putting down their babies for a nap.

Jack had just returned from a trip back to the house. Barbara and Lewis were preparing to take the boys for a drive out to the mill—a public relations strategy, Lewis had said.

Now Jack was explaining, "Some man named Curtis Gregory. And a woman, too. Allie or somethin' funny. Real good lookin'. She said they'd flown in on the 'express orders' of a Mr. Abrams. Somethin' about a phone call from you, Barbara." He glanced her way, then back at Lewis. "This Mr. Abrams wants to know what's goin' on here, she said. Didn't sound real happy about bein' here," Jack added disparagingly. Then, having delivered the entire message straight, he looked satisfied.

Lewis, with the frustration of a man who finds fatherhood and career and love life splintering into three different directions, sighed heavily. "What will Abrams and Bean think of next?"

He implored Barbara with comically angled brows from where he lay stretched out on a picnic bench, a long leg braced on the ground on each side. Beyond them, the boys were kicking the inevitable soccer ball.

Lifting his head, he asked Jack, "How long have they been there?"

Jack fished a pocket watch from his trousers and snapped open the top. "About an hour and a half, I'd say. I've a hunch they're gettin' a mite impatient by now."

Barbara smiled at Lewis with ancient wisdom. "Only fools ignore the strange truths of Jack's hunches."

"No one ever accused Dad of being a genius," Charlie quipped as he darted in for a soft drink and grabbed one from the cooler.

Chuckling, Lewis lunged off the bench and grabbed the boy to playfully wrestle for a moment before he said to Jack, "Thanks, Jack. I'll take care of it."

Charlie had put up his dukes and was dancing about his father like a prizefighter. "One for the money, two for the show," he chanted.

Over his head, Lewis searched for Barbara's eyes. He switched to the sight of Rick scampering around with some of the other children and Steven alone, as usual.

"I guess I'd better drive over and see what's up," he said to her, and Rick, dashing up, skidded to a stop.

"Does this mean we can't go out to the mill?"

"Of course not. We'll go later. But I have to see what's up at the house."

"Trouble," Rick said, and Charlie puckered his mouth and sucked on his braces.

"Not necessarily," Lewis chided. "Say, guys, don' grumble on me. It won't take too long, and then we'll a∥ pile into the Suburban and go."

Steven, seeing everyone in a cluster and assuming the worst, shuffled up to listen quietly. Barbara's heart ache∢ for the oldest son. What mother could shatter a boy' world by telling him that his father was not his father' What absolution could be worth that?

She smiled at him, and Steven smiled shyly back, but he didn't join the group, and he didn't give her any indica tion that she would be welcome as a member of the fam ily.

Rick, however, slipped to Barbara's side and gaze∢ adoringly upward. "I have an idea. Barbara can drive u out in her Mustang. I can steer. Right, Barbara? Huh huh? Can I steer? *Pleeease*..."

Laughing, Barbara shook her head at the child. "Rick I'll make a date with you. Four years from today, whe∩ you're old enough to have a learner's permit, I promise I'∥ take you out and let you drive. Honest."

Someone else probably would have given in to the irre sistible pleading on the boy's face, and Lewis sent her ⸱ visual congratulations. *How can they not love you when love you so much?*

"Okay, okay," Lewis gave in. "Look, you all go on ou to the site, and I'll follow in the Suburban. If worse come⸱ to worst, I'll pack up Curtis and Allie and bring with me."

Barbara's eyelids dropped to half-mast. "Allie is th∢ piranha?"

Cringing, Lewis said in a stage whisper, "Keep your voice down. We live with three parrots who have a way of repeating things at the worst possible times."

As the boys trotted off toward Barbara's little car, Lewis sidled up beside her and bumped his hip to hers.

"Are you sure this is such a good idea?" she asked.

He kissed the air between them. "It'll be good for you. You need some time alone with them. I'll be right behind you."

"I'm not sure I'm ready for this, Lewis."

But they were halfway to her car, and Barbara knew Lewis was right. There were times she wondered if she hadn't fallen in love with the boys before she'd fallen in love with him. But to want something as badly as she wanted their affection was dangerous. The gods went crazy when you wanted things very, very much.

Lewis called out to his children. "You guys behave yourselves."

"What's the matter?" shrilled Rick. "Don't you trust us?"

"No!"

As Barbara drained Lewis's adoring eyes for the last possible drop, Rick and Charlie returned to grab her hands and tow her to the car.

I love you, she signaled Lewis over her shoulder.

I love you, too, he signaled back.

With typical childish abandon, the boys tumbled into her car. Barbara directed them where and where not to put their feet and was congratulating herself as she opened her own door and stooped to get inside. Over the top of the hood, across the narrow strip of tree-shaded asphalt, was a parked truck—only one among dozens, but inside this one sat Simon Bodine, May Lamont and Chino.

A shadow passed over the day. How long had they been watching? What were they thinking behind those leering faces? What words had passed between Lewis and Simon when he recovered her pictures?

"Hey, princess," Simon called as he poked the upper half of his body out the passenger window and braced his hands cockily on the top, a cigarette tucked between his fingers.

She started to step into the car. "I don't have time to talk to you, Simon."

"You got time for everything else," he taunted. "Consortin' with the enemy these days? Huh, princess? Yankee-lover?"

May Lamont giggled, and Chino leered.

With an alarmed glance at the boys, Barbara felt a drop of perspiration drizzling down her back. The boys glanced uneasily at her, their bright laughter hushed now and their smiles waning.

Lewis's car was not in its parking place when Barbara turned to see. It really was time for her to be a mother, wasn't it? She had no intentions of letting her first excursion with the boys be marred by some jerk. She climbed in beneath the wheel and shut the door.

"Who's that?" Steve asked from his place in the front seat.

"Trouble." Barbara twisted the key in the ignition.

"We're not Yankees," Rick said, subdued.

"The man is a boor, Rick," she said. "He likes to insult people. He's angry because he doesn't have a job. He's not worth taking seriously."

During the drive out Spur 109, the boys told her about Manila and about the days Lewis had spent in the hospital after the accident with the boat. They were briefly distracted by the excitement of soccer games, and they ex plained the difference between European sports and American.

Once they arrived at the mill, they took considerable pride in knowing more about the goings-on than she did. They showed her every tiny detail and explained what every small thing would eventually be. They were quite knowledgeable about construction, she saw. The equipment was commonplace to them. Steven climbed aboard a Caterpillar and prepared to demonstrate his expertise.

"I think you'd better get down from there," she advised.

A challenge lay briefly in the boyish brown eyes, as if to remind her that if she wanted to give orders, she would have to earn the right to do it. But eventually he obeyed.

"This is the belly of the whale," Rick announced as he dragged her inside the huge skeletal frame of the mill itself. He demonstrated how the huge panel door dropped out of the ceiling, and they tipped back their heads to look at the skylights.

"And we're all Jonahs," Barbara said into the hollow interior.

Her voice echoed as if they were in a cave. Charlie stopped the door at half closure and wiped his hands on his jeans as he came away. He moved deeper into the interior. "Only one Jonah allowed."

Steve cackled with a laugh that echoed. "Then we'll just have to throw you overboard, nerdo."

That remark set Steve and Charlie to scuffling.

Glad to have Barbara all to himself, Rick clasped her hand and eagerly took her on a tour of the lavatories that weren't finished yet. They drank water out of a hose and inspected the six-foot stacks of lumber and plywood for the interior and the panels of aluminum to be used for office partitions.

It was then, as Rick was climbing onto a stack of two-by-fours, showing off for her benefit, Barbara knew, that the door slammed all the way closed and they were left with only the light from the roof.

"Hey!" yelled Steven, spinning around. "Who did that?"

For some moments they let their eyes adjust, and they looked at each other, thinking little of it. But when the door didn't open as promptly as it had shut, their curiosity turned to concern.

"Get me down from here," yelped Rick from the stack of lumber.

Moving carefully toward him, Barbara now realized that some of their light streamed from a small vent a few feet away near the floor. Reaching up, she pulled Rick down from the lumber, but as she was holding the boy she felt his small body clinging to hers.

"It's your father," she said, laughing. "He's teasing us."

"Hey, Dad!" shouted Steven.

"Dad-ad-ad," his echo answered back.

"Lewis?" Barbara called.

"Lewis-ewis-ewis."

Angry now, Barbara gave Rick a fierce hug and placed him upon his feet. She moved toward the place where the door had dropped down, Rick at her heels and the other two boys making their way toward her. She tried to budge it, but she couldn't.

"Lewis Paccachio?" she called. "This isn't funny. Open that door."

Nothing. Or did they hear sounds from outside?

"Shh!" Steven hissed as he leaned over her shoulder.

"Someone's out there," whispered Charlie.

Steven lunged to the wall and beat it with his fists. Echos collided with his shouts. "Open this door-*oor-oor*. Let us out-*out-out*!"

The irritation Barbara felt evolved into full-blown anger, then changed into fear. Whoever was outside wasn't Lewis. But who would shut the door on them?

Unless the party didn't know anyone was inside. But her car was parked outside. Whoever had shut the door knew they were here.

Simon Bodine's mocking laugh came to mind. *Consortin' with the enemy, princess?*

Her first thought was that they must open the door. "Everyone grab hold," she started to say, but in split seconds a deafening sound rocked the building, rippling through the steel hull like the blast of a warhead and hurling them, stumbling, into each other.

There was a sound like the sucking of a jet, and Barbara instinctively grabbed Rick and jerked him down to the cement floor. The sucking sound came again, and the opposite end of the building was ripped open and filled with blood-red light. Debris showered them.

"Let's get out of here!" screamed Steven.

Barbara struggled to her feet and ran a few feet toward the open end where the explosion had occurred. Her adrenaline surged, her heart thudded painfully in her breast, and her side ached.

But to go near the heat would have been insanity. The flames jerked, orange and yellow, against the sky. The materials stacked nearby had caught like tinder. Thick smoke roiled into the building.

Strangling, Rick began to weep. Charlie, usually so quiet, was coughing and babbling.

"Oh, Lewis," she whispered as the heat struck them in a wave that nearly blistered their cheeks. "We're going to die."

Barbara knew that somewhere in the heart of every person was an incredible strength to survive. But her own survival had always consisted of small battles, of mental and emotional stamina over the long haul. She had never been a mother fighting for the life of her young.

But now, as she reacted by instinct and not logic, as her newly rooted love made her look upon Lewis's children as her own, she became a person she did not know. She jerked the sobbing Rick to his feet and screamed at him.

"Stop it!" She shook the child.

She collared Charlie, and as the smoke burned her eyes she grabbed a handful of his hair and pulled. "Listen to me!" Swiveling, she screamed for Steven. "All of you. Take off your shirts. Wet them and wrap them around your heads. Soak everything. Don't breathe the smoke. Breathe through your shirts."

Almost before she had the words out of her mouth, Charlie was running for the hose. Snatching off her own blouse and holding it beneath the spray, she tied it over her face and head until nothing showed but her eyes. With her lungs aching and eyes burning, she ran frantically through the end of the building that wasn't burning.

Steven was hard on her heels. Putting her mouth to his ear, she yelled, "We have to drag some of the aluminum to the air duct. Build us a shelter."

"We're gonna die in here!"

"No!" she shouted. "Move it!"

He did move it, and Barbara thanked God for Lewis's clarity of purpose that was indelibly imprinted upon his sons. With that same presence of mind, Steven now raced to obey. He read her mind even before she shouted out the orders. Both of them slivered their hands as they dragged the panels and leaned them against an outside wall.

"More of them!" she yelled. "It's the smoke that will kill us."

The flames were far away, but the smoke was so thick she could hardly see through it.

Coughing, gagging, strangling, it seemed like eons until they had the mean little shelter constructed. But it was only minutes. As the dreadful roar of the fire and the shrieking of expanding metal surrounded them, Barbara shouted for them to crawl inside.

"Lie down. Breathe the fresh air," she ordered. "Heat and smoke go to the top. Put your faces on the cement as close to the vent as possible."

As they obeyed, she, choking and praying that she could stay conscious long enough, grabbed the hose Charlie had used to wet down their clothes. She wet down herself and the boys again, and she sluiced water over and over the shelter.

Spotting a sawhorse through the smoke, she dragged it to the sheets of aluminum and braced the hose so that a spray would fall on the life-saving panels. Then, praying for Lewis to please come, she glanced around them for some means of escape she might have overlooked.

Her gaze settled upon the skylights. "Steven!" she shouted.

The boy was instantly at her side. He followed her eyes and saw the same thing. Her voice was frantic. "Can you break it?"

With bleeding hands, they searched for something he could hurl at it. Barbara found a piece of iron that was already hot to the touch.

Steven was a strong, athletic young boy. Time after time he tried to send the iron flying up to the skylight. Finally, as he was wearing down and weeping with despair, he gave one blood-curdling yell and flung with all his might.

Glass showered down upon them as they scrambled for the shelter. "Thank God," Barbara wept. Crawling inside with the younger ones, she opened her arms to hold them.

Rick was sobbing. "I'm scared."

"Don't be scared," she choked.

Charlie was speechless with terror, and she kissed him. "We'll be all right, Charlie. Your dad's coming."

Across the younger boys' heads, through the cloudy air, she met Steven's haunted eyes. "I hope she's sorry," he blurted, weeping openly, his face contorted with grief and fear.

"I know, darling," she said, and pulled his stubborn, hurting blond head down to her own so that their tears ran together.

"It's going to be okay," she muttered, and pressed the clinging arms of them all. "Hold tight. It's going to be okay."

If the fire had been at night, lighting up the sky with orange and crimson, Lewis would have known much sooner than he did what was going on. But with Allie and Curtis talking to him at once—Curtis explained their command appearance while Allie spewed disparaging remarks about Arkansas and complaints about her unwillingness to be in it—Lewis concentrated on controlling his temper and getting out to the mill site.

Pinpointing the source of the smoke that grayed the sky was difficult at first, but when the rutted road brought them closer to its source, Lewis felt the skin tightening on his skull.

A thousand fears loomed on the horizon of his thoughts, and Curtis and Allie exchanged a puzzled query when he grew silent and alarmed. Curtis apparently made the connection between the threatening sky and the sweat that was beginning to pour off Lewis, and he reached into the zippered bag at his feet and took out his camera.

A pickup roared past them going in the opposite direction, and Lewis, with a growled oath, slammed his foot to the brake, sending the Suburban skidding to a halt crossways with the road.

"What's going on?" Allie snapped.

"God damn you!" Lewis yelled as he lunged wildly from the car and took a step into the tornado of dust created by Chino's truck.

With a jerk, Lewis flung himself back into the car, and the wheels spun furiously as he skidded the machine around and sent it shooting down the road to the mill.

Something terrible had happened. Fire was catching some of the nearby treetops, and he aimed the car through the smoke that billowed over the road.

Allie screamed as he swerved into a ditch and out again. "What's happened?" she yelled again. She clawed at Lewis, but he was like a madman as he forced the car through the stands of burning, smoking grass and bounced over the rough land of the site.

"They're out here!" he roared. "I sent them out here!"

Now the building was in sight. "Who? Oh, my God!" Allie cried. "Lewis, what—"

"Shut up!" Lewis screamed, and slammed the car to a stop that threw them all forward.

Allie caught herself on the dash and cursed Lewis, but he was already out of the car and running at top speed toward the burning building. He heard her shout to Curtis, "Give me the camera! Go help him, for God's sake!"

Deep inside the smoky screen, Lewis darted first one way, then another in an attempt to gain access to the building, but the heat forced him back. Frantic, he ran to a bulldozer parked a distance away, climbed on and started the huge machine. Then, like a man possessed, he headed the bulldozer straight for the building.

Chapter Thirteen

"Sweet are the uses of adversity, which, like the toad, ugly and venomous, wears yet a precious jewel in his head." Shakespeare

You know, I never did like this hedge," Emma told Mr. Katt in confidence as she descended the steps of Lewis's house with a tray of lemonade in her hands. "Not even when Josephine Hempstead planted it. I'm glad to see it coming down."

"Which does present a problem," Lewis laughed as he robbed the tray of two glasses and two pretty pink napkins in passing, lifting one of the glasses in a silent toast to the sheriff as he strolled past.

Sheriff Katt smiled. "One problem among many?" He nodded to Max, who was racing back and forth before the hedge in eager anticipation of discovering Tabor crouched, claws bared.

Lewis laughed. He was glad to leave Bumper O'Banyon in charge of hedge disposal. Not that the man didn't have

plenty of help; Julia and her household had been over
since breakfast and were brimming with all kinds of per
tinent advice. A serious family conference was already in
progress.

Beneath the live oak tree, a chaise longue had been se
up, and Lewis felt his heart lurch at the sight of Barbara
sitting curled up on it, her silver hair catching the spec-
kled sunlight through the branches, her smooth legs bare
in her shorts and her hands so belovedly bandaged.

He'd wanted to kill Simon Bodine for what he'd done to
her—and would have done so happily with his own bare
hands—but Bodine was in the custody of the police now
where he belonged. At least Lewis had the satisfaction of
knowing it was his own damning testimony that had put
the bastard in jail.

As he gazed at Barbara, his moodiness lifted. Was it a
hundred times he'd thanked her for his sons' lives? Not
since the fire trucks and the ambulances had come had he
let her out of his sight for more than ten minutes at a time.
If her family had objections when he brought her home
from the hospital to his very own house, they hadn't ex-
pressed them.

"Why do I get this feeling that there's a conspiracy
going on inside that head of yours?" he growled as he
walked over to loom over Barbara.

She tipped her head back to look at him, her blue eyes
as bright as the sky. "Because evil men surmise evil of
others, tough guy."

"Then tell me what I'm thinking, madam." He wickedly
held the dripping glass over her head and flicked a drop of
condensation onto the lenses of her glasses.

Yelping, she raised her bandaged hands, and Lewis
pushed her legs aside and squeezed in beside her to hold

the glass to her lips. "Here, drink your hemlock. There are much more interesting things to talk about."

"Like what?" She sipped all she wanted, and then he sipped the tiny residue from her upper lip.

"Delicious," he murmured.

"You're a very greedy man, Lewis Paccachio," she whispered as Steven strolled out onto the porch in his swimming trunks, soccer ball predictably in hand. The boy spotted her.

Looking up, Lewis groaned. "How would you know? Merely because I have to fight off my own children and stand in line just to get five minutes alone with you these days?"

"It's your own fault."

"*My* fault?" he growled as his son approached with a could-you-give-me-five-dollars? look on his face.

Grinning, Steven asked Barbara, "Do you need anythin', Barbara?"

"No, Steven, not a thing." Barbara adored him.

"Are you sure?"

"Positive."

"Okay. Hey, Dad—"

Lewis reached immediately for his billfold. "How much?"

"Gee, Dad, let a guy finish."

Rolling his eyes skyward, Lewis comically pretended boredom. "Why, hello, Steven, how nice of you to come by. Have a seat, and let's talk."

Groaning, Steve said, "Five dollars'll be enough."

"I thought so."

After Steven collected his brothers and told everyone they would be at the city park, they tromped across the lusciously clipped lawn, fondly insulting each other. Lewis bent his head and took advantage of the moment to caress his bride-to-be. Smiling at the contentment he found simply being close and sharing a lovely summer morning with her, he stroked her cheek.

"They're over there." Rick's voice floated brightly back into the yard. "By the chaise."

"Thank you, son."

Lifting his head, Lewis saw Murray Levitt climbing out of his car and walking up the sidewalk, his heavy shoulders drooping, his clothes hanging as if they'd been placed on the wrong body, his hat pulled limply over his head.

Under his breath, Lewis swore. "Now, what does that shyster want?"

Frowning, Barbara swung her legs off the chaise and met the eyes of her mother, where Julia sat on Lewis's lawn with her pale green skirt wrapped modestly about her legs. Julia had grown still and pale at the sight of the mayor, and even Emma stopped her chattering to watch.

"Be nice, Lewis," Barbara ordered. "Murray Levitt was one of mother's dearest friends."

"I guess I'm not as forgiving as you are, my darling. When someone hurts one of mine, I come out with hammers cocked and fingers on the trigger. I'm sorry, that's the kind of hairpin I am. Now, what movie was that from?"

"I can't remember, but you're not James Cagney."

By now Barbara knew Lewis's faults about as well as she knew her own. Fearing that he might not be above taking a swing at Finley's mayor, she scrambled off the chaise and followed him as he stepped from beneath the live oak.

"What can we do you for, Mr. Levitt?" Lewis said as he approached the man midway in the yard.

They were like two generals coming out to parley, Barbara thought dourly.

But Murray Levitt was a more humble man than before, and he now extended his hand and remarked about how good the old Hempstead place would look with the hedge torn down. "Looks like you plan to stay in Finley for a while, Mr. Paccachio."

Lewis was aware of Barbara moving to stand behind his shoulder. He felt her bandaged hand touch his waist in a gentle wifely reminder to remember his manners. A rush of love made him reach back and draw her to his side.

"I don't really know, Mr. Levitt," he said tightly. "I don't really think of this town as home, if you know what I mean."

Murray inclined his head at Emma, at Gene Katt, at Granna Finley and Edward Wheeler. Evidently he couldn't bring himself to look at Julia. "I, uh . . . I guess you know that I plan to resign as mayor."

"Stands to reason," Lewis said uncharitably.

"Lewis!" Barbara whispered.

Unhappily, Murray smiled at the woman who had spent almost as much time growing up in his house as she had her own. "That's all right, Barbara. I got it coming, you know. I did take the money. Oh, it's all in the escrow account, but I took it, pure and simple, and there's nothing I can do about it now. What I really regret, though, is that I let Tom Woodward and that bunch carry on all that talk about asking you to resign. The city doesn't want your resignation, honey; it wants mine, and now that they've got it, everything will go on as usual. I just wanted you to know that."

Julia had risen, and tears glistened in her eyes as she approached the chastened man. "Hello, Murray."

The aging man turned to her. "Now, don't go giving me one of those looks, Julia. I don't think I could stand it."

"Murray. Poor dear Murray."

Lewis felt a strange empathy drifting between mother and daughter, and he also felt his anger radiating toward the man standing on his lawn. He wanted to knock him to the ground and cram every last word the creep had said about Barbara down his mayorly throat.

He kept Barbara tightly in the curve of his arm. "I assume you've heard that Abrams and Bean is pulling out, Mr. Levitt."

Murray nodded. "I don't know if they can legally do that, but if I were in their shoes, I guess I'd take my chances in court rather than face a bomb scare every day."

"Well..." Lewis shrugged, not knowing what to say.

Shifting around on the sidewalk, the older man took out his handkerchief and mopped his face. "I thought, Mr. Paccachio, I mean, it came to me that I could kind of make up to the town for what I did if I just swallowed my pride and came right out and asked you... Oh, I know it's illogical and all that, but you know, we do have the escrow account, and the people of this town are willing to work. They'll work for almost nothing. We all would, if you would consider... I'm not asking you to make a decision now or anything like that, I'm just asking you to consider staying with us a little while, Mr. Paccachio, and maybe patching things up out there at the mill so we could take over the finishing of it. Barbara knows her way around these kinds of things; maybe she could find us another company that would help out. I don't know, it was just an idea that came to me, and I thought... hell, I don't know what I thought...that maybe Barbara, here, could talk you into it."

He sighed brokenheartedly, and watching the man became so painful that Barbara couldn't stand it. Detaching herself from Lewis, she walked over to the humiliated man and took him into her arms.

"It's all right, Murray," she whispered. "It's all right. Mother, please?"

With her impeccable grace, Julia glided forward and took Murray Levitt by the hand. "You must come along now, Murray. Well, goodness, Emma's made lemonade. You know, when Josephine planted this hedge, I don't know why in the world she had to choose common privet. It's not all that pretty, and the roots go down absolutely forever."

For long moments Barbara and Lewis watched the generation before them, and the generation before that, take the prodigal son to its heart.

"I'll be damned," Lewis said, and watched the ladies pour Murray a glass of lemonade and hand him a napkin.

"Small towns, Lewis." Barbara smiled and, standing on tiptoe, placed a smug kiss upon his scarred cheek. "We have to take care of our own. If we don't, who will?"

"The old coot—he damn near had me crying."

"But not quite, hmm? Mr. Macho Man?"

"Me? Cry? Hell, no. Come back in the shade before you get a sunburn."

Barbara smiled to herself because deep in her heart she knew what he did not. She knew perfectly well that Lewis would stay and build Finley's paper mill. She knew, too, that they would be married in the First Lutheran Church, and that Lewis's sons would finish growing up in this small town of hers, that they would have a beautiful daughter and that her name would be Bella, after Lewis's mother.

"Stop that," he said as they returned to the chaise and he held her elbow while she arranged herself on its cool, scratchy length.

Barbara laughed. "Stop what?"

"Planning my life. I don't have a great yen to go out there and rip down that mill and start all over."

"But you will, won't you?"

"Well, I don't know. It'll take forever teaching those guys how to use all that equipment. That's why the corporation always used their own crews, you know. Costly delays, things that can't meet inspection, to say nothing—"

"Lewis, shut up."

Growling, knowing that he undoubtedly would build the mill and take a tremendous cut in pay, he stretched himself out beside her. "Maybe I'll start my own corporation. Maybe I'll sell stock. Maybe I'll..." He stared at her and drew her glasses down until they rested on the tiny hook of her nose. "You know, Barbara, there's something I've wanted to do ever since the first time I laid eyes on you."

With a happy sigh, she leaned back against the cushion and listened to the busy chatter of everyone at the hedge, expecting to be kissed soundly. "What?"

She dreamily closed her eyes, and when she felt Lewis's fingers burying themselves in her hair and suddenly ruffle it in all directions until she looked like a wild Indian, she screeched and went tumbling off the chaise in a tangle of arms and legs.

All the talk at the hedge stopped until the lawn was so quiet that one could have heard the grass growing. Crouching, doubling up her fists, bandaged hands and all, Barbara drew back and prepared to take a great, looping swing at Lewis's head.

Laughing, he leaned forward and caught her wrist easily in his hand and pulled her up hard against him. "Lewis," she scolded, flushing. "Everyone's watching."

Kissing her nose, he pointed to his scar. "You see this, Barbara Regent? Now, there are one hundred and six stitches in this scar. If you had one hundred and six stitches, I might be inclined to sympathy...."

Barbara sighed as she leaned her head tenderly against his chest. "I don't like you, Lewis. Not one little bit."

"Oh, yes, you do. You can't get enough of me."

"We've got to do something about your lying, Lewis."

"Like what?"

"I'll think of something."

At the hedge, Emma Parker was looking at Mr. Katt, who was scowling at Edward Wheeler, who was watching the tender way the tall, scarred man was holding Barbara in his arms.

"Did I ever tell you, Mr. Katt," Emma said as she touched the brooch at her throat, "that Barbara was one of the finest little piano students I ever had? She could have played in the Tchaikovsky competitions, you know."

* * * * *

Silhouette Special Edition

WHITE LIES*
by
Linda Howard

Bestselling author Linda Howard is back with a story that is exciting, enticing and—most of all—compellingly romantic.

Heroine Jay Granger's life was turned upside down when she was called to her ex-husband's side. Now, injured and unconscious, he needed her more than he ever had during their brief marriage. Finally he awoke, and Jay found him stronger and more fascinating than before. Was she asking too much, or could they have a chance to recapture the past and learn the value of love the second time around?

Find out the answer next month, only in
SILHOUETTE SPECIAL EDITION.

*Previously advertised as MIRRORS.

COMING
IN MAY

SSE452

Silhouette Special Edition

NORA ROBERTS'S 50TH SILHOUETTE NOVEL

In May, SILHOUETTE SPECIAL EDITION celebrates Nora Roberts's "golden anniversary"—her 50th Silhouette novel!

The Last Honest Woman launches a three-book "family portrait" of entrancing triplet sisters. You'll fall in love with all THE O'HURLEYS!

> *The Last Honest Woman*—May
> Hardworking mother Abigail O'Hurley Rockwell finally meets a man she can trust...but she's forced to deceive him to protect her sons.
>
> *Dance to the Piper*—July
> Broadway hoofer Maddy O'Hurley easily lands a plum role, but it takes some fancy footwork to win the man of her dreams.
>
> *Skin Deep*—September
> Hollywood goddess Chantel O'Hurley remains deliberately icy...until she melts in the arms of the man she'd love to hate.

Look for THE O'HURLEYS! And join the excitement of Silhouette Special Edition!

SSE451-1